BEHIND THE GATES

BOOK 2

THE COLLAPSE OF AMERICA SERIES

BOBBY AKART

BOBBY AKART

BEHIND THE GATES

TWO

THANK YOU

Thank you for reading **Behind the Gates Two**,
the second installment in the ***Collapse of America*** series.
Join Bobby Akart's mailing list to learn about upcoming releases,
deals, and appearances. Follow this link to:
BobbyAkart.com

PRAISE FOR BOBBY AKART AND COLLAPSE OF AMERICA

"Bobby Akart's newest thriller is his most horrific yet. We have stepped over the line of Science Fiction into Science Fact and the landscape he draws is so scarily real, you will never feel safe again."
~ Amazon review for Behind The Gates, Book One

"Heart pounding action. Great premise. Real-life characters. All very, very believable and possible." ~ Amazon review for Behind the Gates, Book One

"Love the intensity of his stories, his through research, his creativity, the characterizations and the abundant action and realistic locations."
~ Amazon review of New Madrid Earthquake

"This book is history on the making. I feel like I'm reading today's news. The book's reality and today's reality are the same." ~ Amazon review for Behind The Gates, Book One

"Prepare yourself for another page turner. The master of this genre does it again. Nobody does it like Bobby Akart. Do yourself a huge favor and read every series he has. You won't regret it." ~ Amazon review of Behind The Gates, Book One

"I cry for the injured and defenseless, rage at the bad guys, and scream with impotent rage when one of my favorite characters are hurt or killed! Such is the artistry of the author. Such is the realm of Bobby Akart." ~ Amazon review of Yellowstone

BEHIND THE GATES

BOOK TWO

The Collapse of America Series

by
Bobby Akart

OTHER WORKS BY AMAZON CHARTS TOP 25 AUTHOR BOBBY AKART

The Collapse of America Series
Behind the Gates One
Behind the Gates Two
Behind the Gates Three
Behind the Gates Four

The California Dreamin' Disaster Thrillers
ARkStorm (a standalone, disaster thriller)
Fractured (a standalone, disaster thriller)
Mammoth (a standalone, disaster thriller)

The Perfect Storm Series
Perfect Storm 1
Perfect Storm 2
Perfect Storm 3
Perfect Storm 4

Black Gold (a standalone, terrorism thriller)

Gunner Fox Novels

Made In China (a standalone, terrorism thriller)

The Odessa Trilogy (Gunner Fox)

Odessa Reborn
Odessa Rising
Odessa Strikes

The Asteroid Trilogy (Gunner Fox)

Discovery
Diversion
Destruction

The Nuclear Winter Series

First Strike
Armageddon
Whiteout
Devil Storm
Desolation

New Madrid (a standalone, disaster thriller)

The Virus Hunters

Virus Hunters I
Virus Hunters II
Virus Hunters III

The Geostorm Series

The Shift
The Pulse
The Collapse
The Flood
The Tempest

The Pioneers

The Doomsday Series
Apocalypse
Haven
Anarchy
Minutemen
Civil War

The Yellowstone Series
Hellfire
Inferno
Fallout
Survival

The Lone Star Series
Axis of Evil
Beyond Borders
Lines in the Sand
Texas Strong
Fifth Column
Suicide Six

The Pandemic Series
Beginnings
The Innocents
Level 6
Quietus

The Blackout Series
36 Hours
Zero Hour
Turning Point
Shiloh Ranch
Hornet's Nest
Devil's Homecoming

The Boston Brahmin Series

The Loyal Nine
Cyber Attack
Martial Law
False Flag
The Mechanics
Choose Freedom
Patriot's Farewell (standalone novel)
Black Friday (standalone novel)
Seeds of Liberty (Companion Guide)

The Prepping for Tomorrow Series (non-fiction)
Cyber Warfare
EMP: Electromagnetic Pulse
Economic Collapse

DEDICATIONS

To the love of my life, Dani, and our little princesses in training, Bullie & Boom. Every day, you unselfishly smother me with your love, support, and merriment. I may be the machine that produces these words. You are the glue that holds me together and the fuel that winds me up each day so I can tell these stories. I will love you forever.

To my loyal readers and friends who've patiently awaited the release of the Collapse of America series. Please indulge me as I repeat the words that popped into my head one cold morning at our Tennessee home some twelve years ago:

All empires collapse eventually, and America is no exception.
Their reign ends when they are defeated by a larger and more powerful enemy,
or when their financing runs out.

History is replete with the rise and fall of empires. Are we so arrogant or oblivious to realize we are in a stage of decline and collapse? I began this journey as an author nine years ago and throughout, my goal has been to raise awareness in my readers. Through your encouragement and support, I continue to tell stories of collapse. Yes, all empires will collapse, America included. I hope that my words have changed your perspective. Be ready my friends.

Choose Freedom and Godspeed, Patriots!

ACKNOWLEDGMENTS

Creating a novel that is both informative and entertaining requires a tremendous team effort. Writing is the easy part.

For their efforts in making this novel a reality, I would like to thank Hristo Argirov Kovatliev for his incredible artistic talents in creating my cover art. He and my loving wife, Dani, collaborate (and conspire) to create the most incredible cover art in the publishing business. A huge hug of appreciation goes out to Pauline Nolet, the *Professor*, for her editorial prowess as sure ensures the millions of pages I have in print are near flawless. Thank you, Drew Avera, a United States Navy veteran, who has brought his talented formatting skills from a writer's perspective to create multiple formats for reading my novels. Thank you, Andrew Wehrlen, an incredibly talented voice actor and SOVAS award nominee who performs the audio narration of my stories.

As always, a special thank you to my team of loyal friends and readers who've always supported my work and provided me valuable insight over the years.

Thanks, y'all, and Choose Freedom!

ABOUT THE AUTHOR, BOBBY AKART

Author Bobby Akart has been ranked by Amazon as #25 on the Amazon Charts list of most popular, bestselling authors. He has achieved recognition as the #1 bestselling Horror Author, #1 bestselling Science Fiction Author, #5 bestselling Action & Adventure Author, #7 bestselling Historical Fiction Author and #10 on Amazon's bestselling Thriller Author list.

Mr. Akart has delivered up-all-night thrillers to readers in 245 countries and territories worldwide. With seventy novels in print, he has sold nearly two million books in all formats, which includes over forty international bestsellers, in nearly fifty fiction and nonfiction genres. He has produced more #1 bestselling novels in Science Fiction's post-apocalyptic genre than any author in Amazon's history.

His novel *Yellowstone: Hellfire* reached the Top 25 on the Amazon bestsellers list and earned him multiple Kindle All-Star awards for most pages read in a month and most pages read as an author. The Yellowstone series vaulted him to the #25 bestselling author on Amazon Charts, and the #1 bestselling science fiction author.

Since its release in December 2020, his standalone novel, *New*

Madrid Earthquake, has been ranked #1 on Amazon Charts in multiple countries as a natural disaster thriller.

Mr. Akart is a graduate of the University of Tennessee after pursuing a dual major in economics and political science. He went on to obtain his master's degree in business administration and his doctorate degree in law at Tennessee.

Bobby Akart has provided his readers a diverse range of topics that are both informative and entertaining. His attention to detail and impeccable research has allowed him to capture the imagination of his readers through his fictional works and bring them valuable knowledge through his nonfiction books.

SIGN UP for Bobby Akart's mailing list to learn of special offers, view bonus content, and be the first to receive news about new releases.

Visit www.BobbyAkart.com for details.

REAL WORLD NEWS EXCERPTS

CHINESE DEFENSE MINSTER THREATENS TO ATTACK TAIWAIN 'WITHOUT ANY HESITATION'

~ *Excerpts from speech at Shangri-La Dialogue in Singapore, March 15, 2024*

Chinese National Defense Minister Li Shangfu told attendees at the Shangri-La Dialogue in Singapore that the communist nation's military would attack "without any hesitation" against any allies of Taiwan seeking to support the nation's independence from Beijing.

Li said, "China calls for mutual respect which should prevail over bullying and hegemony, fairness and justice should transcend the law of the jungle, eliminating conflicts and confrontation through mutual trust and consultation and preventing bloc confrontation with openness and inclusiveness."

"If anyone dares to split Taiwan from China, the Chinese military will resolutely safeguard China's national sovereignty and territorial integrity without any hesitation, at all cost, and not fearing any opponent," the Defense Ministry quoted Li as saying. The press statement from the Ministry on Li's speech emphasized his remarks on Taiwan, rather than his called for Chinese communists' definition of "peace."

"How to solve the Taiwan question is Chinese people's own business, which brooks no foreign interference," Li reportedly said. "The authorities of the Democratic Progressive Party (DPP) seek independence by colluding with foreign forces and some external forces use Taiwan to contain China. They are the biggest troublemakers in changing the status quo across the Taiwan Strait."

TAIWAN AIR DEFENSES ACTIVIATED AFTER DOZENS OF CHINESE MILITARY AIRCRAFT FLY NEAR ISLAND

~ *THE HILL, June 8, 2023*

Taiwan on Thursday activated its defense systems after detecting dozens of Chinese warplanes in the island's air defense identification zone (ADIZ).

Starting at 5 a.m. local time, Taiwan's defense ministry detected 37 Chinese air force planes, including J-11 and J-16 fighter jets, H-6 bombers, YU-20 military transport planes and AWACS surveillance aircraft in the island's southwest airspace.

Also as of late, Beijing has taken aggressive new actions in the Taiwan Strait, last week overtaking a U.S. destroyer in an almost unprecedented maneuver.

The incident has escalated Beijing's routine harassment in the international waterway at a low point in diplomatic relations between Beijing and Washington.

FITCH DOWNGRADES THE UNITED STATES' LONG-TERM-RATINGS

TO 'AA+' from 'AAA'

~ FitchRatings.com, August 1, 2023

The rating downgrade of the United States reflects the expected fiscal deterioration over the next three years, a high and growing general government debt burden, and the erosion of governance relative to 'AA' and 'AAA' rated peers over the last two decades that has manifested in repeated debt limit standoffs and last-minute resolutions.

Erosion of Governance: In Fitch's view, there has been a steady deterioration in standards of governance over the last 20 years, including on fiscal and debt matters. The repeated debt-limit political standoffs and last-minute resolutions have eroded confidence in fiscal management. In addition, the government lacks a medium-term fiscal framework, unlike most peers, and has a complex budgeting process.

Rising General Government Deficits: We expect the general government (GG) deficit to rise to 6.3% of GDP in 2023, from 3.7% in 2022, reflecting cyclically weaker federal revenues, new spending initiatives and a higher interest burden.

INCREASING PSYCHOPATHIC BEHAVIOR IS A SIGN THAT SOCIETY IS ON THE VERGE OF BREAKING DOWN

~ Zero Hedge, January 16, 2024

Discussions on collapse often turn to signs and signals - The economy, politics and social tensions have become increasingly unstable for many years now, and much like adding more and more weight to a man standing on a frozen lake, eventually the ice is going to break. The question is, how do we know when that moment will be?

As cultural systems begin to dissolve due to political clashes and economic decline the real evil tends to slither out of the woodwork. It happens slowly at first, then all at once. A sure sign of accelerating collapse is the growing prevalence of psychopaths and psychopathic behavior in the open.

The US appears to have entered the middle stages of such a collapse with many sociopaths and psychopaths beginning to feel that they might be able to act out their worst impulses without consequences. They are beginning to test the waters to see what they can get away with.

AUTHOR'S NOTE

Winter 2024

At the onset of every novel or book series, I ask myself, why am I here? That's usually followed by will anybody else care. This is more important to me, as an author, than anything else as I take a story from concept to publication for my dear readers. Something of interest to me may not necessarily be of interest to you. Thankfully, with much gratitude, I seemed to find the mark every time.

With the *Collapse of America* series, I'm putting into fiction what many of us are experiencing in reality. As I've said for more than a decade, paraphrasing, all empires collapse eventually, and America will be no exception. They're either defeated by a stronger, more powerful enemy or they go bankrupt.

In the case of present day, we are experiencing both. Only, the powerful enemy is attacking America from within. This enemy is responsible for both our societal woes and our teetering on the threshold of economic collapse.

I see the systematic destruction of America, through social and economic collapse. This collapse will likely be triggered by an event that puts the nation over the edge from cyber warfare, a grid-down scenario, or even the collapse of our monetary system.

For now, we're experiencing *death by a thousand cuts*. Here's what that means.

Over a thousand years ago, there was a form of torture and execution practiced in the Far East known as *lingchi*. Lingchi was translated as the slow process of removing portions of the human body eventually resulting in death. Each cut, on its own, was not fatal. Together, the pain would slowly increase until the victim bled to death in an excruciating manner. It became known as *Death by a Thousand Cuts*.

Few of those who now use the phrase "death by a thousand cuts" will be aware of its origins in lingchi. Most, especially those who have no interest in learning history, will attribute its first use to the Taylor Swift song. However, in modern phraseology, it has come to mean a situation where lots of small bad things happen, none of which are fatal in themselves, but which in their totality add up to a slow, painful demise. I believe we are in the throes of America's collapse.

One day, historians will be able to identify the point in the great American experiment when things began to turn for the worst. Some will point to the decade of the 1960s, a period of social unrest, countercultural movements, political assassinations, and the emerging generation gap. Young people wholly embraced the lyrics from the Beatles, *all you need is love,* and nothing else. It was a decade mired in cultural changes following trends directly opposite the laudable values of the forties and fifties.

Just like the fall of the Roman Empire, after the sixties, America seemed to be changing rapidly. Was it for the better? Time will tell.

Now, Fast forward to the present day. We now live in a world where everyone has a voice. The internet and especially, social media, has enabled people to speak out on issues of importance to them. What was once hailed as a means for everyone to look up and interact with friends or classmates, Facebook, once dubbed *Bragbook,* turned into a platform for adversaries to attack one another.

Facebook, Twitter (now X), TikTok, Instagram, and dozens of other social media platforms have become anything but social. They've become the catalyst for dividing Americans along political lines. History has shown that the Revolutionary War and the Civil War were years in the making. Had the internet and social media been available to the Colonists and mid-nineteenth century Americans, the timeline for both conflicts would've been expedited.

Today, the twenty-four-hour news cycle has become the twenty-four minutes news cycle. Breaking news is often live streamed on the internet. Supreme Court rulings are disseminated to millions within seconds of their issuance. Acts of violence around the nation are reported within minutes.

And, in the media's quest to be the first to break the story, oftentimes, they get it wrong. As does the average social media user. The concept of catching a deep breath is lost on everyone.

So is the concept of standing back from the noise to form an opinion of what is happening around us. We can't see the forest for the trees. We cannot see the big picture because we focus too much on the details.

This is a story about a group of Americans who one day realized that something is fundamentally wrong in our country. They start to take random geopolitical and domestic events, piece them together, to come to an awakening, of sorts. They stand back and see the forest.

The collapse of America was unfolding before their eyes and then needed to get ready.

And, fast.

EPIGRAPH

When the people find that they can vote themselves money,
that will herald the end of the Republic.
~ Benjamin Franklin, Founding Father

———

Republics decline into democracies and democracies degenerate into
despotisms.
~ Aristotle, Ancient Greek Philosopher

———

"The further a society drifts from the truth, the more it will hate
those who speak it."
~ George Orwell

———

A rocket won't fly unless somebody lights the fuse.

~ Homer Hickam, NASA Engineer

An evil man will burn his own nation to the ground to rule over the ashes.
~ incorrectly attributed to Sun Tzu, Chinese general and philosopher, but accurate, nonetheless.

AUTHOR'S NOTE TO THE READER

February 22, 2024

While this is a work of fiction, many of the subplots relayed herein are based upon actual events. Sometimes, we're required to look at the mirror to see how mean-spirited we can be. And like Alice in Wonderland, we all need to use a Looking Glass to see what we can become.

And so it begins ...

PART 1

"If violent crime is to be curbed, it is only the intended victim who
can do it.
The felon does not fear the police, and he fears neither judge nor
jury.
Therefore, what he must be taught is to fear his victim."
~ Lt. Col. Jeff Cooper, USMC

ONE

Friday Night Club
The Winchesters' Home
The Colony at Malibu
Malibu, California, USA

Their world changed in an instant. For several seconds after the power grid went down and Malibu was thrust into darkness, Dean Winchester and his guests were frozen in stunned silence. During this surreal moment, Dean recalled the title of one of his last lectures at Pepperdine University: *America would collapse without warning.*

Were they witnessing the inevitable demise of the once mighty nation? Without realizing it, he was the first to break the silence, uttering a rhetorical question under his breath.

"My god, what have they done?"

Grayson McCall, Dean's neighbor and best friend, replied in a calm demeanor that only a trained military operative could have under the circumstances. He gently reached out and addressed each of the members of the Friday Night Club.

"Gather around, everybody," he began after clearing his throat. He'd anticipated this moment but held out hope that the greater Los Angeles area might dodge the proverbial bullet in the form of China's cyberattacks. While they had been discussing the possibility on the Winchesters' deck overlooking the Pacific Ocean, without warning, the lights of the surrounding homes had gone off in unison.

Emmy Foley, Dean's wife, tried to contain her emotions. As a daytime television actress, she was capable of conjuring up all six categories on the emotion wheel to play a role. Love, fear, surprise, happy, sad, numb and angry. Her training and excellent acting skills betrayed her as she wrapped her arm through Dean's. Her body shook with nervousness as the significance of what was happening overcame her.

"Grayson, is this it? Are we out of power like all of those people?" She pointed down the ridge toward the stream of refugees' cars on the Pacific Coast Highway.

Throughout the day, thousands of vehicles had descended upon Los Angeles County. Refugees from power outages that stretched from the San Francisco Bay area to Seattle, Washington. All the major coastal cities of Central and Northern California were without power at the same time as they were inundated with a series of atmospheric rivers that dropped record amounts of rainfall on the region and massive snow accumulations in the mountains. LA was the only major city on the West Coast that had been spared. It had become an oasis in the desert for the refugees. Now, everyone had suffered the same fate.

Grayson, whose mind was prioritizing a mental checklist of things to do, replied calmly, "Emmy, we don't know for certain. That said, we have to assume this is what we've been preparing for."

"We can do this," said Lee Wong, a Los Angeles police detective. He and his wife, Nicole Hermann, had found themselves in many a tense, life-threatening moment in their pasts. Their friends in the

Friday Night Club had no idea what the couple had faced before they'd met. Although the loss of the power grid might present new, unimaginable horrors beyond what they'd survived years ago. Nicole took her husband's hand.

Suddenly, Liza Pryce broke down crying. The usually amiable, unflappable advertising executive had been a nervous wreck since the day the subject of preparing for some kind of collapse event had come up during their regular Friday night gatherings. The Friday Night Club had always been an opportunity for the three couples plus Grayson to share the events of their week, discuss current events, and throw back some cocktails. Indications that America was dying by a thousand cuts, as Dean had described the way society had begun to collapse, had given the group a new sense of purpose. Liza and her husband, Judson, a civil engineer, were concerned about whether they could survive a catastrophic event like the one unfolding in front of them. They'd never considered the possibility of losing power for many years, potentially. Now reality was setting in.

Judson tried to comfort her, but it was Liza's best friend, Emmy, who gathered the strength to come to her friend's aid. Emmy pulled her away from the group and spoke softly to her, coddling her in an effort to keep Liza from hyperventilating. Judson turned to Grayson.

"I agree with Lee," Judson began. "Grayson, you've apparently envisioned this scenario in detail. What do we need to do first?"

Grayson paused before responding. He walked to the railing of the upper deck and surveyed the neighborhood as well as the traffic on the PCH. He pulled his cell phone out of the thigh pocket of his cargo pants. As he brusquely tore the Velcro, he startled Nicole, who'd not spoken since the lights went out. She let go of Lee's hand and wrapped her arms across the front of her body, subconsciously hugging herself as a form of protection. The attractive real estate broker had always exuded confidence. Now she was showing a vulnerable side Grayson had never seen. He illuminated his cell phone and apologized to Nicole.

"I'm sorry. I didn't mean to startle you."

She simply shrugged and stared toward the ocean.

Grayson studied the display and navigated to the contact list in the phone app. He chose Dean's number and dialed it, but nothing happened. He studied the iPhone's display. At the top left of the display were the words SOS *only*. He tried dialing 9-1-1, but he received *an all circuits are busy* response.

"Are the phones working?" asked Lee.

Grayson shook his head. "No, apparently emergency calls only. There's good news in this." By the looks he received from his friends, he knew an explanation was necessary. Grayson continued, "The power grid can be taken down for a couple of reasons. One is a cyber-attack, which is what I think has been happening to the other major West Coast cities. The other is by an electromagnetic pulse."

"We talked about this," interjected Judson. "Either from a nuke or a solar flare. My money would be on China nuking us."

Grayson finished his thought. "Except the cell phones are still operable, and SOS only is still an option, although the system is overwhelmed. This is not the worst-case scenario. A bad one, but not the worst."

The group was startled when they heard a woman scream in the distance, followed by horns honking. Then the sound of steel scraping on steel as two or more vehicles ran into each other. It forced them all back into the present.

Grayson took a deep breath. "Here's the plan."

TWO

Friday Night Club
Dean and Emmy's Home
The Colony at Malibu

A cacophony of horns blaring in the background urged Grayson to take the group inside to explain the initial stages of the collapse. However, he noticed other residents carrying flashlights milling about in the distance. He kept them outside so he could keep a wary eye on their surroundings. He needed to get the group started immediately.

"For tonight, we're gonna keep it simple. Most importantly, make it until tomorrow without incident. Daylight is the enemy of intruders, which is what we're most concerned about right now. Especially since we've stockpiled a lot of supplies over the last few weeks."

"If we go home, what do we do if we need help?" asked Liza. Her eyes were wide, barely blinking, as a myriad of scenarios entered her mind. She glanced toward the empty houses on both sides of

Grayson's and Emmy's. She suddenly wished they lived right next door.

Grayson nodded as he replied, "I've got that covered. As you know, I have a small solar array on my roof."

Nicole, who seemed to have recovered from the initial shock, added, "Yeah, the neighborhood pitched a fit about it. You just ignored their threats of litigation."

Grayson smiled. "I did. It's not a big system, and it's not attached to the electric meter like most people do to save money. It goes straight to an inverter and a rack of batteries in my garage."

"I've seen them," added Dean. "Don't you have all of your power tools plugged into it?"

"Yeah, but only for convenience or situations like this. I also bought each of us a Midland long-range radio. I have them charging now. They already have presets for us to reach one another. Channel seven, chosen because there are seven of us, is our primary contact channel. I want us to keep in touch throughout the night. At least every thirty minutes but without excessive chatter. Never use names or locations. These radios are easily monitored, but they'll serve the purpose of allowing us to stay in touch."

Lee added, "I have my police radios, one handheld and the other in the car. I'll monitor them throughout the night and charge the portable at your place."

Dean had been fairly quiet throughout the conversation. He asked Grayson, "Can you use your satellite phone to find out what has happened? I mean, how widespread and permanent is this?"

"I'll try. I have limited contacts available to me. The Midland two-way radios will be helpful, too. We can pick up conversations from as far away as thirty-five miles. I also have the Baofeng portable ham radio. It would require someone who doesn't mind scrolling through a lot of channels in search of chatter."

"I'll do it," volunteered Emmy.

Grayson continued, "That said, we need to be wary of our battery life. I don't know what the next several hours will bring."

Emmy noticed more people in the street at the entrance to their cul-de-sac. The beams from their flashlights were dancing around as they greeted their neighbors. "Listen to them. They're freaking out." The excited voices carried in the near silence of the night as the motorists honking their horns took a respite.

"All the more reason to get started," said Grayson. "Listen up, please."

"Okay, we're ready," said Liza.

"After I fetch your radios, you need to hurry home. Each of you needs to pick a single entry to use when you come and go. Preferably not the front, where your neighbors will see you. Pick a side or back entrance out of direct view.

"Once that is done, barricade the other exterior doors, keeping in mind that you might need to leave your home in a hurry. If you move heavy pieces of furniture to prevent entry, just know that you can't move them out of the way if you gotta evacuate. Do the same thing with first-floor windows that are accessible to anyone wanting to enter.

"Ordinarily, I would urge you to maintain light discipline. That means keeping lanterns, flashlights, or candles out of sight from anyone peering into your home. Not tonight. I want people to know you are home. Upstairs windows only, but away from your exterior decks. You're gonna want to keep watch from those. In that instance, darkness is your friend."

"Guns?" asked Dean.

"Absolutely, but don't make a mistake. Only fire upon someone if they're breaking into your house. A reminder to everyone. And Lee knows this. Don't point a gun at someone unless you intend to use it. Drawing down on another person is an overt act that will force them to react with force of their own."

"This is crazy!" exclaimed Liza. "Are we gonna be shooting at people? Our neighbors?"

"Only if they try to break into your house," said Emmy.

"What if Toby or his minions come around?" asked Judson.

Grayson sighed and looked to Dean. They'd focused so much on gathering food and supplies that they hadn't established a game plan for dealing with the HOA president and his newly hired security team.

"We can't hide from them," said Dean. "I don't know what they'd ask from any of us, but I do know they have plans that neither Emmy nor Nicole are privy to despite the fact they're on the HOA board."

Grayson thought for a moment before responding, "I can't imagine they'd venture out into the dark and go door-to-door. That's a good way to get shot by a panicked resident. I believe we'll have until morning before we have to deal with them. The most important rule with Toby, his people, or anyone else, for that matter, is to keep your level of preparedness to yourself. Tell them nothing about your food storage, your supplies, weapons, or any of the tools we've purchase to deal with this scenario. It's none of their business."

"We can't remain completely aloof," said Nicole. "Toby and his guy, Tom Zelmanski, will see right through it."

Dean took a deep breath and nodded his head. "She's right. We've gotta come up with a response they'll accept, or which will at least stall them until we can figure out what's going on."

The horns began to blare again, and shouting could be heard emanating up the ridge from the beaches. "Lee, can you give me a hand?" asked Grayson, who didn't really need it. He wanted to speak to Lee alone.

"Let's go," said Lee as he gestured for Grayson to lead the way.

The two men walked through the dark house, using their cell phones to illuminate the way. Dean trailed close behind, curious as to why Lee had been singled out to help Grayson. He didn't think it would take much to carry half a dozen walkie-talkies.

"Is everything okay?" Dean asked.

Grayson turned to Dean and whispered. He was frank in his assessment. "I have concerns about Liza and Judson. They're not ready for this."

"We could move them in here," said Dean.

"I don't know if they'll leave their home unattended," said Grayson.

Lee motioned for the men to go down the stairs to the second floor. "I can see their front lawn from our upstairs garage balcony. I can help watch over them."

"That's what I was hopin' you'd say," said Grayson. "Also, I have something for you that might help."

"What's that?" Lee asked.

"An AR-10 and a full ammo can of NATO rounds," he replied before turning to Dean. "I don't have an extra one for you. Because we're next door to one another, I can use mine to defend our homes. Those guys are gonna need their own."

Dean held up his hands as he spoke. "Understandable. No doubt Lee can handle a weapon like that better than I can."

Grayson turned back to Lee. "I'm gonna send you back with the radios. I need to try to find out what's going on. As soon as you can, break it up and head to your homes. But stop by next door and get the rifle first."

"Got it." Lee nodded as he spoke.

Grayson took a step back up the stairs. "I'm gonna go back and join the group. I'll pull Judson aside and talk to him about staying with us. At least through the night."

The guys went their separate ways. Dean stopped at the top of the stairs and took a deep breath. He shook his head in disbelief. He contemplated if the threat they faced was greater from behind the gates than beyond them.

THREE

Friday
Toby Davenport's Residence
The Colony at Malibu

Toby Davenport had always craved power. However, he never was willing to step out of his comfort zone to achieve it. But then, what was real power, anyway? After the initial shock of the electric grid going down wore off, he had the opportunity to gather his thoughts.

He endured his wife's meltdown for a minute or two before dismissing her so he could think. A stiff drink helped him steady his nerves. The clarity he achieved during those initial moments of silence as the alcohol coursed through his veins set him on a path that would change his life forever.

He stood in his study and stared through the bay window that provided a view of his front lawn and the main street winding its way through the Colony. He imagined that within minutes, his neighbors

—no, his constituents, his flock, in a way—would be coming to his front door in search of comfort and guidance. He expected it to be a seminal moment in his life. His moment of greatness.

His mind was filled with the concept of power. Many assume power comes from the outside in, bestowed upon them by a government, a powerful individual, or the residents of a community association. They see power as a position or title, which comes with authority and control, and a belief in the form of supremacy over others. Toby was willing to accept that premise. However, in this moment, he felt something else rising within him.

He believed real power came from the inside out. It was a power innate in each individual. One they could cultivate by themselves. Real power, Toby thought, was increased within a person simply by the choices they made, the actions they took, and the thoughts they created.

Toby, in those critical moments after the grid went down, defined power differently. It didn't matter whose name was at the top of the Colony's organizational chart of officers and directors. Power was available to everyone, no matter their position or title. And as a result, there would be those who might try to assert themselves to wrestle it away from him. He had to act energetically and with confidence.

"Toby!" his wife hollered for him from the dining room, where she'd lit candles. She'd been standing at the window, looking for signs of movement outside. She was not confident that her husband could control their panicked neighbors. "There are people coming this way. Lots of them. With flashlights!"

Toby rolled his eyes as he reached into the top desk drawer of his desk to retrieve a pistol. The .38-caliber firearm, used by many police departments for much of the twentieth century, had been handed down to him from his uncle, a former court bailiff. Toby only had a couple of boxes of .38 Specials made by Smith & Wesson, also a standard service bullet used by cops until the nineties. He checked to make sure it was loaded and then tucked it into the waistband of his jeans. He didn't expect to need it when greeting his constituents, but one never knew. It reminded him that he needed to address using some of the neighborhood's security patrols for his own safety detail. He was about to become a very important man in the Colony, if not all of Malibu.

First things first, he thought to himself as he approached the front door. It hadn't been that long ago he'd had to address the neighbors about the rising crime in idyllic Malibu, including an attack of a woman in the Colony. The events taking place in LA and the rest of the West Coast proved he was correct in the need for enhanced security measures, as he called them.

He flipped the switch for the front porch light out of habit. Naturally, it didn't work. "Idiot," he muttered to himself with a smile. "It's a different world now, pal." One he'd fantasized about. One that he role-played before he fell asleep at night. One in which the weak relied upon him to lead the way through the peril and mayhem.

When he opened the door, he expected the residents to greet him with adoration befitting someone of his stature. Instead, they screamed their displeasure over the inconvenience of it all. He'd barely stepped through the door when the barrage of voices struck him.

"What's going on, Toby?"

"Our cell phones and my internet don't work."

"My television quit working, and I have a satellite dish. I don't even have cable!"

"Who cares about all of that!" a man who'd just arrived bellowed from the back of the pack. "There are people trying to get through our gates. They've been stranded on the PCH, and now they want in here."

"Why?" a woman turned to ask the man. The other residents stepped aside so the man could approach Toby to speak.

"They're hungry and tired," he explained. "I came through the gate just as the power went out. The gate's arm was stuck open. Our people were struggling to lower it. The idiots broke it in the process. I told them to use their cars to block the entry. You know, like in *The Godfather*."

Toby loved *The Godfather* movies. He could visualize the fifties-era sedans blocking the entrance to Don Corleone's compound during Connie's wedding, followed by Sonny Corleone beating up the media who were trying to get pictures. Oddly, this thought led Toby to wonder where Tom Zelmanski was, his head of neighborhood security. His Sonny Corleone.

"Did they get the gates blocked?" asked Toby.

"Yeah, but it's a pain in the you-know-what for the residents returning from dinner and such. The guys at the gate can't tell who belongs here and who doesn't. Morons."

Suddenly, another voice joined the conversation. It was Zelmanski. "They're doing the best they can under the circumstances." His annoyance with the man was obvious, especially when he added, "You could've stuck around to help them secure the neighborhood instead of running up here to tell Mr. Davenport about the situation."

The man immediately cowered under Zelmanski's stern tone of voice. Other residents who'd been prepared to throw in their two cents' worth also opted to stay silent. Zelmanski pushed his way through the crowd to join Toby.

"We need to talk," he growled in Toby's ear.

Toby scowled. *What's he pissed at me about? I didn't do anything.* "Fine, but I need to tell these people something."

Zelmanski suddenly turned around and faced the burgeoning crowd. "Everybody needs to go home and lock your doors. The block captains will be around soon to give you instructions."

Now Toby was perturbed. Zelmanski was usurping his authority by addressing the residents directly. Toby needed to show his people that he was in control. In charge of the situation. Ready to act. They didn't need to be taking orders from an underling like Zelmanski.

"Yes, everyone. Please get home to safety. We can't protect you if you are wandering the streets. Plus, in a tense situation like this one, mistaken identity can result in serious consequences."

"When are we gonna hear something?" asked a distraught woman.

For a few seconds, Toby didn't respond. Mainly because he couldn't. He knew as little as they did. It had only been an hour since the power went out. For all he knew, it was temporary. *Heaven forbid,* he said to himself, stifling a chuckle. *That won't do, now, will it?*

FOUR

Friday
Toby Davenport's Residence
The Colony at Malibu

Toby spoke briefly to a couple of his closest neighbors and then realized none of the HOA board members had come to his home. Naturally, he didn't expect to see Emmy Foley or Nicole Hermann, the two outcasts of the seven-member board. However, where were the rest of them? He knew them to frequently dine out. Had they all been beyond the gates when the power went out? What if he had to make a decision that required a board vote? Did any of that even matter now? After all, he was the authority. The man in charge.

He turned to invite Zelmanski inside and found the front door open and the former alarm-system salesman ordering a drink from his wife. Toby became flustered, and when another resident shouted a question to him, he spun around quickly, causing his jeans to adjust on his waist. The pistol he'd stuck in his waistband dislodged and fell onto the concrete porch with a loud thud before bounding down the stairs onto the sidewalk.

"Is that a gun?" asked one woman. "It could have shot one of us!"

"Toby, is that really necessary?" asked another.

"Nobody said anything about needing guns," added an older man who'd returned to the front of the crowd.

Toby hustled down the steps and fumbled around in the dark for the weapon. Finally, one of the neighbors assisted him by illuminating the concrete with his flashlight. He held it there for a couple of seconds that felt like hours. The group of Davenport's most faithful residents were mesmerized by the weapon. Then it dawned on them that Toby owned it.

"Do you need a permit for that?"

"Is it loaded?"

"Toby, you've never mentioned to any of us that you have a gun."

"I didn't know either. Wow. Who knew?"

Toby snatched the gun off the sidewalk and inadvertently waved it around toward the remaining neighbors. All of them spontaneously jumped back as they reacted to his unexpected movements. A couple in the rear took off running, their hard-soled shoes clomping along the pavement.

Toby turned and rushed inside, slamming the front door behind him. He was greeted by his wife.

"Are you okay? Can I get you a drink?"

"No!" he barked in response out of frustration. "I can fix my own damn drink. Here, do something with this." He handed his wife the gun. Her hands shaking, she touched the barrel with two fingers and held the pistol like it was a dead mouse.

"What, um, what do I do with it?"

Toby closed his eyes. All he could think of was a drink. And then another after that. "I don't care. Just don't lose it. Where's Tom?"

"In here," Zelmanski replied from Toby's study.

His study. His sanctum sanctorum. The off-limits-to-everyone room except by rare invitation only. Zelmanski had taken up a seat in front of Toby's desk, with his feet propped up on the corner. He was sipping a glass of Toby's twenty-six-year-old Glenfiddich scotch. It had cost him six hundred dollars a bottle and was only meant for his lips.

"What do you think you're doing?" Toby asked.

Zelmanski let out a huff. "Hey, don't take that tone with me, Davenport. I've had to deal with a helluva mess at the gate. We've got real trouble brewing."

"Like what?" asked Toby. He grabbed the scotch bottle away from Zelmanski's reach and stuck the cork back in it. After placing it behind his desk on the credenza, he replaced it with a bottle of Johnnie Walker Red Label, the guest scotch as he called it.

"Seriously? You have to ask that question? We've got a thousand travelers outside our gates who come from all walks of life. Most of them look broke. Everything they own is crammed into their cars. I've watched them. They all stare at our gatehouse, pointing. Wondering. What's in there? Maybe they've got something we need or want? I can feel 'em, Toby. If this power thing is permanent or even long-lasting, they're gonna come for us."

Toby sat behind his desk. His wife had lit a couple of candles when Zelmanski came into the study. The light flickered in the darkness, casting an orangish glow across the room. Toby imagined his face looked sinister to Zelmanski. Determined. In charge. In reality, Zelmanski saw a cherublike man who was weak and insecure. Hence the reason he treated his boss with disrespect in private. This evening was the first time Zelmanski had treated Toby with open contempt. This was disconcerting for Toby.

"I don't understand what the problem is," Toby began. "Didn't you block the gates with vehicles? Nobody can get through those."

Zelmanski laughed and shook his head. "They can walk around them. Over them. Dozens at a time. More than my people can handle. If they bum-rush the gates, we're screwed. If those refugees, or whatever you wanna call them, decide to storm the gates, they'll swarm through this neighborhood like out-of-control, ravenous locusts."

Toby got the visual. "Okay, I get it. So what do you need to secure the gates?" *In other words, subordinate, what do you need to do the job I pay you for?*

"Manpower. I can't pull the block captains to do gate duty. If I do, I can't deal with the residents. Also, one of my top guys told me the hourly guards feel the need to go home to take care of their own families. The only thing keeping them here right now is the traffic on the highway. It doesn't help that we live in a place with only one road in and one road out."

"Tell them I'll double their pay if they stay," suggested Toby.

"Double their pay with what? A rubber check? Monopoly money? They're probably wondering how they're gonna get paid for the hours they've worked so far. And if they stay, where do they sleep? Who feeds them? When can they leave if we don't have replacements?"

Suddenly, Toby had an insatiable urge for a little blow. A line of coke would do him a world of good. Except it was part of a different world for him. One that he'd managed to escape before his success led him to the Colony. Still, the high from snorting cocaine would help him cope with all of this.

"I need to think," said Toby.

Zelmanski laughed sarcastically. He walked around the desk and took a firm hold on the bottle of Glenfiddich. In an act of defiance and disrespect, he poured a full glass of the expensive whiskey and slugged it down.

"Well, you do that, Toby. Think about it. In the meantime, I'll be down on the front line, holding my team together while we protect the neighborhood."

Zelmanski spun around, slammed the empty glass on Toby's desk, and walked out of the house with the Glenfiddich in hand.

FIVE

Friday
The Colony at Malibu

Lee wrapped the AR-10 rifle in a beach towel and tucked it under his arm. During daylight hours, he wouldn't be fooling anyone. He chuckled to himself as he led his wife and the Pryces down the street toward their homes. He imagined a couple of beefy mafioso types carrying a rolled-up carpet out of a New York City flat. The rug, with a noticeable bulge in the middle of it, carried some poor sap who had crossed the mob. A rifle rolled up in a beach towel was no different. Although it was better than carrying it at low ready, Lee thought to himself. The sight of it would probably send his neighbors screaming into the night.

Before the grid went down, he and Judson had been working on obtaining voter rolls and gun registration records from state agencies. Lee had been successful and had started the process of identifying the residents of the Colony who possessed firearms. He was also able to determine what types of weapons they owned.

As for the voter rolls, that had turned into a real shit show. One that got both Judson and Lee embroiled in a federal investigation of a young man who'd entered the United States Capitol on January 6, 2021. The man, a co-chairman of the Los Angeles Republican Party, had spent around a minute inside before exiting. That was enough to warrant his arrest in the eyes of the Department of Justice.

FBI agents had been sent to toss the man's home pursuant to a search warrant. Apparently, Lee surmised, they'd discovered an email from Judson to the man, asking for the voter rolls. In it, unfortunately, Judson had mentioned Lee by name and the fact he'd accessed the California Gun Registry data. Lee had been called into Internal Affairs as a result for a face-to-face meeting with an FBI investigator. He didn't know where it was going to lead, but when the power went out, one of his first thoughts was the feds probably had bigger fish to fry than jamming him up.

"Let's cut through the houses here," Lee instructed the others. They scurried up a driveway and dashed between some shrubbery separating the two closely spaced homes. One of the benefits of living at the end of a cul-de-sac was the larger, pie-shaped lots. Judson and Liza had one of those lots, while Lee and Nicole lived two doors down on a regular lot closer to the entrance to the cul-de-sac.

Nicole hustled to catch up with Lee as he guided them onto their street. "Liza is freaking out," she began as they approached the clearing. "She's afraid they don't have enough food to survive for long. Also, she's concerned about being a burden on the rest of us."

"That's nonsense," whispered Lee. "We're all in this together."

"I know. I told her the same thing. I'll try to help her through this, but honestly, Emmy has a more calming effect on her than I do."

Lee stopped short of walking through the planting beds. There was a group of people standing at the end of their street, talking with one another. He and Nicole had to cross the street to get to their home. They'd be clearly visible to the group of neighbors.

"We'll show Liza and Judson they are a valuable part of our group," he said.

The two of them caught up to Lee and Nicole. Liza was apprehensive. "What's going on? Is it safe to go home?"

Lee held his index finger to his lips, indicating Liza should lower her voice. "I can't let them see me cross the street with this." He raised the rifle slightly to prove his point.

Liza leaned forward to study the group. "I think I see our neighbor Jamie. She lives on the corner opposite of our place."

Judson leaned forward, too. "Yeah. That's her husband."

Lee asked, "Can you guys go speak with them? Position yourselves on the opposite side so they're looking away from the cul-de-sac. That way we can cross quickly without them noticing the gun."

Judson looked again and then shrugged. "Sure. I mean, you're putting a lot of emphasis on hiding the gun. Wouldn't it be better that they know you've got it so they don't mess with you?"

"Trust me," replied Lee. "They'd be all over us if they saw this thing. It's better they don't know."

"What do you want us to say?" asked Liza.

Lee leaned into them as he responded, "Ask questions. Pretend to be clueless. Gather as much information from them as you can."

"Knowledge is power, right?" said Liza rhetorically. Nicole could see her confidence build as she began to see a way to benefit the group. She quickly helped boost her confidence.

"Exactly. Emmy and I can't approach anyone. We're board members, so many people might be guarded. Not to mention half these people are Toby's butt-buddies. They won't speak to us anyway."

"Looks like they're breaking up," interjected Lee. "You need to get moving."

Liza and Judson held hands as they casually stepped on the sidewalk. They strolled toward the group while Lee and Nicole waited for their opportunity to scurry across the street.

"She's gonna be all right," said Nicole. "This seems to be hitting her harder than the rest of us."

Lee nodded. As part of the Los Angeles Interagency Gang Task Force, he'd had to put together teams to raid drug cartel's strongholds throughout the county. He wanted to believe that every member of the team was as capable as he was. However, there was always one weak link. It was incumbent upon the rest of the team to have each other's backs, including the weakest link among them.

They could hear Liza raise her voice to get the attention of the neighbors before they walked back to their homes. Seconds later, she and Judson performed their task admirably.

"Let's go," said Lee. He and Nicole scampered across the street toward their house, where they'd left their front door unlocked. Despite what had happened to a resident who'd recently been a victim of a home invasion, Lee had been comfortable enough to visit Dean and Emmy's home without locking up.

That had changed.

SIX

Friday
The Colony at Malibu

"Hey, everybody!" greeted Liza. She was channeling her inner Emmy Foley, playing the part of the confident and strong neighbor in the face of TEOTWAWKI—the end of the world as we know it. "Whadya make of this mess?"

Her neighbor Jamie wasn't quite as chipper. "Hi, Liza."

Judson stepped forward to shake hands with the men. One man, younger than his neighbors, was wearing the security patrol uniform issued by Zelmanski. Judson hadn't met any of the new people other than those working the entrance gate. He'd purposefully avoided them, even the block captain, who'd left them notes several times.

"My name is Julian Manson," the man said as he shook Judson's hand. His deep, gravelly voice was disconcerting and his missing teeth even more so. "I've been trying to get in touch with the two of you."

Instinctively, Liza scooted closer to her husband. She was going to try to keep up the calm, cool demeanor. But the man's voice unnerved her.

"Yeah, we travel a lot," lied Judson. "I guess we're meeting under the oddest of circumstances. Have you guys figured out what's happened?"

"They think LA has been hit with the same kind of cyberattack as the other cities along the West Coast."

"Who is they?" asked Liza abruptly. In her desire to help the group by asking questions, she came across as rude. She tried to fix it. "Well, um, I mean, there's a lot of speculation as to what's going on with those other cities. Is there any chance this might be temporary?"

Her neighbor Jamie replied, "That would be nice, Liza. But I don't think so. This is gonna take a few days to fix."

"At least," said the block captain. "We need to be prepared for a long-term outage. So I need to get some information from you."

Judson dodged the request with a question. "How long is long? We eat out all the time."

Their neighbor added, "We do, too. In fact, Saturday is my regular shopping day. Our cupboard is kinda bare."

"Same here," added a neighbor who lived on the main street leading from the front gate to the top of the ridge. "We never imagined something like this happening. I mean, we did some calculations, and if we skimp on our meals, we'll only have enough for a week."

The block captain spoke up, revealing information that caused a chill to run up Judson's spine. "My boss, Mr. Zelmanski, has already considered this problem. He plans on speaking to your HOA president, Mr. Davenport. My boss thinks it would be best for everyone to pool their resources in order to make sure everyone gets fed."

Liza was about to speak up, but Judson squeezed her hand. He hoped one of the other neighbors would say something first, but they didn't, leading him to believe they already knew of this grand plan. He needed to change the subject.

"How are things going at the entrance to the neighborhood? I know there are a lot of cars on the PCH trying to get into the city."

"It's been a challenge," the block captain replied. "We don't have enough manpower to keep those on foot from attempting to run past our guards. We've got cars blocking the entrance and exits. Nobody can come or go in their vehicles. But if we get rushed by a mob trying to enter the neighborhood, we can't stop them with the number of guards we still have on duty."

"Wait," said Judson. "The way you said that last part. Still have on duty. Have members of the security team left?"

"Yes. Quite a few, actually," he responded. He inched closer to Judson. Judson recoiled slightly at the man's bad breath. "They're talking about a resolution for this. It might include bringing on volunteers."

"Oh, okay," said Judson. Liza sensed it was time to extricate themselves from the conversation.

"Honey, I have to use the bathroom." Liza paused and then whispered to her neighbor. *If you're gonna lie, make it a whopper*, she thought to herself. "We had Mexican food tonight, and I think it's hitting me."

"All right, guys," began Judson as he allowed Liza to pull him toward the house. "Nature calls, as they say. Um, Julian, I'll catch up with you tomorrow."

The block captain stood with his hands on his hips as he watched the Pryces move quickly toward their home. He shouted after them, "Count on it! I also need to get with another resident on the cul-de-sac after you!"

Judson waved his arm as they briskly walked up the sidewalk toward their front door. He mumbled to Liza, "Good luck with that."

She added, "We gotta warn the others. Toby and his people are moving way faster than I imagined."

SEVEN

Friday
Entrance Gatehouse
The Colony at Malibu

Tom Zelmanski closed his eyes, looked upward, and let out a deep exhale as he urinated on the side of Toby Davenport's house. After he emptied his bladder of the expensive scotch he'd consumed on top of the cheap stuff in his own bar, he zipped up his pants and leaned backward to glance into the bay windows of Toby's study. A smile came across his face.

Toby was pacing back and forth in front of his desk, running his fingers through his thinning hair. The stress was oozing out of the man's pores. He'd stop periodically to take a sip of whiskey before resuming his nervous pacing. This was exactly what Zelmanski had hoped for.

He'd been around Toby enough to know the man was weak, but power hungry. He used his status as HOA president like a bully pulpit. He wielded all the authority using the tools afforded him by the bylaws and restrictions.

Yet Zelmanski saw an opportunity with the collapse of the power grid. He'd compiled a massive binder with information on every household, from names and ages and occupations to social media posts. As he strode away from the Davenport home toward the entry gate, he patted himself on the back for never disclosing the magnitude of information to Toby. The universe had dropped a helluva sweet opportunity in Zelmanski's lap, and he planned on seizing the day.

His days of paying rent on an apartment were over. The car payments, which seemed to keep him in debt, were a thing of the past. He could kiss goodbye the California spousal support and the accompanying collection efforts that seemed to hound him. What had been laid before him was the opportunity to move into one of these multimillion-dollar homes. Perhaps a couple of new cars. Maybe even a new lady friend who was already single and needed protection. Or whose husband never made it home from a trip and was in need of comforting.

While Toby *the wimp* Davenport was wringing his hands, worrying about how to deal with his constituents, as he liked to call the residents of the Colony, Zelmanski was shopping for empty properties and any signs of weakness found within the information on residents he'd compiled.

While he was anxious to better his lot in life, he knew he had to secure the neighborhood from outsiders while identifying friends and foes within it. The one thing he didn't need was an invasion from beyond the gates, which appeared to be building as midnight approached.

He arrived at a scrum, of sorts, on the other side of the gate arms. His men were lined up like police who create a skirmish line in response to a riot. A war of words had ensued between travelers descending upon LA at the time the power grid went down and his security personnel, who were already exhausted from working twelve-plus hours. Not to mention they were shorthanded, as several of his crew had managed to leave to protect their families.

Zelmanski rested his hand on his pistol grip, allowing the sidearm and holster to protrude outside of his sweatshirt. Riot police had tools and weapons at their disposal to deal with crowds like this. Zelmanski wished he had rubber bullets, bean-bag rounds, pepper balls, or tear gas to send the interlopers on their way. However, he knew there would be another wave of refugees right behind them.

He knew Toby would have no idea how to address the problems of keeping the Colony secure. Zelmanski would do it his way. First, like any commander who needed to quarter an army, he had to give his people a place to live and food to eat. He had three levels of hierarchy in his security personnel. Himself, the top dog. Block captains with two gate captains, his close friends. Neighborhood patrols and gate sentries, hourly people with dubious backgrounds.

He would identify housing for each of them. Squatters had taken up residency throughout LA's affluent neighborhoods. Recently, a multimillion-dollar property in the Hollywood Hills had been overtaken by a group of squatters. The property, fully furnished and used as an Airbnb, had been on the market. The Realtor's lock box had been broken into and removed, giving the squatters easy access inside. The locks were changed, a fake lease was created, and utilities were transferred into the squatters' names. The lawsuit to disgorge the squatters took nine months to resolve. By then, the home had been abandoned and stripped of its luxury furnishings.

Once his men were comfortable with their new housing arrangements, he'd convince Toby to create a neighborhood pantry. The plan was to have the residents willingly contribute food and supplies to a communal stockpile. Then everyone would share and share alike. After he and his team got theirs first, of course.

As for companionship, he'd admonished his men not to force themselves on anyone. He'd cautioned them not to squander this opportunity to build a future out of disaster.

The former security-alarm salesman had a little more spring in his step as he made his way to the gates. His plan was solid. With a little manipulation, he'd be in the perfect position to profit off the fears of the Colony residents. But when an argument erupted, coupled with the sound of glass breaking at the gatehouse, he began to wonder if he and his people would make it through the night.

EIGHT

Friday
Entrance Gatehouse
The Colony at Malibu

"Stay back, or we'll shoot!" shouted the gate captain, who was standing on the hood of a BMW sedan. He was flashing the ultra-bright beam from his powerful Gearlight flashlight. The nine hundred thousand lumens temporarily blinded the people who were pushing against the fiberglass gate arms at the entrance to the Colony. Its brightness obscured the fact he was unarmed.

"When did this start?" asked Zelmanski as he hastily approached his men.

"They were milling around, and then all of a sudden, they got more ballsy. A couple of guys got mouthy with ours, and there was some shoving. The next thing we knew, there were dozens of them pushing forward, trying to get in."

Zelmanski knew he needed the residents to help with gate duty.

They were only a few hours into the collapse, and it was dark. Most of the residents remained in their homes with the doors locked. His block captains had had little success in recruiting help. And even then, the residents were relegated to walking their streets, looking for anyone who didn't belong in the neighborhood.

He surveilled the situation. The battery backup lighting provided plenty of illumination. It also enabled the refugees to see how few men were guarding the entrance. If they set their mind to it, they could overwhelm his people easily.

He checked his watch. Just past midnight. Six hours or so to sunup. Toby needed to see this. Zelmanski took one of the block captain's golf carts and drove up the hill to Toby's house as fast as the gas-powered Cushman would take him.

He drove across the front lawn, through a bed of pansies and primroses, and came to a skidding stop on the sidewalk near the front stoop.

Zelmanski announced himself by yelling, "Toby! It's Tom! I need you out here!" Without waiting for Toby to come to the door, Zelmanski began pounding on it.

A sleepy-eyed, half-drunk HOA president opened the door. His disheveled look told the whole story. The man had passed out in a chair or on the couch.

"Come on. You need to see this."

"See what?" Toby mumbled as he wiped the sawdust out of his eyes. "Wait, okay. Let me get my shoes."

"You don't need shoes. Let's go!"

Zelmanski used the same tactics with Toby as he'd used earlier. Bullying. Create a sense of urgency. Offer solutions so Toby would accept them.

"Okay, fine," said Toby as he half-stumbled down the steps. He slid onto the bench seat of the golf cart and held onto the roof's steel frame. "Go."

Zelmanski purposefully slammed the gas pedal to the floorboard, causing Toby's neck to snap backwards. When he approached the street curb, he slammed on the brakes, throwing Toby forward. This was followed by another mash of the gas. He glanced over at Toby to see he was about to vomit, an unintended consequence of Zelmanski's bullying behavior.

"What is all the yelling about?" Toby asked after he regained his composure.

"They want what you have, Toby," replied Zelmanski as he came to another abrupt stop near the gatehouse. "If you don't get me some help from the residents, our security people won't have enough to defend against these locusts."

Toby exited the golf cart and looked from right to left. The crowd was six or eight people deep. They were shouting and waving their arms, demanding food and water.

"It seems to me they're just hungry and thirsty. Cold and scared."

"Yeah. And there are tens of thousands just like 'em up and down the PCH."

Toby walked slowly to the left, wishing he'd ignored Zelmanski and grabbed a pair of shoes. It was too cool to go barefoot, but the shock to his system helped sober him up.

There was a group of neighbors standing adjacent to the wall where a pickup was parked to block access. They were Hispanic residents and were talking with a group of women holding children. Because they were speaking Spanish, he couldn't understand what they were saying, so he moved closer.

Just before he arrived, a child appeared from underneath the Ford F-150's bumper. And then another crawled through.

"Hey, what are you doing?" Toby shouted at the couple who were helping the kids to their feet.

"They're looking for a place to sleep. We have three extra bedrooms since our kids are off at college."

"No way!" shouted Zelmanski. "Send them back!"

"What do you mean? We will not send them back. They can stay at our home as our guests."

Zelmanski shoved his way past Toby. He was reaching for one of the children when a man scrambled out from under the pickup. He was cursing at Zelmanski in Spanish and then grabbed his arm to pull it away from the child. This caused Zelmanski to fall to one knee as the child ran to her father.

Zelmanski, still high from consuming half a bottle of scotch, jumped to his feet and pulled his handgun just as his gate captain swung the high-powered flashlight onto him. Any of the refugees with a view could see him pointing the gun at the man and child.

"Pistola! Pistola!"

The other child broke away from the resident and crawled back under the pickup. The man shielded his daughter from the taller Zelmanski, who was holding his weapon menacingly over their heads.

"Javy!" a woman screamed as she wailed in fear. She climbed onto the hood of the pickup and began to climb up the windshield.

Startled, Zelmanski swung his pistol toward her and fired without thinking. The single bullet sounded like cannon fire, and when it struck the back window of the truck, the glass exploded with a thunderous clap.

Panic and mayhem ensued. The man and child hit the ground, where they crawled to safety under the truck. The crowd immediately dispersed, running back toward the slowly moving caravan of cars that continued toward the city, dodging traffic as they sought the safety of the beach on the other side of the highway.

With a single gunshot, Zelmanski had cleared the threat from the Colony's gate. However, a new threat would arise, as the refugees' fear would turn to anger.

PART 2

"After midnight, we're gonna let it all hang down.
After midnight, we're gonna chug-a-lug and shout.
We're gonna stimulate some action.
We're gonna get some satisfaction."
~ J. J. Cale, American Songwriter, 1966

NINE

Saturday, After Midnight
Malibu Beach

On Malibu Beach, the bonfires were raging as the surf crashed ashore, both fueled by high winds sweeping across the coastline. Hundreds of stranded motorists milled about, commiserating over their fate. Some sat in stunned silence. Others traded conspiracy theories as to what had caused the power outages along the West Coast. Some argued with one another, as they wanted to find a boogieman. A person, or government, to blame for their woes. As Friday turned to Saturday, a collective groundswell of fear for their futures swept across the refugees.

Then they heard the gunshot. It was a single report from a large-caliber handgun that echoed in all directions, momentarily stifling the sound of the waves rushing onshore. In unison, their voices were muted as their minds tried to comprehend what they were certain they'd heard. Was it a gunshot? Was it the backfire of a vehicle's exhaust? Was it their imagination?

All of their questions were answered as dozens of people came rushing through the stalled cars and trucks onto the beach. Panicked women dragged their crying children. Men attempted to run backwards in an attempt to shield their loved ones from harm, only to stumble and fall through the dunes.

Mayhem ensued and rapidly spread for a quarter mile in either direction as the displaced refugees sought safety, fearful for their lives. Then their terror subsided when the shooting didn't continue. With trepidation, they returned to their part of the beach. Next to their bonfire. Near their belongings. The only home they had, for the moment.

That was when they learned what had happened. Across the highway from the beach, the evening before, the millionaires had looked down upon them from their spacious properties. The poor and downtrodden, forced to abandon their homes, could only dream of such a lavish lifestyle. And now, to make matters worse, they were shooting at them.

A family from Eureka Valley in Central San Francisco had been caught in the crosshairs. Their children were cold and tired. They simply wanted a place for the kids to sleep until daybreak, when they promised they'd move along. That was when the guards of the fancy neighborhood tried to kill their mother and father, so the story began.

Like any tale, as it was told and retold, it grew in magnitude and scope. What began as an inadvertent, wildly-off-the-mark gunshot turned into patrolling guards with automatic weapons attempting to kill people with brown skin.

Fear turned to anger.

More and more men descended upon the beach directly opposite the gated entry to the Colony. They passed their liquor. They smoked their weed. They stoked the fires of hate by directing their ire at the residents of the Colony.

Anger turned to fury.

One man's ill-advised attempt to frighten away intruders to the neighborhood coupled with his poor handling of a firearm had created a mob who were now plotting their revenge. They would teach the rich a lesson. They would show them what pain and suffering looked like. They would take what they wanted. They would protect their own.

Ironically, the family directly affected by the confrontation wanted nothing to do with the vigilante justice the other men wanted to obtain. Javy tried to calm the men. He explained that they, the refugees, should not become monsters in order to fight monsters. There was still law enforcement to handle such matters, he presumed. Cooler heads should prevail, and the entire incident should be forgotten.

Where was the fun in that? An actual question asked by a young man from Portland. He hated fascists, and he was certain the Colony was full of them. He was ready to extract his pound of flesh.

Sometimes, evil meets opportunity. It was happening behind the gates as well as beyond them.

TEN

Saturday
Dean and Emmy's Home
The Colony at Malibu

"There's no way I can sleep," said Emmy, who emerged on the upper deck to join Dean. She wrapped her arms around his waist and cuddled him from behind. She could feel the tension in his body. The collapse of the power grid was the culmination of a really bad week or so for the couple and their friends.

First, there had been the attack on Pepperdine by the gunman who'd carried out a crime of passion by killing his ex-girlfriend and then himself outside Dean's classroom. Dean had carried a weapon in violation of school policy and had been prepared to use it to protect his students. He had been suspended for his good intentions.

Then, in an ongoing trend of lawlessness in LA, Emmy had been the victim of an attempted carjacking. She'd barely escaped and then scrambled for cover as the would-be carjackers had engaged in a shoot-out with undercover detectives.

Finally, in an attempt to help their Friday Night Club group of friends, Judson and Lee had become embroiled in a federal investigation of a local Republican party executive.

All of that paled in comparison to their worst fears being realized. They felt it coming. She'd described Dean and Grayson's belief that they, and the country, were in grave danger as an intuitive power. A sixth sense inexplicable to others, but clear as day to the guys who were attuned to geopolitical affairs and the gradual collapse of America.

Grayson had once casually stated the most likely peril they'd face if the power grid were to go down for an extended period of time would not be starvation. Rather, the greatest threat was their fellow man. After her experience during the carjacking attempt, Emmy feared he was right.

Now, here they stood together on their upper deck, where barely eight hours ago, the group had shared drinks and appetizers as they contemplated their futures. Instead of sleeping in their bed, they were staring into the darkness of the Colony and wondering what would happen next.

"I get it," mumbled Dean as he turned to kiss his wife on the cheek. He pulled her to his side and squeezed her waist. He would never admit to her how afraid he was. He had to wear a cloak of confidence and strength. While he was alone, he focused his senses on sounds. Once, he thought he heard a rustle in the bushes in front of the vacant house to their left. He almost went to check on it but opted to stay at his post.

Earlier, he and Emmy had barricaded the back of the house the best they could. There were four sets of patio doors leading from their home into the backyard, where a lagoon-shaped pool was located. They'd built a spa-like oasis to unwind from their busy days. Now it had become a point of weakness where intruders could easily break in and attack them.

He debated whether he should patrol the upstairs Juliette balcony located at the second-floor landing as opposed to the upper deck overlooking the front of the house. For a while, they both stood watch on opposite sides of the sprawling structure. After an hour or so, Dean begged Emmy to get some sleep. She tried, but it was impossible to turn her brain off.

The two-way radio squawked to life, startling them both. Emmy jumped a little, and Dean hastily fumbled for the Midland, which he'd attached to his jeans' waistband. It was Judson, who was checking in at the top of the hour as agreed.

Earlier, Judson had made his way to Lee's house and then to the upper deck to relay what he'd learned from the conversation with the block captain of his street. Grayson had gone over as well and soaked in the information. None of them were surprised by the revelation. They'd seen Toby's demeanor change as he began to seize control over the neighbors by using the recent events to frighten them. "Fear is a great motivator," Dean had reminded the group, to which Emmy had replied, "Stubbornness is the antidote for Toby's overreach. We don't have to participate in his games if we don't want to."

After they'd all heard the single gunshot coming from the entry gates, they became keenly aware that either Zelmanski and his men were armed, or the streams of refugees included armed criminals. Or both. For that reason, no member of the Friday Night Club found sleep that evening.

Emmy pulled away and walked along the railing overlooking the cul-de-sac. She laughed to herself as she realized she never looked down into their yard or driveway. Although it was dark, their solar-powered landscape lighting provided some illumination even at three in the morning. Whenever they were on the deck, their focus of attention was usually on the beach and the vast Pacific Ocean beyond. The view was mesmerizing as the human mind tried to comprehend the immeasurable size of the ocean. She rolled her neck on her shoulders and arched her back to shake away the stiffness caused by stress. She returned to her husband's side.

"Dean, I have to ask you a question, and I hope you'll be honest with me."

"Yeah, of course."

"Truthfully, when you and Grayson talked about stuff like this in the past, usually with Judson chiming in, I wasn't totally interested. You know? Of course, I love when you tell me about your lecture topics and the feedback you get from the students. I just looked at all of that stuff as out of my control. If there was nothing I could do about it, then why let it invade my already overcrowded brain?"

"You're not alone," Dean said as he turned his attention completely to his wife. After the events of the last couple of weeks, they'd had several serious, intimate conversations about whether they were placing too much emphasis on preparing for something that might never happen. Now that they were living in the throes of collapse, it was logical their lives would be focused on survival rather than the stresses of their jobs, such as they were.

He continued, "I've seen studies that only a few percent of the population can effectively multitask. Our brains are simply not wired to focus on more than one thing at a time. At least, we can't do it well.

"I had this conversation with my students when I busted one browsing their Instagram account during one of my lectures. I quizzed her on the basics of what I was discussing that day, and she failed miserably.

"Here's what I learned from my personal experience and a little research online. The problem is that excessive focus exhausts the focus circuits in your brain. It can drain your energy and make you lose self-control. This energy drain can also make you more impulsive and less deliberate. As a result, decisions are poorly thought out."

Emmy nodded. She glanced toward Grayson's home and then to their street as she spoke. "When we were hustling around buying stuff to get ready for this crappy situation, I didn't think about the why. I was merely using logic. I thought about how we started our day. What did we do in the bathroom? What did we eat for our meals? What did we need to clean on a daily or weekly basis? Then I bought plenty for everybody.

"Now our shopping is over. I, um, we don't have jobs anymore. There are no social events with the studio. No basketball games at Firestone Fieldhouse. No planned afternoons at the beach. All I can think about is what might happen to us next or how much food we can eat each day before we run out. It's pretty damn gloomy, to be honest."

Dean sighed. "It's certainly not what we ever imagined our life looking like."

"Honey, that's my point. Somehow, you and Grayson imagined it. You guys stopped talking about a collapse as hypothetical. It was if you *knew*."

"I wish I could explain it, Emmy. I can't."

"Well, I said all of that to ask this. I know you. You understand all the policy and politics of it. You can identify the unintended consequences of politicians' otherwise good intentions. It's fascinating to me, and I love you for it.

"But Grayson is different. He's always kinda been an enigma to me. Because you love him like a brother and I admire your relationship, I've never pressed either of you about his background or career. I'm not like the rest of these nosy people who intrude on somebody's life by searching their name on Google. I always thought that was rude and invasive."

"I have to admit, we're seeing a different side of Grayson. It's crazy how he has an answer for everything. When we began talking about getting prepared, he never had to hesitate to propose a solution or a plan of action."

"I know," said Emmy a little too loudly. She brought her voice down to just above a whisper. "He has friends with guns. Lots of guns of the exact same type to give to us. I mean, even Lee couldn't pull that off."

"Yeah, that kinda surprised me, too. That said, I appreciate what he was able to do, so I didn't press him."

Emmy asked, "And who has a satellite telephone? One that has a military base or officer on speed dial."

"It's a friend of his in Georgia," interjected Dean.

Emmy became animated as she spoke. She began to use her hands and arms to make her points. "Who has friends like that? Friends who can equip us with an arsenal and ammo. And a satellite phone. Maybe even intelligence to find out what the hell is going on."

Dean laughed and reached out to gently grasp her hands. "Um, the guy next door? He probably has an OnlyFans account to tease all the suburban housewives."

Emmy furrowed her brow and scowled at Dean. She didn't like him teasing her right now, so she threw it back at him. "I'd pay. You know he's a hunk. Admit it."

Dean stammered as he spoke. "Huh? No, Emmy. He doesn't, um. Maybe? Listen, at least I don't think so."

She playfully slugged him. "See what I'm saying. He's an enigma, I'm telling ya."

Dean laughed and stared across the darkened homes between them and the PCH. "Well, he's our enigma."

ELEVEN

Saturday
Entrance Gatehouse
The Colony at Malibu

Zelmanski, the gate captain, and one of his friends whom he'd hired to be a block captain were sitting around the gatehouse, drinking bourbon. They were his closest confidants and also the highest paid of his men. After the adrenaline rush wore off from the chaos created by his firing his weapon at the family trying to enter the neighborhood, they found an opportunity to relax. None of the refugees dared approach the entrance to the Colony, as apparently word had spread that the security guards meant business when they ordered people to stay away.

Zelmanski laid out his plan for his friends and the rest of his crew. The three men had already identified the homes they planned to commandeer as well as a few of the neighborhood women they planned to approach.

The conversation then turned to the residents who had been uncooperative or otherwise unresponsive. While Zelmanski had never shared the contents of his research binders with anyone, including his most trusted allies, he shared some of what he knew with these two men, as he needed them to do his dirty work if necessary.

"We've got this group of four families who apparently get together every Friday night," began the block captain. "The professor and his wife, the actress, have shucked and jived every time I see them. In fact, this weekend I was gonna put the full-court press on them and their next-door neighbor, Grayson McCall."

The gate captain asked, "Whadya know about him, boss? He never comes through the visitors' gate. His schedule isn't regular. When I can get a look at him, he has a serious scowl across his face."

"Angry?" asked the block captain.

"Nah, more like deep in thought."

"Dude's wound too tight," said the block captain, drawing a laugh from his boss.

Zelmanski had been intrigued by Grayson as well. "There was absolutely nothing about him on the internet. No social media. No LinkedIn. Nothing job related. No criminal record. No marriage, in Cali at least. It was as if his name had been made up completely. Except he did show up as the record owner of his home. A home with no mortgage. Ever. Paid over a million dollars in cash fifteen years ago, I think."

The block captain turned on the swivel chair to address the gate captain. "Has he had any visitors?"

"Not since I've been here. I even searched the archived logs. Nobody. Not even freakin' Uber Eats."

Zelmanski asked, "What about women? Or, hell, men? Have you ever seen him bring somebody into the neighborhood in his car?"

"Nope. Nada."

Zelmanski stood to stretch. He'd had plenty to drink and really felt like he needed sleep. With the activity at the gate stopping an hour or so ago, he felt like he could slip away to catch a few hours' sleep.

"Can you guys hold down the fort?" he asked.

His men eagerly said yes. Zelmanski adjusted his pants and repositioned his holstered weapon. He straightened his back and imagined himself wearing a holster with pistols on both sides. A grin came across his face as he fashioned himself the new sheriff in town.

He opened the door leading to the residents' exit lane when suddenly a baseball-sized stone crashed through the door's window, throwing shards of glass across his back. Seconds later, he was pelted with rocks, and the screams of banshees sent chills up his spine.

Zelmanski fell to the ground and began crawling back into the gatehouse. He screamed as a piece of glass embedded in the palm of his right hand. Pain shot into his arm as he tried to shake it out.

Gunshots rang out as one of his men began firing. Someone beyond the gates fired a shotgun. The enormous boom the weapon made was unmistakable. This sent a shock wave through his nervous system, as none of his men had a shotgun.

"What the hell is going on?" he asked his two captains. Neither responded. They'd left through the other side of the gatehouse. Zelmanski was alone.

He found a roll of paper towels and unfurled it to create a bandage for his injured hand. The blood soaked it in seconds, and the stinging sensation made him wince.

BOOM!

Another shotgun blast rocked the building. Shotgun pellets smacked the side and cracked the glass overlooking the highway. Zelmanski was too afraid to rise to see what was happening. He crawled toward the open door with a view of the entry gate.

Two shots were fired by his man. There was screaming. Not in pain or agony. But angry. Defiant. Like a group leading a charge.

And charge they did.

"Come on!" shouted the young man from Portland, Oregon. "They can't shoot us all."

He was right. The guards were overwhelmed. Afraid for their lives, they made their way near the gatehouse, standing aside as several dozen men ran over and through the blockade of vehicles. They didn't stop to engage the cowering guards. Instead, they raced into the darkened streets of the Colony, carrying rocks and sticks and balled-up fists.

Zelmanski stood and forced his way past one of his men blocking the exit of the gatehouse. He had his pistol drawn. He aimed at the man who'd claimed they couldn't shoot them all. Zelmanski plugged him in the back, throwing his body forward onto the pavement.

"We shot you, asshole," Zelmanski mumbled under his breath. He'd killed without hesitation or remorse. In fact, he was emboldened by it. Oddly, it felt good. Empowering. He used his newfound chutzpah to issue orders to his men.

"Get them!" he demanded. However, nobody made a move. "Let's go, people! Are ya gonna let 'em run loose in the neighborhood?"

His aggravation with his men made him forget the flesh wound caused by the shard of glass. Zelmanski drew his pistol and began waving wildly in all directions.

"Tom, we aren't armed. Remember Davenport's rules."

"Well, he is!" shouted Zelmanski as he pointed at the lone guard, who was carrying a Glock nine-millimeter handgun. "I've got more at the house. First, nobody else gets through. Understand? Shoot 'em. Beat 'em. I don't care."

"Okay," said the man who was armed.

Zelmanski continued to bark his orders. "Second, we need to round up those who got through and get 'em out of here. Hurry, follow me to my condo. We're gonna track them down and take them out, even if they're in body bags."

"Should we call the cops?" asked one poor soul, who immediately regretted asking the question.

"We are the damn cops!" Zelmanski screamed in response in anger.

Zelmanski began jogging toward the condo complex, which was immediately adjacent to the Colony's entrance. Several men followed while others remained at the gate. He'd planned on arming his guys over Toby's objection. It was difficult to purchase weapons in California without raising eyebrows, so he'd made his purchases in Las Vegas during his frequent gambling trips. He'd purchased only nine-millimeter handguns because they used the same ammunition that could be shared by his crew. There were more weapons on his wish list, but he'd never had the opportunity to make the purchases before everything fell apart.

It was yet another reason to pressure the homeowners to reveal what weapons they owned. Then, for the good of the neighborhood, turn them over to the security team, who would then defend them. This jailbreak into the neighborhood would bolster his argument unless it got him fired and banished from the Colony.

TWELVE

Saturday
Dean and Emmy's Home
The Colony at Malibu

Grayson had been pacing the floor, annoyed that his contacts at U.S. Cyber Command at Fort Eisenhower in Augusta, Georgia, hadn't responded to his phone calls. Even his superiors were maintaining radio silence. Being in the dark, literally and figuratively, was not something he was accustomed to. He relied upon contacts through all levels of government for information. This was beyond belief that he'd be ignored.

The quiet of the evening was disconcerting. After hearing the gunshot around midnight, he'd been on edge, as he sensed something was coming. He desperately wanted to stroll down to the entry gates to see how Zelmanski and his guards were keeping people out of the neighborhood.

Traffic had come to a complete standstill, and vehicles heading into LA had taken up every lane in both directions, the turn lanes, and the medians. It looked like a twenty-four-car pileup at the Daytona 500. The inability to make progress resulted in drivers shutting off their engines, turning off the headlights, and abandoning their vehicles.

All the pedestrian traffic was sure to create headaches for the gate personnel. Food, water, a place to pee. The basic necessities were not available to the refugees. Undoubtedly, they asked for all of the above as they passed the Colony's entry gates.

Grayson was wearing his dark camo cargo pants and a long-sleeve black tee shirt. While he didn't have any intention of roaming around the neighborhood in stealthy apparel, he had to be ready for every eventuality. Readiness was his thing, always had been. His father had been a legendary member of the Task Group Taji X Quick Response Force stationed in Iraq. He'd instilled the concept of readiness in the minds of the Australian Army Soldiers he'd trained while he was embedded with them. He'd taught Grayson the same values.

He put on his utility belt, holstered his weapon, and counted his magazines for the third time that night. He knew the importance of ammo discipline and maintaining a count. When Grayson engaged in a firefight, even with multiple hostiles, he was adept at keeping up with the number of shots he fired as well as the number fired by the enemy. It had saved his life on more than one occasion.

After the group checked in via two-way at the top of the hour, he radioed Dean to ask if he could come over. He wanted to discuss what they'd learned from Judson about Zelmanski's plans. They were talking quietly on the upper deck when the shooting at the front began.

The menacing screams of the people storming the entry gate could easily be heard due to the dead silence of the night. Then the gunfire began.

Grayson's body stiffened. He tilted his head slightly to assess what was happening. "They're returning fire! That was a shotgun."

Lee's eerily calm voice over their radios added to the tenseness of the moment. "Guys, we've got trouble coming. From what I can see through this scope, the entry gate's been breached, and people are rushing up the main street."

"How many?" asked Dean over the radio.

"Too many to count." As he spoke, during the brief moment that he released the mic, another single gunshot rang out, followed by shrieks and cursing.

"How close are they?" Judson's voice revealed his apprehension.

Lee's next transmission was frantic. "Gotta go. Running through the yards on our street, checking doors. Judson, comin' your way, too!"

Both of their radios fell silent as they focused on the threats approaching their homes.

Dean turned to his friend. "Grayson, Lee can handle himself. Judson and Liza are not ready for something like this."

Grayson briskly walked back and forth along the upper deck, debating what to do. He couldn't be several places at once. Suddenly, Grayson turned as the sound of an automatic weapon unleashed a barrage of bullets at its intended target.

"Dammit! That'd better be Lee. If not, we've got trouble." He reached for his utility belt and yanked the satellite phone free. He handed it to Dean.

"What do you want me to do with this?"

Grayson put his hand on his shoulder and spoke in a low voice. "Listen to me. If it rings, answer it and simply say *reckless flame*. Nothing else."

"Reckless flame," Dean confirmed. "Nothing else. Just listen."

"Correct. This is important, Dean. Okay?"

"Yeah. What are you gonna do?"

"Help our friends."

THIRTEEN

Saturday
Lee and Nicole's House
The Colony at Malibu

Lee, who'd led many arrest-warrant raids on drug dealers, oftentimes requiring forced entry followed by a gun battle, tried to maintain his cool under pressure. Although, flushing out criminals was far different from defending his home against them. As soon as they'd observed the dozens of people racing past the entry gate, preceded by the gunshots, he and Nicole met at the top of their stairs on the landing overlooking the entry foyer.

"Nicole, you stay upstairs. Bounce back and forth between the bedroom deck and the front window. You'll be able to cover the front and back, but I need you to focus on the back. Also, if they bust through the front door, you'll have the upper ground."

"Okay," said Nicole, her voice weak with apprehension. She cleared her throat and repeated herself. "Okay. Do I shoot at them?"

"Absolutely. Without hesitation. I don't care if you hit them or not. I don't know what we're dealing with here, but if they know we're armed, they'll move on to a softer target."

She nodded and hugged her husband. "Please be careful."

Lee couldn't make any promises, so he continued giving her instructions. "If they try to break in, don't hesitate. If they just run around the yard or something, leave them be. If they are armed, we don't want to invite their return fire."

She nodded. He broke their embrace and rushed down the stairs, the AR-10 in one arm and his hand grasping the handrail with the other as he took the steps two at a time. He wanted to create a cross-fire scenario that would pin down any would-be intruders. Above the family's three-car garage was a bonus room that they'd converted into an adult playroom complete with a bar, pool table, plus old-school arcade games like pinball and *Galaga*. He even had a slot machine they'd purchased on a weekend trip to Las Vegas.

The bonus room had Juliette balconies on both the side yard adjacent to the neighbor and on the opposite side overlooking the front yard. He could guard against anyone approaching from the rear as well as the front.

Lee rushed through the kitchen and into the garage, where a spiral staircase led upstairs. The bonus room was dark except for the faint glow emitted by a battery-powered smoke detector's LED light. He never understood the purpose of the LED light, but now he was thankful it was there.

He opened the doors on both sides of the garage's second story and checked his surroundings. Loud voices could be heard throughout the neighborhood, primarily in Spanish. Lee understood a few basic phrases, mainly commands, that he used in his law enforcement duties. Nicole was fluent in Spanish, a necessity in her former line of work. A prior life during which she'd witnessed incomprehensible violence both before and after the couple had met.

Lee was leaning over the side balcony when he saw a group of men marching through the middle of the street. One was carrying a shotgun while two others had tire irons. On both sides of the three men, children, maybe in their early teens, were running to the front doors of the homes at the entrance to the cul-de-sac. They were trying the doorknobs in an attempt to get in. While the men waited in the street, the teens ran around the side of the house, ostensibly trying other points of entry.

Lee was puzzled as to why the men didn't break into the homes that were, at first glance, unoccupied. His only thought was the homes became larger and more opulent the deeper they got into the cul-de-sac. In fact, Justin and Liza, who'd lived in the neighborhood for many years, had one of the larger homes. Lee imagined it would be a prized target for the thugs who'd invaded the Colony.

The men passed the first couple of houses until they arrived in front of theirs. Lee rushed to the other side of the bonus room and readied the AR-10. He kept his body within the shadows to avoid the ambient light the moon provided that night. He hoped the men didn't notice the open patio doors directly above the driveway.

The boys were instructed to check the front door. They ran up the steps and turned the handle. Lee scowled, and his mouth fell open.

"Shit!" he whispered loudly. They'd barricaded the door with a China hutch and a settee. However, they'd forgotten to lock the door. He shouted at himself in his mind. *Idiot! Freakin' idiot!*

"*Está abierto!*" the taller boy shouted in Spanish. *It's open.*

"*Vamos!*" the man carrying the shotgun responded. Suddenly, he and the two tire-iron-wielding men rushed toward the house. The boys began to push against the door, using their shoulders to move the furniture blockade.

Lee was debating within himself. In those precious seconds during which the men advanced on their home, with Nicole likely frightened inside, he had to make a decision whether to kill them. Inexplicably, and for reasons he was never able to explain, the law enforcement officer chose to warn them off.

He released a barrage of bullets that stitched the front lawn and tore into the concrete sidewalk leading to their porch. The dozen or so rounds from the powerful automatic rifle ripped up the turf halfway between the approaching adults and the two teens shoving their shoulders against the door.

"Go!" he bellowed at the group.

He pointed the rifle directly at the man holding the shotgun. The two locked eyes for a moment. Without saying a word, the man bolted for the shrubbery of the neighboring yard. The other two adults were frozen momentarily. Their eyes darted between Lee and the two teens on the front porch. Lee immediately detected a connection between them.

"*Andale!*" The man's excited voice forced the boys into action. They tried to jump off the front porch, skipping the stairs. They both landed hard in the landscape beds, face-planting in the pea gravel base. It didn't slow their escape, however. They quickly regained their footing and ran toward the next-door neighbor's house, passing the adults in the process.

Lee returned to the side yard balcony. He looked through the scope of the rifle to see in the distance. People were running from their homes on the main street rising up the ridge into the neighborhood, while others were looting the abandoned properties. Gunfire was sporadic, other than what he'd unleashed.

He took a chance and hurried down the spiral staircase. He slowly opened the door from the garage into the utility room. He was certain Nicole was nervous, so he called out her name.

"Nicole! Are you okay? Those men left."

Out of habit, he tried to flip the switches in the kitchen. In the tense situation, it was easy to forget the power grid was down. She hadn't responded. Was she on a balcony? Had someone broken through the back door while he was distracted at the front? He shouted for her again.

"Nicole? They're gone!"

He passed through the kitchen and entered the hallway leading to the foyer. Enough light emanated into the space from above for him to see his statuesque wife. She was standing tall, body rigid, with both arms extended.

He slowly approached her. "Babe, it's me. They left."

She didn't respond.

Lee shouldered his rifle and cautiously approached her. When he was barely a few feet away, he heard a scraping sound coming from the front door.

Nicole began firing both handguns, stopping just short of a full-blown mag dump. The bullets ripped through the solid wood door and struck a body outside. It fell against the door, its arm stuck in the crack pried open by the teens.

Lee cursed himself for leaving his post. He ran up the stairs to the upstairs balcony overlooking the front yard. There was no sign of anyone except for a woman running away, sprinting across the yard into the street to avoid being killed.

FOURTEEN

Saturday
Grayson's House
The Colony at Malibu

Grayson turned toward the door, where Emmy was standing against the wall. She was cradling a rifle in her arms. Her eyes were wide as she stared at Grayson. He leaned into her and spoke softly, "You're playing a role, Emmy. Just act."

She nodded and whispered in response, "Thank you."

Less than a minute later, Grayson had entered his home through a side door leading to his garage. He rushed into the house and toward a closet door located inside the pantry. Earlier, he'd cleared it of boxes of toilet paper, bleach, and water that had been stacked to the ceiling. With his right hand, he pressed the wall, which responded with a clicking sound before it moved open like a large cabinet door.

Grayson stepped inside a small room, which became illuminated after sensing his motion. Inside were the tools of his trade and his own savings bank. He approached a gun safe. He pressed a panel on the wall next to the handle of the safe, revealing a biometric keyboard. He punched in a four-digit-code representing his father's birthday, and a green light illuminated. Next to the keyboard was a glass reader awaiting his index finger to be pressed against it. A second light illuminated. A series of clicks occurred as the gun safe opened.

He had all the tools for modern warfare, including some experimental weapons that he'd been asked to test for the military. He never imagined he'd have to break open the safe, especially this early in the collapse. He and Dean had discussed how close society was to falling apart.

Grayson shook his head and vocalized his disbelief. "But come on, people. We're only eight hours into this thing."

He put on his tactical vest and filled the pocket with magazines for his AR-10. The powerful NATO 7.62 cartridges packed a punch not likely to be matched on the streets. He hadn't hesitated to provide Lee his other AR-10. He was the only member of the group who had the capability of handling its power.

In less than two minutes, Grayson was fully equipped and out the side door after securing his secret vault. Sporadic gunfire could be heard around the neighborhood, including the unmistakable gunfire from Lee's rifle. Grayson ran at a low crouch down the street and then darted between houses, following the same path the group had used earlier.

"I've got people shooting out our glass," said Judson over the radio. Grayson heard several gunshots coming from the cul-de-sac at the Pryces' home.

He had to be careful to avoid friendly fire. He imagined that Judson and Liza were shooting at anything that moved. He wished he'd had more time to work with them, but the collapse had happened so suddenly.

Grayson had to act quickly to help the Pryces. Without hesitation, he entered a clearing in the yards, where he was rudely greeted by the attackers.

FIFTEEN

Saturday
Judson and Liza's House
The Colony at Malibu

"Judson! I saw two boys running into Nicole's front yard. There were three men standing in the street. They just walked toward their house." Liza, who'd opted to watch through the upstairs windows of their home, had been hustling from room to room since they'd first heard gunfire coming from the front gate. From their home's location at the end of the cul-de-sac, they were only able to have an unobstructed view of the street. Even their backyard was set against the base of the cliff and was bordered by the neighborhood's block and stucco wall capped with Mediterranean-style roofing tiles.

Moments earlier, Lee had warned the group that the men were on their street. Judson had fallen complacent after hours of inactivity. Now he found himself panicked, as he and Liza had not expected something like this to occur. At least not so soon, anyway.

They'd taken steps to block their doors to deter the entry of any attackers. Their home, however, was full of windows. *Bring the outside in,* the architect had said when they were designing their home. *Yes, bright and airy,* Liza had commented during their design meetings. She never imagined those many years ago that all of these beautiful, tall windows that created that open feeling would become a target for what was about to happen.

She and Judson didn't have the experience Lee had in dealing with the criminal element. Although Judson had been accused of engaging with a political criminal, men with guns approaching under the cover of darkness were totally different. What was worse, the types of television programming and movies they watched were rarely Action Jackson, shoot-'em-up movies, as Judson liked to call them. He and Liza couldn't even emulate what was portrayed on-screen.

"I see somebody!" Judson shouted to his wife. "Two men just came across our neighbor's yard and into the street. Wait! There's a third man. They're hiding behind the front of our neighbor's Expedition."

Judson had taken the lower level. He was wandering throughout the downstairs, checking their pie-shaped lot. The Pryces took pride in their pristine lawn. The flower beds were kept to knee-depth. It was their lawn that they admired the most. As Nicole once said, it was the envy of all their neighbors, quipping that it appeared their landscape crew crawled around and clipped every blade of glass with scissors.

On this night, it provided no cover for the teen boys who were sent to their front door. Judson, who was on edge, didn't wait until they reached the stoop. He forced open a window and began firing his pistol at them. He struck one of the boys in the arm, spinning him around until he landed in the cool grass.

"Arrrggghhh!" the boy screamed in pain. The taller boy helped the youngster to his feet, and they began running down the street.

Liza had opened an upstairs window and fired at them, missing wildly as her weapon's recoil caused the bullets to sail high over their heads.

Judson shouted up the stairs, "They're leaving, Liza! Let 'em go!"

"You shot one of them!" she shouted back.

"I know! I didn't mean to. It was just supposed to be a warning—" The rest of his words were muted by the blast of a shotgun, followed by glass shattering in their dining room.

"*El cabrón!*" a man growled loudly. He racked another round into his shotgun and fired at the upper level of their home. The glass in the couple's bedroom was obliterated.

"Leave us alone!" shouted Liza, who fired back toward the street. She had no idea where the shooter was. She simply wanted to retaliate. She gave away her position, earning another shotgun blast that pelted the side of their house and broke out the upper panes in the living room windows below her.

It was Judson's turn to return fire. He'd caught a glimpse of a shadow near the parked SUV. His bullets ricocheted off the fenders and back hatch door.

"They're running away!" exclaimed Liza victoriously. Then her voice changed to alarm. "Duck!"

The shooter broke cover and unleashed two successive blasts, both of which blew out windows in the Pryces' home. Pieces of glass rained down upon the couple, stinging them with small cuts in their skin. With his weapon held at his hip, he racked another round and prepared to shoot again.

BOOM!

Another explosive blast from the shotgun shook them to their core. Only this time, the shooter wasn't directing the attack at them. Oddly, Judson thought, the neighbor's shrubbery appeared to be his next target.

Then a powerful rifle entered the fray.

First, there was a short burst of bullets. Seconds later, a longer volley exploded into the night, finding its target. They heard a man groaning in the distance, followed by footsteps running down the street.

"Liza, are you okay?"

"Yeah. I got hit with glass, but I'm okay. Where are you?"

Judson's heavy footsteps pounded the marble staircase leading to the second-floor landing.

"Here," she replied softly. Liza met him at the top of the stairs, their bodies crashing together in a comforting embrace. Tears streamed down her face as the fear subsided and the reality of being close to death overwhelmed her. She was both thankful for being safe with Judson and worrisome that it wasn't over.

Lee's voice could be heard over the two-way radio, which was downstairs.

"They're leaving!" His voice reflected his excitement. "I see people running down the streets toward the gate."

Judson kissed his wife's tear-filled cheeks. "Let me find the radio. I'll check in."

"Let me come with you," she began but stopped herself. *Take nothing for granted*, she told herself. "No. I'll keep watching. You never know."

In that moment, a change came over Liza. She refused to be a victim. She knew there was evil outside their home. They were entering a phase of their lives, unexpectedly, where they had to fear being killed by everyone they met. It would require nerves of steel she wasn't sure she possessed but was certain she could acquire.

SIXTEEN

Saturday
Dean and Emmy's Home
The Colony at Malibu

BOOM!

The shooter was crouched behind an SUV and racking another round before randomly blasting the buckshot into the windows of the Pryce home.

He heard the distinctive sound of the shooter loading another shell to fire upon his friends again. The man must've caught a glimpse of movement when Grayson slipped into the landscape. Grayson ducked as the shotgun blast came from across the street, barely fifty yards from where he was moving through the yard.

Grayson didn't hesitate. He broke cover and entered the cul-de-sac. With the confidence of a trained operative, he kept his sights trained on the shooter and another man who stood by his side. He squeezed the trigger, firing off a short burst of four to six rounds at first. The windows of the vehicle were obliterated, and the left front tire exploded as a round struck its sidewall.

The man was not hit. He turned and fired the shotgun wildly, peppering the trees behind Grayson. His lack of control of the shotgun caused him to lose his balance. Grayson let loose another, longer burst. Each of the five bullets riddled the shooter's body, killing him instantly.

His partner, fearing for his life, was screaming, "Don't shoot," with his hands held high in the air as he turned and ran away. The man was unarmed, so Grayson let him go. Lee, however, could not.

Using his pistol, he fired several shots at the man as he raced down the sidewalk in front of their home. Bullets ricocheted off the concrete, throwing sparks into the air. The attacker was running like the wind as he reached the street corner. So fast that he tripped over his feet. He tumbled over and over until his body hit the concrete curb on the other side of the street.

Quiet consumed the neighborhood now. Grayson keyed the mic attached to his vest near his shoulder. "Everyone check in."

Dean was first, followed by Lee. After Lee responded, Grayson instructed him to secure the entrance to the cul-de-sac, which Lee acknowledged.

Grayson slowly backed out of the street, his eyes roving in all directions in search of potential targets. Judson had not responded. Grayson glanced over at the front of their home, which looked like Swiss cheese. There were gaping holes in the walls, and the windows were completely obliterated. Even the front door had been hit by the double-aught buckshot.

"Check in, please."

A meek voice responded. It was Liza. "Um, he's okay. We're okay."

Grayson managed a smile as he eased into the dark shadows of their neighbor's house. He kept his weapon ready as Nicole rushed out their front door toward the Pryces'. Lee confirmed the threat was over and raced down the cul-de-sac. He stopped to check the shooter, kicking the dead man in the thigh before following Nicole toward the Pryces' to check on them.

Once again, Grayson, the sheepdog, wanted to protect everyone, not just his close friends. However, with the amount of sporadic gunfire he'd heard in the last hour coupled with Zelmanski's merry men roaming about, possibly armed and nervous, he didn't want to become an unwilling victim of friendly fire.

He hustled back to his house, checking every entryway and possible hiding place as he did. However, because he wasn't certain the threat was over, he kept his gear and weapons intact. He shouted out to Dean, a heads-up that he was coming toward the house.

"Hey! I'm headed your way."

"I'll cover you," Dean shouted back.

Grayson's eyes grew wide as he shook his head. *Um, no thanks, pal.* "No, don't! I'm fine." He didn't want his best friend to shoot him either.

Several minutes later, after Emmy fixed the guys a drink, the three gathered on the upper deck as the first signs of dawn appeared on the ridge behind them. Dean was anxious to speak with Grayson.

He handed him the satellite phone. "A call came through. Just about the time you were firing in the cul-de-sac."

Grayson set his drink on the railing and turned to Dean. "What did he say?"

"Winter Wonderland. Omaha."

"You've got to be kidding me," said Grayson as he pounded his fist on the top of the railing. His glass of whiskey hopped slightly under the pressure he'd exerted. He quickly grabbed the glass and downed it.

"What does it mean?" asked Emmy.

"Winter Wonderland is the generally accepted code phrase for a domestic false flag, and Omaha means the code words are being changed daily because there are trust issues within the government."

"What?" Emmy was genuinely confused. "False flag? What kind of trust issues?"

Grayson and Dean stared at one another. Grayson was shaking his head in disbelief. "You wanna take that one, Professor Winchester?"

"Emmy, a false-flag operation can take many forms, but typically it's a covert governmental action designed to deceive the public into thinking some other entity or government is responsible. They want the finger of blame pointed elsewhere."

She was still confused. She directed her questions to Grayson. "What's the point? And what, um, what are you saying?"

Once again, it was Dean who responded. "The point is to change public opinion about something. In this case, if Washington wants to start a war with Beijing, they need Congress and the will of the people on their side. Even with the power outages in other major cities on the West Coast, it is still not certain China was behind it. We can assume that to be the case, but there's probably no definitive proof. That's the nature of cyber warfare."

"Exactly," added Grayson. "We must want to initiate a hot war with China over Taiwan. The cyberattacks taking down the grid may have been done by DC, not China."

"Just so we can fight another war?" asked Emmy.

"*Another* is the key point, darling," said Dean. "The American people are war-weary. We finally pulled out of Iraq and Afghanistan, only to find ourselves embroiled in Ukraine, Israel, and Taiwan. Most Americans think none of that is any of our business."

"So they cut off our power to get us mad at China?" she asked.

Grayson nodded. "There you have it. Only they underestimated the thin veneer of society that we live in. It doesn't take much to light the fuse of anger in this country. Look at what has happened to us tonight."

The trio grew quiet as they leaned on the railing overlooking the neighborhood. The faint glow of candles could be seen in some of the homes. People along the PCH had restarted their cars and were attempting to move away from the entrance to the Colony. There was still the sound of activity occurring at the gates.

Dean took a deep breath and exhaled, allowing the stress of the night to flow out of his body. He studied Grayson, who'd remained relatively calm throughout. In fact, Dean noticed, the most agitated he'd become was when he'd delivered the news about Winter Wonderland. Dean studied his friend. His attire. His gear. His demeanor. He was becoming suspicious of his longtime neighbor. Not in a bad way. But, rather, in a who-are-you-really way. He took another deep breath and gathered the courage to confront his friend.

Then suddenly, the lights came back on.

PART 3

"Maybe you have to know the darkness before you can appreciate the light."
~ Madeleine L'Engle, American writer

SEVENTEEN

Dateline: Washington
Associated Press

The Associated Press is now reporting that White House officials have openly held the Chinese government responsible for the overnight power outage in the greater Los Angeles area.

A White House spokesman is quoted as saying, "The Chinese government's attempts to virtually attack U.S. infrastructure has reached new levels. Their actions are beyond the pale of accepted norms of international relations."

In addition, FBI Director Carla Hughes released a statement that the cyberattacks are on "a scale greater than we've seen before," calling them a "defining threat to national security and arguably an act of war."

According to the White House, based on FBI investigations, Volt Typhoon, the Chinese hacking network that was revealed last year to be dormant inside U.S. critical infrastructure, with malware that needed only to be triggered to disrupt that infrastructure, is the suspected culprit of the Los Angeles outage.

"It's the tip of the iceberg. ... It's one of many such efforts by the Chinese," Director Hughes said.

China, the White House spokesman said earlier in the week, is increasingly inserting "offensive weapons within our critical infrastructure, poised to attack whenever Beijing decides the time is right."

The president, who was unavailable for comment, pointed to the FBI's report several days ago after Microsoft announced they had disrupted attempts by state-sponsored hackers from China and four other countries who had tried to use OpenAI's artificial intelligence (AI) technology for malicious purposes. The White House spokesman today claimed the escalation was more than malicious. He said the Chinese military clearly has included cyber warfare as a tool to weaken America before a planned attack on Taiwan.

"Although the capabilities of our current models for malicious cybersecurity tasks are limited, we believe it's important to stay ahead of significant and evolving threats," OpenAI officials said on its blog. "To respond to the threat, we are taking a multipronged approach to combating malicious state-affiliate actors' use of our platform."

Congressional leaders have called for a full investigation of yesterday's blackout.

EIGHTEEN

Saturday
The Colony at Malibu

As dawn came, the power was restored. Darkness had been replaced with lights. The dozens of interlopers who'd passed the Colony's security team at the entry gates had dispersed. Some had found a way to climb over the stucco wall surrounding the community. Others had dodged bullets as they'd run for the exits past the neighborhood's security personnel.

At least one man wasn't so lucky. His body, riddled with bullets, was discovered by residents as they poked their heads out of their homes and ventured into the streets. The shotgun many assumed he'd used to terrorize the cul-de-sac where he died was nowhere to be found.

A small crowd gathered around the corpse as Toby and Zelmanski approached the block captain assigned to the street. The block captain ordered the residents to move back. When they reluctantly did so, he bellowed at them, frightening one woman to tears. They hastily walked away, leaving the three men alone with the dead.

The block captain, who'd worked for a security patrol firm once, had had some training when he'd received his associate degree in criminal justice from Phoenix University, the online school. He was the closest thing the neighborhood had to a crime scene investigator other than Lee. Toby and Zelmanski had identified the detective as somebody hostile to Toby's so-called administration. Therefore, he wasn't included in the analysis of the shooting scene.

The block captain was adept at stating the obvious.

"Whadya think?" asked Toby.

Earlier, the man had picked up the shotgun without regard to preserving the crime scene. It was bundled in a tarp in the back of his Cushman EZ-GO cart. He unveiled the tarp to reveal the shotgun.

"This is a Mossberg 590. It's a nine-shot weapon." He paused to look around. There were seven empty shot shells lying on the pavement nearby. "It's empty, and it appears seven of the nine shots took place here. I tucked it away for safekeeping, so nobody ran off with it."

Toby grinned. He saw that as an opportunity to add to his team's arsenal. "Good. Please take it to my home without anyone noticing."

The block captain nodded.

"I believe there were two shots at the gate when they broke past our people."

"Okay, that would account for the nine shots fired," the block captain said. He looked at the homes in the cul-de-sac. "Swiss cheese, gentlemen. They took most of the brunt of the attack."

Zelmanski kicked at the dead shooter. "This guy took half a dozen rounds. High powered, too. Pretty gruesome."

Toby walked toward the center of the road. "Nine shots, you say?"

"Yeah, assuming it was fully loaded," the block captain responded.

"Based on that, he was unarmed at the time he was shot. Correct?"

Zelmanski frowned and stood between Toby and his block captain. He whispered, "What are you driving at, Toby?"

"What I'm saying is we have somebody in this neighborhood with a high-power weapon that tore this guy to pieces while he was unarmed. That goes beyond self-defense, don't you think, Tom?"

Zelmanski half-shrugged and waved his upper body back and forth. Unsure, he responded honestly, "I don't know, Toby. In a court of law, you could easily make the case for self-defense. I mean, look at what this guy did to the house."

"This is not about a court of law," Toby hissed. He walked several steps toward Zelmanski, getting close enough for Zelmanski to smell the leftover liquor on Toby's breath. "This is about convincing the people of the Colony to toe the line. We have a murderer in our midst, and we'll move forward as if that is the case."

Zelmanski stared down Toby for a brief moment. He didn't like being challenged like that. However, he admired the devious mind of the HOA president. Toby never ceased to amaze him with his ability to come up with ways to screw his neighbors. In the end, as long as he could benefit from it, Zelmanski would come up with a narrative to support Toby's ploys.

He turned to the block captain. "Go interview those folks. Last name is Pryce. Be gentle. Helpful. Tell them it's over. Then get them to talk about what happened. I've looked into their background. They don't strike me as a couple who would own a high-powered rifle."

"Yes, sir." The block captain walked deliberately toward Judson's home with his hands high over his head, calling out for the Pryces and identifying himself as a block captain.

Toby stood for a moment in the middle of the cul-de-sac. He tried to visualize where the shots had come from that killed the intruder. The SUV's bullet holes led him across the street toward a heavily landscaped part of the home's yard. The sun was higher in the sky now, enough to fully clear the ridge. Its bright rays reflected off something in the grass that caught Toby's attention.

He rushed over to the yard and located one of the bullet casings. He picked it up to study its bottle-necked shape and its length, which he estimated to be two inches. He smelled it as if to confirm there was an odor of gunpowder. As he was deep in thought, Zelmanski arrived by his side.

"What did you find?"

Toby was somewhat startled but caught himself. "Check this out. Two inches, roughly."

Zelmanski took the brass casing and rolled it through his fingertips. He looked past Toby and saw two more. Then another. Soon, without speaking, the two men picked up a dozen or more spent cartridges.

"He had to be using a large-capacity magazine," muttered Zelmanski. "Sacramento passed a law limiting the magazine capacity to ten, but a judge overturned it. Still, this is a hunting-rifle round. Large animals like deer or elk. To fire this many so quickly, it would have to be a rifle with a bump stock, or it's an assault weapon capable of automatic fire."

Toby looked around. People were gathering at the entrance to the street and pointing toward the crime scene. He'd have to address them soon. Plus, he wanted to survey the rest of the neighborhood. He turned to Zelmanski.

"Tom, what are we dealing with here?"

"Best guess?"

"Yeah."

"The Colony has a resident who has the extraordinary capability of reloading a hunting rifle in rapid succession, or he owns an assault rifle. It would be capable of killing dozens in short order."

They walked back into the street and were joined by their block captain. His first words were, "I think they know the shooter, but they wouldn't tell me his name." He went on to relay the entirety of their conversation.

"Okay," began Zelmanski. "Go to the other homes on the street and see what else you can find out. However, not that one." He paused and pointed toward Lee and Nicole's.

"Well, okay." The block captain left the two men in the street and went to the closest house to the dead body to knock on their door.

"Isn't that Nicole's house?" asked Toby.

"Yeah. Either the detective has a rifle capable of handling these bullets, or he might know who does. They're part of this close-knit group who get together every Friday night. So are they." Zelmanski pointed at the Pryces' home.

"Let's go talk to them," said Toby as he straightened his back and took a step toward Lee and Nicole's.

"Don't bother," said Zelmanski. "They're accomplished liars. Detectives are, and so are Realtors. Besides, he wouldn't admit it anyway."

"Do you think it's the professor?" asked Toby.

"That's my first thought. We know he's a gun owner, and he admittedly was prepared to use it during the Pepperdine shooting. He may have a house full of guns and came down the hill to protect his friends the Pryces."

Toby studied the growing crowd of onlookers down the street. "What should we do about it?"

Zelmanski furrowed his brow as his mind weighed the options. "Well, let's see how the day progresses. First, we gotta find out why the power went out in the first place, and was it widespread? Then we'll use the event to encourage compliance with your directives. Finally, we'll give this group of friends an opportunity to be forthcoming. If not, we'll contact law enforcement and suggest Professor Dean Winchester is armed and dangerous. We'll even give them these shell casings to run for fingerprints. That'll give them all they need to get a search warrant, probably with a full-blown SWAT team involved."

"Armed and dangerous. I love it," cooed Toby. "It'll blow up their little clique of friends, and it will also show the residents we have their best interests at heart by eliminating a danger to our community."

The two men exchanged high fives before marching confidently to address the neighbors.

NINETEEN

Saturday
Dean and Emmy's Home
The Colony at Malibu

Emmy convinced Dean the house was safe now that the power was back on, and the sun was shining. She desperately wanted to check on Liza. While Judson had done his best to assure everyone they were fine over the radio, Emmy wanted to look into Liza's eyes and make her own assessment.

After notifying Grayson of their plans, Dean locked up the house and set the alarm, something they hadn't done in almost a year. The Colony wasn't the kind of neighborhood that made one fearful of a break-in. Even the recent home invasion of a neighbor hadn't prompted him to arm the system. Last night changed everything.

They walked the sidewalks instead of cutting through the yards. Hand in hand, they exchanged pleasantries with neighbors, who commiserated over the events. Dean and Emmy had a secret certainly worthy of sharing. However, that was not their place. Besides, revealing the information would only raise more questions. Questions that might expose their group to others, not to mention drawing scrutiny of Grayson as a person who had a direct line to military intelligence.

The last thing Grayson had said to Dean before he left the house a few minutes ago was, "I don't think this is over." Dean was anxious to expand on his thoughts, but he needed to allow Emmy a chance to visit with her best friend. They'd turned down the street toward the next cul-de-sac when Dean noticed Karen Javitz peeking through the curtains at them. She held them open for a long look before easing away from the window facing them. Dean made a mental note to call on her on their return to the house.

They were halfway into the cul-de-sac when they noticed a crudely cordoned-off area halfway between Lee's and Judson's. Grayson had provided a few details of the shooting, so Dean wasn't surprised at the location. It was the gruesomeness of it all. Even Emmy, who'd shot scenes for *General Hospital* in which she was caught in the crossfire of rival mobsters, was shocked at the sight of real blood and a really dead body.

"Hey! You need to return to your homes!" a man's voice barked at them from the other side of the fluorescent orange survey tape used to close off the area.

"What? Who are you?" asked Emmy.

"I am the authority here. You need to return to your homes immediately."

Emmy bowed up. Nothing was going to stop her from seeing Liza. "Well, I am a member of the association's board of directors. That would make me your boss, sir." She grasped Dean by the hand and ducked under the orange ribbon. Out of respect for the dead, they steered clear of the corpse.

The man stepped between them and the Pryces' home. He rested his hand on his hip as if he wanted to draw a weapon. Dean actually got a chuckle out of the attempt to intimidate him. This

Barney Fife character clearly didn't have a gun. Dean, however, did.

"Listen, there's no need for trouble," said Dean, who took a conciliatory approach. "We're gonna check on our friends, and then we'll leave."

"What's your name?" the man demanded, his voice threatening.

"Nunya," replied Emmy.

Once again, Dean attempted to stifle a laugh as he and Emmy strode past Zelmanski's man. He was still yammering at the couple when Liza opened the front door and ran into Emmy's arms.

Judson was right behind her. "What's he bitchin' about?"

"Peon power," said Dean as the two men shared a bro hug. "Are you guys okay?" asked Dean as he studied the front façade of their once beautiful residence.

Judson stood next to Dean, with his hands on his hips. "We are. Shaken, but not broken. The house, however, didn't fare so well."

"Geez," was all Dean could muster. Every window in the front of the home had been shot out by the shotgun-wielding marauder.

"What are the chances we can get a window company out here to fix it?" asked Judson with a smile. He was clearly joking.

Dean shrugged. "From what I saw on the main drag, the neighborhood could negotiate a bulk discount."

The two men adoringly watched their wives discuss the events. Liza's tears of relief oddly turned to laughter as she and Emmy discussed the condition of their home. Liza wondered aloud as to whether it would be a bad time to put it on the market, drawing hilarious laughter from the two women. They almost fetched Nicole to get her opinion, but the dead guy's watchdog was giving the foursome an evil death stare.

Dean wanted to disclose to Judson what he'd learned from the satellite phone call. However, Grayson had cautioned him against it. There was more to learn, and with the power restored, he was in a better position to do so. Until he had all the facts, he thought it would be best to wait until later in the day.

"Grayson wants to get together this afternoon," said Dean. "There's lots to discuss."

Judson looked at his house and then stared up the ridge to where Dean and Emmy lived. "Weren't some building materials delivered to the Matlock job site?" Several weeks prior, Nicole had sold the last available building sites in the Colony to the star rookie quarterback for the Los Angeles Chargers, J. T. Matlock. It had been fast-tracked through permitting, and construction had begun with the digging of footers.

"Yeah, Grayson and I saw them the other day while running. Two-by-fours and plywood, in fact."

Judson smiled. "Are you busy today, old buddy?"

Dean shook his head and laughed. "Nope. Let's load up our trucks with plywood and board up your windows."

"Do you think we need to get HOA approval from Toby?" asked Judson.

"Yeah, right," said Dean.

Emmy turned to address the guys. "Honey, I'm gonna help Liza clean up. Is that cool?"

"Absolutely. We've already hatched a plan to board up the openings. I'm gonna pop in at Lee and Nicole's, then grab my truck. Plus, I'll let Grayson know the plan."

Judson joined the women, and Dean turned toward Lee's home. He was confronted once again by Zelmanski's man.

"I need your name," the man said.

Dean shook his head and laughed. "No. No, you don't." He walked past him and kept going. He wasn't interested in putting up with Toby's bullies. Although, he suspected that time would come.

TWENTY

Saturday
The Colony at Malibu

Dean was not surprised that Lee and Nicole came through the onslaught unfazed. As a cop who'd fought the drug wars in Los Angeles County his entire career, Lee had faced a lot worse. Nicole had always struck Dean as someone who was cool under pressure. Her beauty and poise might cause some to underestimate her. However, in Malibu, the real estate business was known to be cutthroat, and there were many of her peers who felt like she hadn't earned her seat at the table years ago when she'd inherited the brokerage firm where she worked. Her dealings with the other brokers seemed to have hardened her, at least from a business perspective. That apparently had paid off last night.

After some cleanup of their own, Nicole promised to assist the Pryces in boarding up their windows. Also, Lee had already placed a call to the sheriff's department to get a crime scene investigative unit to the neighborhood with investigators. He explained what had happened, and the homicide detectives showed little interest in getting involved, as it was a clear case of self-defense.

Besides, the Colony wasn't the only part of the county that had suffered during the outage. Murder and mayhem were the norm rather than the exception. Lee was ordered into the task force's office to assist in the investigations of several gun battles between the Canoga Park Alabama 13 street gang, also known as CPA-13, and the Vineland Boys, who'd been waging a turf war against one another over the West Valley in LA county.

The power outage had been seen as an opportunity for both sides to make a strong move against the other. Unfortunately, as was often the case, civilians were caught up in the war. Dozens of soldiers and citizens alike had been shot overnight. Hospitals in the West Valley were full of gang members, which required a strong police presence to keep the peace. As a result, there were fewer cops on the street to control the looting.

Stores and businesses were broken into at will. Looters were undeterred as they stole from shop owners, some of whom dared to stand up to the thieves. Several died trying. To make matters worse, vandals randomly set fires around the valley, burning cars, buildings, and even a fire hall that had been emptied of firefighters on a call. It was lawlessness, and it had been triggered by the power outage.

Dean absorbed all of the information provided by Lee and shook his head in disgust. Although, he wasn't surprised. The thin veneer of civilization had been ripped wide open overnight as a result of the power grid going down. Everyone, including himself, had assumed they were facing a long-term outage similar to what had happened in the other West Coast metropolitan areas. Some had used it as an opportunity to do harm. Others, like Dean and his friends, had presumed it meant lawlessness would rule the day, and therefore, they'd have to take whatever steps necessary to protect themselves. Including, as Grayson had done, killing their fellow man.

He slowed his pace as he reached the yard of Karen Javitz. Like the Barlows across the street from her corner lot, Dean knew very little about her. Over the years, other than exchanging pleasantries, they'd never had a deep conversation of a personal nature.

Mrs. Javitz had lived in the Colony before Dean and Emmy had built their home. Her husband had passed away more than ten years ago. Dean had never seen any regular visitors, so he doubted she had any children. That, and the fact she had impeccable flower beds, was the extent of his knowledge about the elderly woman.

Yet he felt compelled to call on her. Last night had been traumatic for the entire neighborhood, especially someone of advanced years who lived alone. Mrs. Javitz had been known to keep an eye on the happenings within her field of vision, so to speak. Dean often wondered if her peering through the curtains of her home was out of nosiness or fear.

As he approached the front door, his eyes darted around the exterior of her home, searching for any signs of an attempted break-in. When he and Emmy had walked past earlier, he seemed to be focused on the homes up and down the Colony's primary street. Should a catastrophe like they experienced last night happen again, he'd have to learn how to refocus his mindset on all the details, not just the ones he was looking for.

He slowly approached her front door and gently knocked. "Mrs. Javitz? This is Dean. Um, Dean Winchester from down the street. I just wanted to stop by and see how you're doing." Dean imagined that she already knew he was at the front door before he knocked. It seemed she had a sense of awareness like that.

The bolt lock popped, followed by the heavy wooden door slowly opening. Before him stood a proud, seventy-something-year-old woman, impeccably dressed, holding a mug of coffee that was still steaming.

"Good morning, Professor. Please come in."

Her voice was strong, and her diction impeccable. There was no sign of nervousness or anxiety following the prior evening's events.

"Thanks. Um, Emmy wanted to join us, but one of our neighbors had their, well, they need a lot of repairs to their home after last night."

Mrs. Javitz smiled and nodded. "It's okay, Professor. I heard the gunshots. You don't have to dance around the subject for fear I'll become a blubbering ball of bawling mush."

"Okay. But please call me Dean. I'm not exactly a professor at the moment."

"I'm aware, young man. And although I will always be Mrs. Javitz, please call me Karen." She paused, then waggled her finger at Dean. "However, make no mistake. I am not one of *those* Karens."

Dean spontaneously burst out laughing. The sight of this sweet old lady making the distinction between herself and the *Karens* of society, a slang term typically used to refer to middle-aged white women who were perceived as entitled or demanding.

"Okay, Karen."

"And, Professor, or Dean, as you wish, I am familiar with your plight, and I for one call bullshit."

Dean lost it again. The sound of this sweet woman cursing caught him off guard as if it were uttered by a four-year-old. Cute, in an odd sort of way. The laughter felt good, and Mrs. Javitz apparently was pleased to take the seriousness out of her morning.

"How about some coffee? I just put on a fresh pot."

Dean hadn't taken the time for coffee, and he was enjoying the relaxed state of mind she'd put him in. "Absolutely. Black is fine."

He followed her into the kitchen, admiring her home as he strolled behind her. It was impeccable, just like her flower beds. There were photographs of her with her husband. Dean had only met the man once. He had been friendly enough. Heavy New York accent, if he recalled. She turned toward him with the mug and caught him staring at the photos.

"That's my Bernie, God rest his soul. He was a good man, Dean. Like you."

"Oh, I imagine he was a far better man than I am. I regret that I didn't get to know him better. Or you, for that matter."

She waved her arm at him. "Pshaw. Yes, Bernie was a good man and a great husband. He was a retired cop, you know. Former NYPD Chief of Transit. Stressful job, believe it or not. Six million people a day rode those subways. When it got to where his patrols couldn't arrest people anymore, he called it quits. He died just a few years after we moved here to sunny California."

She led Dean into the family room, where he was stunned by what he saw. On one wall was a curio case with her husband's awards, hat and uniform on display. Commendations filled every available part of the drywall. Another wall was filled with four television monitors, each filled with a different news network reporting on the events of last night.

Dean wasn't sure what to address first. "Your husband was highly decorated, Karen. I bet you're proud of him."

"More than you know. To be honest, I felt bad for him at the end of his career. He didn't want to retire. He could've worked his way to at least DC, um, deputy commissioner. It just became so political. And cops became the bad guys. It was something that puzzled him so much he became consumed by it. His people risked their lives every day to protect others and put away criminals. Instead, they became hamstrung by cop haters and the media. That's part of what brought us all the way out here. We didn't know anybody in California, or on the West Coast, for that matter. He just wanted to get as far away as he could from New York to forget what was happening to our beloved city."

"Makes sense," added Dean as he listened to Mrs. Javitz pour her heart out about her husband. Then, as she apparently enjoyed doing, she caught him off guard.

"I wanted to move to Hawaii. I've always been a big fan of pu pu platters."

Dean couldn't take it anymore. He almost snorted out his coffee as she once again disarmed him with humor. He needn't worry about her in the case of a break-in. He pitied the poor fool who had to sit with her for coffee.

"You're in a pretty good mood considering what's happening on the news," he said, pointing at the televisions.

"Well, maybe so. After experiencing the melee in our neighborhood last night and around LA, I consider myself lucky. Besides, I'd have something for them if they broke in." She pointed at a weapon on the table near the television remotes. Before last night, Dean had questioned which weapon was more lethal, the gun or the remote. "His service revolver was retired in 2018 just after he received his retirement shield."

The news networks kept the images of death and destruction rolling across the screens. Three of the televisions were tuned to local networks, and the fourth was turned to Newsmax. This was revealing to Dean. Newsmax had become a network made popular by conservatives who had become disillusioned with Fox News. *Hard-core*, he thought to himself. Even he didn't watch Newsmax.

"Looks pretty bad," he said.

"Well, I only turned it on because all of the stations are consumed by it. They keep repeating the same thing over and over again. Then the talking heads come on and tell us what we should think. That's infuriating. I wish they'd just report, like the old days, and let us decide for ourselves. We're not stupid. I hate the news."

Dean frowned and tilted his head. His puzzled look was easily noticed by Mrs. Javitz, so she continued.

"So, you're asking yourself why I have so many televisions, right?" she asked rhetorically before answering her own question. "Well, Bernie was always a newshound while we lived in New York. He claimed it was part of his job to know what the media was saying. But he hated them with a passion. He even had those Nerf bricks. Are you too young to know what a Nerf brick is?"

Dean shrugged. Apparently, Mrs. Javitz was very good at carrying the conversation at a cocktail party, had she attended one.

So she continued, "It was, quite simply, a piece of foam molded and colored to look like a brick. He had a whole stack of them on the side table next to his La-Z-Boy recliner. He needed four, one for each television. He'd chuck them at the screen when he got mad about the news. Then, out of need, of course, he adopted a K-9 transit dog named Rex, a glorious German shepherd. While the pup was well trained, he had difficulty grasping the concept of fetching the Nerf bricks after one of Bernie's tirades. It was quite comical, actually."

Mrs. Javitz paused to catch her breath. Dean took a sip of coffee and was about to speak when she abruptly stood from the sofa.

"May I get you another cup? I need a refill."

No, you don't. Dean stifled a laugh. "Um, sure. Thanks." He finished off the mug and stood to hand it to her.

"Keep your seat, Dean. Yours is easy to fix."

She snatched the mug from his hand and made her way to the kitchen, where she continued to talk.

"Now, I hate the news, too. I love sports. During the summer, I can watch my Yankees play. I show the Mets games just so I can enjoy them losing. Locally, I get my fill of the Dodgers and then whatever ESPN is showing. Same thing in the fall with football. NFL Sundays are a lot of fun. We've been longtime Jets fans. You know, in the city, the upper West Side crowd who eat salmon on their bagels supported the Giants. The rest of us Jets fans would always say to the Giants fans, screw you and your bagels."

Dean wiped away the tears as he tried to remain upright on the sofa. He couldn't take any more. When he relayed this conversation to the Friday Night Club, they'd think he was either lying or he was high.

"Here you go," she said as she returned. Thankfully, she hadn't noticed that he'd lost his composure. Or she had and decided not to let on. Dean doubted Mrs. Bernie Javitz missed a trick.

"Karen, I'm so glad I stopped by to see you," Dean began. "I regret that I haven't taken the time to visit. I believe that you could turn the gloomiest of days to one full of sunshine."

She grinned and sipped her coffee. She studied Dean over her glasses. "Very profound, Dean. You should be an author."

"I may have to. Jury's out as to whether I'll get reinstated."

She set her coffee mug on the table next to her. Her demeanor turned serious. "I'm glad we've spoken as well, Dean. I want you to know something. I see things. Not in some kind of new age clairvoyant sense. I'm just observant. The proverbial fly on the wall of our neighborhood." She paused.

Dean felt the need to fill the void of silence, encouraging her to continue. "Okay. There's nothing wrong with that."

"I know about your get-togethers almost every Friday night. You, your neighbor, Grayson, and the two couples from the street behind me. Sometimes, you get a little loud up on that deck, and I can hear you from my backyard. It's not annoying. Actually, it's somewhat comforting, as it reminds me of our neighborhood in Queens."

"We have a good time, but I didn't realize you could hear us all the way down the street."

"Voices carry. Like the song said. Anyway, I want you to know that I was somewhat afraid last night. Fear of the unknown is the worst. Also, lack of a partner doesn't help. Bernie always instilled in me the importance of his officers having backup. Well, he was my backup until he died. After that, I had to find my own way. I've done fine, don't get me wrong. But last night was different. It reminded me that I don't have a partner to back me up like you people back each other up. Do you follow?"

Dean set his mug down and stood to sit next to her. He gently took her hands and looked her in the eyes. "Karen, I will take steps to ease your mind. You will have a partner. I and my friends could never replace Bernie. We can try to do everything we can to give you peace of mind and protection."

A tear came to her eye, and she managed a smile as she shyly looked downward. "Please, Dean. Tell them I can contribute, too. Like I said, I know things that can help you. There's a dark cloud that has descended upon the Colony. We have to be prepared."

Her ominous words hung in the air as Dean contemplated what she meant. The observant Karen Javitz might not have been a psychic, but she could see the threat looming behind the gates.

TWENTY-ONE

Saturday
Grayson's Home
The Colony at Malibu

Grayson paced the living room floor as he changed the channels on his big-screen television. Having grown up in rural Georgia, he was a NASCAR fan. It was his only reason for owning a television. Nothing else appealed to him, especially the news. Today, however, was an exception.

The lack of information other than the local footage from the Los Angeles networks was frustrating. It led to rampant speculation on the part of the talking heads. On a national level, everything had been overly politicized. A tragedy would immediately become a game full of finger-pointing in order to score political points. In a presidential election cycle, this was especially the case.

Grayson wanted to get his information directly from people in the know, not just the know-it-all, biased pundits. He'd placed calls to a number of friends and in the intelligence community in an attempt to determine the true cause of the outage.

Winter Wonderland, a false flag, was not surprising to Grayson. The current occupier of the Oval House was trailing badly in the polls. His approval rating among voters was horribly upside down. The so-called Right Track/Wrong Track metric revealed sixty-eight percent of Americans thought the nation was on the wrong track.

The fall election was shaping up to be a slaughter. Grayson, a student of history, knew one thing. A nation, including America, was reluctant to change their Commander-in-Chief in the middle of a war. That said, the war had to be popular with the media and the citizenry. Americans had proven themselves to get war-weary in the past. Vietnam. Iraq. Afghanistan. Ukraine. These were just a few of the examples that changed the face of politics as a result of prolonged conflicts the U.S. was involved in that eventually became toxic.

If the administration was pining for a war with China, before Beijing ordered a full-on assault of Taiwan, what better way than to blame their infamous cyber hacking unit for the power outages up and down the West Coast. If the president could rally the American people around revenge for the power outages, then a potential reelection could turn in his favor.

While he waited for a return call from any of his contacts, Grayson's mind wandered to the revelation from Friday that Toby and Zelmanski were looking for ways to force residents to reveal the weapons they owned and the supplies they'd stored. Of course, they had no legal basis for entering the private homes of the residents. Although, the events of last night might embolden them. If they broke into a house to confiscate guns and ammunition, what would a homeowner's recourse be? Sue? Yeah, right.

He wandered through his home and garage, trying to look at everything from a different perspective. With his secret room hidden within the pantry, the most valuable assets he owned—his weapons stash, alternative identifications, and cash or cash equivalents—were hidden behind a biometric locked door. Inside the house, he had a single Glock nine-millimeter handgun in his dresser drawer. He imagined there were several other neighbors who had the same.

No, what Grayson found out of place about his home was that it didn't have that lived-in look. Dean and Emmy's home looked like, well, a home. There was stuff everywhere. Television scripts. Dean's classroom things. Magazines. Family photos. Throw pillows that looked like they'd been thrown onto a chair and left for dead.

Grayson's house was almost sterile. It was too perfect. It was devoid of his personal life because he didn't have one except for the Friday Night Club and his relationship with Dean. Grayson fought off a wave of sadness that overcame him. Who was he, really?

Was he that Georgia boy who joined the Army because he didn't have any better options? Was he that exceptionally talented soldier who grabbed the attention of his superiors, eventually landing him in special operations training within the U.S. Army's 75th Ranger Regiment? Or was he the shadowy phantom operative who rarely went by his real name?

One who couldn't tell his best friends the truth about himself. One who couldn't maintain a relationship that lasted beyond that early phase during which exploring each other's bodies was more important than talk of the future. One who had no family photos in the living room, or anywhere else for that matter, for fear of causing harm to them if the wrong people came into his residence.

As he often did to overcome a morose moment of weakness, he applied logic to fix the problem. He vowed to take the time that week to adopt a family. Not somebody he knew. He'd find one in Google images to adopt. Then he'd feed a bunch of information about people he knew in Georgia into one of the artificial intelligence programs to generate a phony life for himself. One that he could commit to memory to share when pressed by a lover or a friend or a captor.

His cell phone rang, jolting him out of his musings. The specific ringtone assigned to the Gray Fox team, which he'd just been recruited into, caused him to scowl. *Duty calls*, he thought to himself.

"Yes," he replied sharply.

"Sitrep?" the woman's voice asked.

Grayson kept the response simple. "Standing by. Ready. Local situation is FUBAR."

"Roger that," she said. "Out." The call was abruptly disconnected.

Grayson stared in disbelief at the blank display on his iPhone. "That's all I get? You wanna make sure I'm okay?"

Grayson had been recruited into the Gray Fox team, a covert special operations unit based in Fort Belvoir, Virginia. He'd only conducted a few missions for the unit, the most important of which had taken place in the bowels of the Ukrainian government buildings just a month ago. He was still finding his way within the unit.

He'd only been to Fort Belvoir once to meet the former Air Force colonel who went by the name Ghost. Grayson had been impressed by Ghost and the entire operation, although he found it odd that he hadn't been introduced to any of the other operatives. The offer presented to him had been made the day of his visit, and he'd had two minutes to accept it or leave. He'd agreed in less than thirty seconds. It was the career move he'd hoped for. One that enabled him to use his talents without constraint or fear of interagency oversight. The Gray Fox team operated outside of the CIA and FBI or any of the other special ops units under the DOJ or the Department of Homeland Security. It was almost a paramilitary unit with near-unlimited resources.

The television caught his eye as the director of the National Security Agency entered the briefing room at the White House. He was introduced by the White House spokesman before he took to the podium. Grayson turned up the volume.

"Ladies and gentlemen, I will be making a statement, which will be supplemented by a more complete written explanation within the hour. The president has asked me to take the lead because of the complex, technical nature of this matter." The NSA director paused to review his notes before he continued.

"Yesterday evening, the communication infrastructure for the major power suppliers in Southern California was infiltrated by elements of the Chinese government. Using the internet as its gateway, we have evidence the Beijing government ordered their military team of hackers to infiltrate the process control networks of Southern California Edison and other local electricity suppliers to the city.

"Once they gained control of the PCN, the hackers manipulated traffic and data sharing between the servers at the utility's control room and the gateways to the major substations in the Los Angeles area. They were able to target the smaller utilities first, the so-called weakest links. Because of the interconnectivity of the power grid between local suppliers of energy and larger ones like Southern California Edison, the hackers were then able to attack vectors of the system to disrupt transmissions. The result was a power outage of approximately twelve hours overnight."

He paused again, which provided reporters with an opening to begin shouting questions. The White House communications team stepped in to quiet the reporters and remind them that no questions would be taken at this time.

The NSA director continued, "Just before dawn, working in concert with our own teams of cyber experts, Southern California Edison was able to regain control of the system and restore power to the region. While the Department of Homeland Security is pleased with the quick resolution, they are fully aware of the continued challenges experienced by other major metropolitan areas in Washington State, Oregon, Northern California and San Diego. All parties are working nonstop toward a resolution.

"Like I said in the beginning, a more detailed statement will be released to the media forthwith."

Grayson turned down the volume when the news network turned to their roundtable of experts for analysis. He didn't care what they thought. He needed to think alone.

If Winter Wonderland was real, the question for Grayson was whether it was over. Would Washington wait until they could get the poll numbers they needed to take on China, a country that could arguably fight us on an equal footing, especially in the Asian theater?

Grayson glanced at his watch. It was just after four. He needed to call a session of the Friday Night Club, on a Saturday.

TWENTY-TWO

Saturday
The Colony at Malibu

It took almost ten hours for the sheriff's department's crime scene unit to arrive at the entry gates to the Colony. Because power had been restored, Zelmanski had ordered the vehicles used to block the gates from intruders to be removed. Traffic was moving steadily along the PCH toward the city. After the statement released by the NSA director, Toby and Zelmanski were confident the power would remain on or be quickly rectified if there was a temporary outage.

Property damage by the mob who'd stormed the gate was simply unreportable. It was impossible to identify who the culprits were, and even if they could, the suspects had left. There were several intruders who had been shot. One had died from being shot in the back near the front gate. Zelmanski and his team had met about the event and agreed that the shot was friendly fire from another intruder who was attempting to shoot one of the Colony's guards.

The dead man in the cul-de-sac was another matter. The discussions with detectives would be handled only by Zelmanski and Toby. It was a delicate situation that required a single voice to drive the narrative.

Toby had recruited many residents to help with the cleanup. He made sure as many of his constituents as possible received the word that, while the breach of the entry gates was unfortunate, it could have been much worse. He credited Zelmanski and his brave men with blocking out hundreds of others who'd planned to follow the dozen or so who got through. It was an exaggeration, of course, but one that was plausible to those in the neighborhood.

In addition, Toby conveyed to the other HOA board members, excluding Emmy and Nicole, of course, that an investigation would be undertaken into the shooting death of the man in the cul-de-sac. Several had already expressed concern about the sound of an assault weapon. The rapid-fire capability was disconcerting, to say the least, to the other members of the board. Toby assured them they, and the police, would get to the bottom of it.

The two men upgraded their appearance to greet the sheriff's department's investigative team. Toby donned a suit and tie. Zelmanski wore his best security detail uniform. They wanted to put forth an air of professionalism and, hopefully, credibility.

After introductions were made, the sheriff's department got to work. Zelmanski took them on a tour of the scene and explained what he'd done in the aftermath of the shooting to secure the scene for investigators. He admitted he and Toby had handled the brass casings fired upon the man who still lay dead in the street, covered by a blood-soaked sheet. They were told to get fingerprinted for the forensics team.

Toby was left with two uniformed deputies. "Um, are you the detectives?"

The deputies continued to survey the scene. One of them replied, "No. Dispatch sent us. It was determined this was not a homicide matter."

"What?" Toby asked, stunned by the revelation. "How could they make that decision without coming out here?"

The deputy shrugged. "Apparently, the person who called in the body was in law enforcement and said it was not a homicide."

Toby immediately glanced at Lee's house. It had to be Lee Wong. "They took his word for it?" He was trying to contain his incredulity. This was not going as he planned.

Fortunately, he and Zelmanski had discussed this possibility from the moment they came upon the scene. If asked about the shotgun, Toby would say, in the interest of neighborhood safety, they thought it best to remove the shotgun from the crime scene for safekeeping. After all, they didn't want the neighborhood children picking it up like it was a toy.

"I don't know why the caller would make that assertion. An unarmed man was killed here this morning. A man probably looking for food or shelter for his family."

The other deputy surveyed the scene again and wandered off in search of a weapon. The senior deputy glanced back and forth between the corpse being processed and Toby.

"I thought they busted through your gates?" he asked.

"Yes, that is true. And most of them simply got caught up in the moment. They thought the power outage was permanent. You have to understand. They are refugees from as far north as Seattle or Portland. Most are Californians from the Bay Area. They've been victimized by the Chinese trying to attack us. That's not their fault."

The other deputy returned. "The vic appears to be unarmed. I count seven spent shotgun shells, but no shotgun. And the ME says his body took multiple, high-powered rounds center mass. Whoever shot the guy was a helluva marksman to drill a target like that, human or stationary."

Toby wanted to jump and thrust his arm into the air. The deputy had referred to the dead man as a victim. He was turning their thinking around.

"A hunting rifle couldn't drill center mass like that without a rapid-fire capability. Are they thinking one of the AR platforms?"

"Yeah. Their hunch is an AR-10, likely full auto."

"Jesus," the senior deputy said under his breath. "And there's no shotgun? I mean, look at that house down there. It's torn up pretty good."

"No doubt a shotgun was fired. But it's not near the vic."

"Okay, maybe one of his buddies picked it up and ran. It still doesn't change this from a clear-cut case of self-defense. Those people had a right to fire back."

The younger deputy furrowed his brow. "Yeah, um, that's the thing. There are bullet holes in the SUV. Smaller caliber. I found one and bagged it. It looked like a nine."

"Trajectory?"

"From the house," the younger deputy replied. "And another thing. These two gentlemen cordoned off the crime scene and found shell casings over there in the yard. They're .308s or NATO 7.62 rounds." He turned over his left shoulder and pointed at the home next door to the Pryces'.

The senior deputy walked away from Toby and his partner. Toby tried to contain his excitement. However, there was more information to be delivered to law enforcement now that they were reconsidering the circumstances behind the shooting. He had to remain calm, giving them the opportunity to bring up the subject.

The senior deputy walked back to Toby. "Did you say you're the HOA president?"

"Yes, that's correct."

He pointed at the yard where the shell casings had been found. "Have you spoken to these people?"

"They're not home. We have quite a few part-timers who own properties here."

The deputy thought for a moment, looked around once again, and then asked the question Toby was waiting for.

"Are you aware of anyone in the neighborhood who might be in possession of an assault rifle? You know, one that looks like an AR-15? Do you know what I'm referring to?"

Toby nodded, trying to hold back his exuberance. "I've seen them on television. And, well, while I don't claim to know the private lives and proclivities of every resident, there is one person who comes to mind."

"Who?"

"His name is Professor Dean Winchester. You might recognize his name from the Pepperdine shooting a few weeks ago. He was suspended by the university for carrying a weapon onto school grounds in violation of their stated policies. He lives on the street directly behind that house." Toby pointed directly to the location where the brass casings were found.

The deputy studied Toby and then asked, "What else do you know about this professor?"

"Well, while I haven't personally spoken to him, I know that he's very angry about his suspension. He even threatened reporters a few days afterwards when his wife was involved in a carjacking of some kind. Like my neighbors, we kinda steer clear of the guy, if you know what I mean."

The senior deputy turned to his partner. "Call it in. There's more to this shooting than meets the eye."

Well played, Toby congratulated himself. *Well played.*

TWENTY-THREE

Saturday
Dean and Emmy's Home
The Colony at Malibu

It would be yet another special session of the Friday Night Club. Last night's get-together on the upper deck had been a real doozy. Dean hoped this gathering was neither special nor eventful. Hastily called by Grayson, Dean presumed there was more information to be shared regarding the power outage. Plus, the group needed to determine their new direction, if any.

Out of respect for those who had not yet arrived, Dean, Emmy, and Grayson forced themselves not to discuss the information the operative planned on sharing. He was anxious to get started, glancing frequently at his watch and becoming somewhat annoyed that the others had not arrived.

Finally, it was Nicole who announced her arrival with Judson and Liza in tow. "Hey, guys, sorry we're late. I'd hoped that Lee could make it home in time to meet tonight, but he got called to yet another crime scene as he was driving back to the house. He told me the streets of the West Valley look like a war zone."

"Damn," muttered Dean. "Last night, we were a microcosm of the rest of the city."

Nicole continued, "Here were Lee's words: indiscriminate killing. Honestly, I've never heard him distraught. You know Lee Wong, Mr. Unflappable."

Emmy fixed them drinks, and they settled on the sectional sofas inside the third-floor great room. Dean stepped onto the balcony and took a quick look around, not that he expected there to be any more barbarians at the gate. Well, not from beyond the gates, anyway. Behind was another matter.

Liza spoke next as they got settled into their seats. "For what it's worth, Judson closed his offices indefinitely until the unrest settles down. I've taken a leave of absence, as well. My bosses completely understood."

"Same here," said Emmy. "The entire industry has shut down until they're certain the unrest will simmer down. Believe it or not, they broke into Universal Studios Hollywood. The theme park, not the studios. The place was trashed, and looters took artifacts. They stole a life-size replica of Super Mario, for Pete's sake."

Dean laughed, then apologized. "I'm sorry. I'm not laughing about Super Mario although I can certainly see how that might help someone with a lack of food and water during the apocalypse, right? Anyway, I was laughing at the irony of you guys shutting down. You watch. Pepperdine will hire me back first thing Monday morning."

"Yeah, they'll put you in charge of security," quipped Judson.

Emmy leaned into her husband and kissed him on the cheek. "It would be nice to see them eat their words. You were right all along."

Dean gave his wife a loving smile. "Well, thanks but no thanks. Besides, the last thing those snowflakes are gonna do is reopen the campus. I watched buses brought in to haul stranded students to the airport or bus stations. If history repeats, it'll be a long time before they start classes again. Hell, they didn't retire their COVID proto-cols until May 2023!"

The conversation paused as everyone took a drink. Suddenly, all eyes were on Grayson. He swigged down the last of his Samuel Adams and made his way to the bar for another. He was too hyped to sit, anyway.

"Okay, I need to tell you what I've learned from friends. The information was not fully explained, but that's how these people operate. Sometimes, though, a few words can speak volumes."

"What were they?" asked Judson.

Grayson hesitated. He couldn't divulge them to anyone else, especially Judson, who'd been accosted by the FBI in his offices last week.

"They were code words, and they mean nothing to anybody outside the intelligence community. In fact, one of the code words, Omaha, is used because of Peyton Manning, the NFL quarterback. Whenever he would change a play at the line of scrimmage, he'd holler the word Omaha. This meant to switch to the second play he'd called, or plan B."

Nicole lowered her eyes as she studied Grayson. "Yet you know what they mean."

Dammit! Grayson screamed in his head. He had to think fast. "Yeah, well, my huntin' buddies like to swig Jack Daniel's when we're reezing' in the woods, waitin' on a buck. It gets boring, and they talk a little too much, forgetting that I'm in the deer hide with them."

The group seemed to be comfortable with the explanation although Nicole's eyes studied him a little longer than he wanted them to. He sensed street smarts about her that were hidden by that polished, broker-to-the-stars exterior.

"So what does it mean?" asked Liza.

Grayson wandered through the room as he spoke. Like Dean, he glanced through the windows to survey the cul-de-sac for signs of activity. "It's called a false flag. If you read about it on X or any social media platform, you'd think it was a conspiracy theory. However, the events of the last twenty-four hours coupled with the ongoing war of words between the administration and Beijing give it plausibility."

Judson added, "I've seen it in blogs all the time. Our government is trying to manipulate us into going along with their already-laid plans. They want us to believe China is responsible for what happened to us last night. Right?"

"That's it in a nutshell," said Grayson.

"Are you saying our government did this to us?" asked Liza. She raised her voice. "We could've been killed!"

"Many were," added Nicole. "Hundreds, if not more, according to Lee. He was not exaggerating. There are dead bodies all over the place in LA county. Not just from the violence. People on life support or home health devices died when respirators failed or dialysis equipment turned off."

Judson shook his head in disbelief. "I've read about these things, Grayson. Would they really do this kind of damage to humanity to sway public opinion? For what purpose? Sway an election in their favor? Or start a war?"

"All of the above," he replied dryly.

"They'll never get away with it," mumbled Judson, who rose out of his seat to make another drink. A stiff one.

"Yes, they will because they'll have the media to cover for them," added Emmy. Then she turned to her husband. "But is a cyberattack an act of war? Would Congress approve something like that?"

Judson refilled Dean's glass, and he promptly took a sip. He allowed the whiskey to coat his throat and clear his mind.

"This argument rages in Washington and think tanks around the world. Basically, most state that a cyberattack cannot be considered an act of war because it does not directly cause human casualties."

"Did they not see the death toll from last night?" asked Nicole.

"They did, but they always qualify their statements with the word *directly*," replied Dean.

"It's a distinction without a difference," interjected Judson.

"I can't disagree," Dean said before continuing, "Here's the other side of the argument. With any type of attack, whether bombs, bullets, or cyber, there is a political decision made by a government. In the world today, the most likely culprits are China, Russia, Iran, and North Korea. Now, a decision is made to attack the U.S. And, so you know, that decision was made many years ago. Since then, every minute of every day, these rogue nations are trying to infiltrate our critical infrastructure and military apparatus to bring America to its knees."

"I believe that is what has happened along the West Coast," said Grayson. "Last night, that was our logical assumption, as well."

"We did it to ourselves, according to Grayson's friend," said Judson.

"Right, and if you think about it, the timing and method couldn't be more perfect," explained Dean. "The news has been full of punditry blaming the Chinese for this. Taking down LA and the last remaining operable ports on the West Coast would be devastating to the American economy. Not to mention, as last night proved, our society would implode.

"That's why many argue that what matters, as with all acts of warfare, is the political intent by a bad actor to cause some level of harm to a country or society without attribution."

"What do you mean by that?" asked Nicole. "We all know who did it."

Grayson raised his hand. "This is important. We all think we know. But cyberattacks can be difficult if not impossible to prove. Can Washington start a hot war with China over a cyberattack that we have no definitive proof they caused? Would Americans go for that?"

"You have to also consider this," added Dean. "We're doing the same thing to all of those countries. We have an entire cyber command capable of hacking into their governments and critical infrastructure. That said, I have a theory, and it's one that escalates into a genuine concern."

"What's that, Dean?" asked Judson.

"Assuming Grayson's information is correct, then our government is garnering public support to attack China over Taiwan, using these power outages as their excuse to fire the first shots. That may be in the works, or the military may be ready when the timing is right.

"However, in the past, cyberattacks have been used as a means of signaling, and possibly degrading a government's geopolitical maneuvers without triggering an all-out escalation."

Grayson stopped his pacing and turned to Dean. "I see your point. The Chinese aren't stupid. They don't have a mouthy bunch of politicians to convince or a war-weary public. They do what they wanna do. If they don't want Washington to gain the upper hand, they may strike first to warn us off."

Dean slowly nodded his head. "Yes. Another cyberattack. Next time, LA's grid may go the way of the rest of the West Coast."

TWENTY-FOUR

Saturday
Dean and Emmy's Home
The Colony at Malibu

The group fell into silence as they contemplated the information given to them by Dean and Grayson. The two men had already processed this scenario and weren't quite as shell-shocked as the others. Even Emmy, who'd discussed it with Dean, seemed to be affected.

Liza adopted an upbeat tone. "Okay, so we're not done yet. We started down this path a month ago. I still maintain we're better off, or better prepared, than ninety-five percent of our neighbors. Maybe, with all this unexpected free time we seem to have on our hands, we should step up our preps."

"I agree," said Emmy. "Now that they've scared the crap out of us with a dry run last night, we can reassess where we are."

Judson spoke next. "Well, we're almost done boarding up our

windows. With everyone's help, we cleaned out the glass. We successfully raided the Matlock property up the hill before anyone else thought to." He gestured toward the back of Grayson's home, where the Matlock property sat atop the ridge.

"Is it worth the effort to pick up more of his lumber?" asked Emmy. "You know, just in case."

Dean and Judson agreed and vowed to take their SUVs up to the jobsite and secure more two-by-eights and plywood as long as nobody was around to bust them. They began planning their weekend when Nicole took the floor.

"Lee is very concerned about what he's seen outside the neighborhood. He was surprised at how quickly a bunch of misfit, displaced travelers could band together to organize an assault on our entry gate. Not to mention their methodical approach to looting the homes.

"For example, there were three men who entered our cul-de-sac with teenage boys assisting them. They'd send the boys to knock on the front doors and wait for a response. Lee's theory is the men would be considered a threat to the homeowner and possibly get shot at. The boys would get a pass. Nobody shoots a kid, right?" she asked and then immediately wished she could swallow her words. Judson had, and in hindsight, he felt immense guilt. Not only because he'd shot a boy out of fright but because it had caused them to endure the wrath of the boy's father or acquaintance, resulting in the man's death.

Nicole quickly continued so the group wouldn't dwell on the unfortunate turn of events. "If nobody answered, they'd try the door handle to see if it was unlocked. We'd followed Grayson's advice and barricaded the door. But we forgot to lock it. Stupid, I know. Anyway, once they tried the door and pushed it open, the men rushed the house. One was carrying a shotgun. Lee was at the balcony in our garage bonus room. He didn't hesitate to fire warning shots at them. It worked to scare them away."

"Yeah, straight to our house," said Liza. She tried to conceal how perturbed she was at the turn of events.

Judson continued to lay out what had transpired. "What happened next was not Lee's fault. It was mine. I got scared and started shooting. When I grazed one of the boys, the man lost it. He just started blasting the windows out of our house with his shotgun."

Grayson kept his comments to himself. The entire group knew he was the one who'd torn the man to pieces with his rifle. There was no reason to state the obvious aloud.

Nicole continued, "From what Lee has told me when we've been able to connect by phone today, outside of the gangs waging war against one another, the violence and property damage was one hundred percent about looting. They weren't interested in finding food or shelter. Their actions focused on looting and stealing, with drugs being a much sought-after commodity."

"Guns, too. I imagine," added Emmy.

"Oh, yeah. About that," interjected Nicole. "I kinda kept an eye on the sheriff's department this afternoon when they came out to get the dead guy in our cul-de-sac. It was hard for me to hear what they were saying, so I eased along the viburnum separating our yard from the neighbor's to listen. I swear I heard them talking about the man being unarmed. The shotgun was gone, from what I could gather."

"Whadya mean gone?" asked Grayson. "What did they say, exactly?"

"I got there at the tail end of the conversation. All I heard them say was the man was unarmed."

Grayson took a deep breath and exhaled. There were several ramifications of Nicole's revelations. Some legal, others practical. He stayed away from the legal issues, for now.

"Somebody in the neighborhood picked up that shotgun."

"Lee and I continued to keep watch after the power came back and the sun was up, but we didn't go near the dead guy. We didn't have a direct line of sight from our house."

"What about you, Liza?" asked Emmy.

"We were so relieved it was over. I don't think we cared what happened to the jerk as long as he was dead."

"I'll say this," Nicole began. "There was some activity near the front of our cul-de-sac as the neighbors came out of hiding. The first group I noticed heading towards Liza's house was Toby, Zelmanski, and one of his men. The rest remained at a respectful distance."

Dean leaned onto the edge of the sofa. "Well, undoubtedly one of those three took the gun for their own use. This is how they operate."

Grayson nodded, although he was suspicious as to their real intentions. "No surprise, really. Let's talk about what's next. We can only focus and expend our mental resources on what we can control. Washington is gonna do what Washington wants to do. All we have is the ability to react when the time comes. We're just pawns in their chess game that can be sacrificed for their plans. I say we continue to move forward preparing, just in case."

"We've been spending a lot of time shopping," said Emmy. "We can always add to our stockpiles of food, water, and everyday household supplies."

Nicole brought them back to reality. "I hope you guys understand. At least from what Lee has seen in the West Valley, every grocery store and drugstore has been ransacked. Sure, some were stupid and stole big-screen TVs from Best Buy. But others were more practical and loaded up shopping carts to take home with them."

"How long do we think it will take the stores to make repairs and restock?" asked Liza.

"Weeks, at least," opined Dean. "This will be like cleaning up after a hurricane. Everyone will be in search of building materials and builders to fix the damage. Then trucks will need to be able to get to the stores without fear of being looted en route. It's a real mess."

"Not to mention a lot of resources have already been allocated to other parts of the state," added Judson.

Grayson thought for a moment and made a suggestion. "Let's consider lesser-known places that might have food and other supplies. Are you guys familiar with salvage food stores? They sell out-of-date products at half the price of a regular grocery store. Granted, none of us would shop there on a regular basis, but they got popular as inflation went through the roof this past year."

"I've seen them around town," said Dean. "There's Misfits Market. Imperfect Foods. There's a store called Too Good to Go that just opened up on the other side of the ridge near the 101. It's off the beaten path in a warehouse district next to a parts dealer for vintage Jeeps like the G-Wagoneer."

"It's worth a try," said Judson. "Don't you think we should make food a priority?"

"What about the expiration dates?" asked Liza. "Is it safe?"

"Most foods have a *best if used by* date or *sell by* date," said Dean. "That doesn't mean the food is spoiled. It just means it might not taste as good. There are no national standards for food expiration dates, which is why stores like the ones Grayson brought up exist. So I agree that we should make food a priority, and this might be a little-known resource to try. We may get one opportunity to restock before, you know." His voice trailed off. Dean's words conveyed his opinion. The possibility of a repeat performance of last night's blackout was very real.

"Worth a try," replied Grayson. "It's gonna be tough, though."

Dean stood. "Okay, we'll come up with a game plan for Monday. I'm sure everything will be closed tomorrow."

"We need to go in teams, with at least somebody staying behind to watch over things," said Grayson. "I don't trust Toby and Zelmanski. I can absolutely see them breaking into our homes. You know, under his bogus, totally inflated authority as the HOA president."

"We need to find allies," added Judson. "I think it's time to review the list Lee obtained, and I'll cross-reference it against anything I can find online since I never got the voter rolls."

"In that regard, I might have a resource who knows almost everybody and their business. One nobody would ever consider."

"Who?"

"Mrs. Karen Javitz."

TWENTY-FIVE

Sunday
Dean and Emmy's Home
The Colony at Malibu

The Friday Night Club had been spending a lot of time together these days. Only Lee went to work daily as he outwardly investigated homicides that grew in frequency as the gangs fought one another, while, inwardly, he continued his quest to maintain the balance between the two strongest in the West Valley—CPA-13 and the Vineland Boys. Nicole spent a little time in the office, but after the blackout, the real estate market had dried up.

Sunday morning, with Lee working, the ladies decided to make brunch. Mimosas and Bloody Marys were the cocktails of choice. While the trio of women enjoyed each other's company in the kitchen, the guys commiserated on the upper deck.

Judson passed around cigars to Grayson and Dean. He was a regular golfer and enjoyed cigars while playing. Golf was not really an option at the moment, so he decided to share them with his friends. As the men puffed away and sipped their drinks, they made small talk.

"What do you think about these preppers?" asked Judson.

Grayson laughed and sipped his Bloody Mary. "We're all preppers now."

"I know, right?" Judson said as he raised his mimosa to toast. "I mean, who are they, really? Are they the doomsday preppers that the media makes them out to be? Tinfoil-hat-wearing wack-a-doos getting ready for the zombie apocalypse? Or are they like us? Common-sense, middle-class libertarians with a tendency toward independent thinking and a strong desire to protect themselves in the event of something like the blackout."

Dean rendered his opinion. "Believe it or not, I think the entire spectrum of social and economic status could be considered preppers. You've got billionaires and big-name movie stars building bunkers on their properties in New Zealand or Hawaii. You've got farmers who are curing their meats or canning their harvests rather than selling them at market. You've got housewives who are learning to defend themselves from an attacker and even carrying a concealed weapon."

Grayson chimed in, "The media wants America to believe that preppers are those bumbling extremists who refuse to trust the government to take care of them. They're always portrayed in a negative light. How many times have you see a rural, white person commit a crime and the media immediately paints him with a broad brush as a doomsday prepper."

Dean agreed. "The elitists in New York and Washington have no idea what preppers really think. What motivates them. We are told a lot of things that aren't true about the prepper subculture."

"Which brings me back to why do they do it?" asked Judson.

"Why do *we* do it?" asked Grayson, placing an emphasis on the word *we*. "Coming from Georgia, the preparedness community stretches far and wide except in the cities like Atlanta and Augusta. Most preppers I know have a healthy sense of skepticism when it comes to establishment claims and mainstream media narratives. They're not extremists, mostly. They just don't trust the government to tell them the truth."

"Is that why they prep?" asked Judson.

"In part," replied Grayson. "It mainly has to do with self-reliance. It's in their genes. Their grandfathers lived off the land. They lived through world wars when food was scarce. They witnessed supply-chain disruptions during geopolitical uncertainty. Hell, we lived through a pandemic that emptied the grocery shelves, starting with toilet paper and Lysol wipes."

Dean stood to fetch the Bloody Mary pitcher from the bar cart. He offered to top off Grayson's glass, and then he refilled his own.

"I, for one, was not prepared to sit idly by listening to the band play while the *Titanic* sinks. I've had this gut feeling that what was happening in this country was unsustainable. Through conversation, I learned Grayson felt the same way. Guys, for me, it's about realism, not pessimism. I don't live under a cloud of constant doom, although the last couple of weeks may be a wakeup call for me. For me, I'm still optimistic that free-thinking people have a chance to turn the tide and dismantle the negative influences that have created the economic and societal instabilities we face."

Judson nodded. "I realize I'm late to this way of thinking. Liza and I are still trying to find our way when it comes to preparedness. Every time she gets upset that we don't have enough supplies or are not as proficient using weapons as you guys, I remind her we're probably ahead of ninety percent of the people living around us."

Dean took a long draw on his cigar and puffed rings of smoke into the air. For a nonsmoker, he enjoyed a cigar like a pro. He tried to reassure his friend. "Here's what you guys have, Judson. You're dedicated to freedom, and you have a strong will to live. You have a foundation and philosophy that is both patriotic and contains an element of survivalist thinking."

"I agree with Dean," added Grayson. "You have to start your preparedness lifestyle somewhere. Once you've adopted a prepper mindset, the rest falls in place with research and a plan. From my experiences, and because of my strong belief in liberty, here are the rules I kinda follow.

"One, prepare for others, not just me. I apologize to you both for not having this discussion years ago. It just seems that what's happened the last few years in Ukraine, Israel, and now with Taiwan gave me a new sense of urgency."

"Same here," interjected Dean.

Grayson continued, "Two, and this relates to your concern that you and Liza are late to the game. Many people's lives are ruled by fear. That fear is transitory, coming and going with the passage of time. Regret, however, is forever. If we had chosen to sit on our asses when our discussions first started on this subject those many weeks ago, can you imagine the consequences?"

The three men contemplated Grayson's words. The consequences could've been deadly for Judson and Liza. Maybe Lee and Nicole, too.

"That said," Grayson continued. He swallowed hard before he spoke. He oftentimes asked himself if he'd broken this rule. "You don't need to become a monster to defeat the monster. Without question, war is hell. We got a little taste of that during the blackout. Somehow, if it happens again, we have to maintain who we are. There's a fine line between righteous indifference to violence and becoming a monstrous killer with no moral compass."

Dean looked through the railing of his deck to confirm nobody was nearby eavesdropping. He lowered his voice, somewhat hesitant to ask the question. He worded it carefully so he didn't offend his friend. "Did you think along these lines when you defended Judson and Liza?"

"Absolutely," Grayson replied. "When I approached the shooter, I fully intended to administer a flesh wound. One that wouldn't kill him, but simply stop his assault on these guys. When he shot at me first, I had no choice. I've said this before. When defending yourself against somebody trying to kill you, do not hesitate. Take him out."

Judson stood to make another mimosa. He heard Liza call for the guys to come down and eat. After putting out his cigar and passing on the message, he added a final thought.

"Let me add another couple of rules, if I may?" he asked.

Grayson stood and gestured for him to continue. "By all means."

"Our experience in the Colony has taught me there are times that you should be visible and times you should not. Before the blackout, we tried to be visible by Nicole and Emmy standing up for what's right against Toby. Now, we need to remain invisible. Blend in. Try our best to fly under the radar.

"However, I will say this. We should never forget the neighbors who've shunned us. The employer, like Pepperdine, who suspended you. Never forget those bureaucrats who tried to force masks and vaccines on us, or the doctors who refused to treat us because we didn't comply. I will never forget what authoritarians like them did to us, and in the future, I won't dare let them pretend it never happened."

The men toasted one another and joined the ladies, trying their best to put on a happy face.

TWENTY-SIX

Monday
Los Angeles County Sheriff's Department
Homicide Division

It was the start of the week. To be sure, the homicide division of any major city was inundated with new case files on Mondays. In Chicago, for example, on any given weekend, forty plus would be shot and half a dozen killed. LA had similar numbers. The previous Friday night, however, would go down as the deadliest since the Rodney King riots of 1992 when sixty-three people died during protests. Thus far, law enforcement in LA had received reports of seventy-one homicides.

To help, the governor of California activated the National Guard in the region. Already stretched to capacity statewide due to the other power outages and the massive storms sweeping across the northern half of the state, guardsmen did all they could to protect the government properties during the power outage. They were not fully mobilized until daybreak, when the power was restored.

As for the homicide detectives, they were unsure of where to start. Many of the murders were gang-related, so those cases were punted to the gang task force. The remainder inexplicably got the mayor's office involved.

At the behest of the governor, the mayor was asked to put pressure on law enforcement officials to protect those who had been killed in underserved communities as well as the refugees, the displaced individuals seeking shelter from the chaos taking place in the Bay Area and nearby parts of Northern California. For that reason, any killings that took place along Interstate 5, U.S. 101, and the Pacific Coast Highway were included in the list of priorities.

Detectives were reviewing the cases when the death of a man within the affluent, well-known community of the Colony caught their attention. LaRon Johnson, a native Angeleno who grew up in South Central LA, reviewed the police reports related to the incident. There were a few witness statements obtained by the deputies who responded to a 911 call made by Lee Wong, a detective on the Interagency Gang Task Force. Johnson didn't know Wong, but he made a mental note to reach out to the man to determine what he could add to the reports, as he noticed Wong had not been interviewed by the deputies who responded to the call.

There were several aspects about the case that troubled Johnson. The missing weapon was one. The fact that the victim had not broken into any of the homes in the Colony was another. While one home was clearly riddled with shotgun pellets, there was nothing that tied the weapon to the victim.

Then there was the matter of vigilante justice. The vigilante self-assigns the role of judge, jury and executioner, deciding who is breaking the law and exacting their own form of punishment without oversight of the criminal justice system. Further, Johnson knew from personal experience, vigilante violence disproportionately harmed marginalized communities like South Central LA.

Johnson believed America's history of terrorizing the black community with lynchings and other violence was a prime example of vigilantism's racist roots. A lynching was designed to send a message of unacceptable behavior to others. The vigilante wanted to show who was in power. Who was *the man.*

Certainly, the unarmed victim, by the reports of the deputies, deserved a day in court. Not eight powerful NATO 7.62-millimeter rounds ripping a hole open in his body via an automatic weapon. Nothing justified that.

Johnson studied the photographs of the victim. The man had a rap sheet, although there was no violence. Petty theft. Breaking and entering. Violation of probation. He'd spent less than thirty days in jail in his forty-four years of life.

The victim was divorced with one son. A teenage boy who apparently had been struck in the upper arm by a bullet fired from the house that had taken the brunt of the shotgun being fired. He had been found at a local hospital, where he was interviewed before being released. The boy had seen his father killed and had run in search of his mother. What touched Johnson the most was the young man's apology. He said he was sorry for going into the neighborhood. He said he was cold and tired. Nothing more.

Johnson laid his glasses on top of the file and rubbed his temple. He processed everything he knew about the crime scene and the participants. To be sure, the victim had no business leading two dozen refugees into the neighborhood against the warning of the community security team. Undoubtedly, he was guilty of trespassing. That didn't warrant a death sentence.

Second, while it was clear he was in a position to fire a shotgun at the house at the end of the cul-de-sac, nobody came forward to confirm he was the shooter. The weapon was missing. The victim did not own any weapons, according to the California Firearms Registry database. Even if he was the shooter, the perp fired his weapon from another yard directly to the right of the victim's position. Maybe a defense of others case could be made, but those were difficult to prove in California.

Detective Johnson was both intrigued by the case and bothered due to the vigilante nature of it. He'd seen it before. In his own neighborhood. When his father had been gunned down by a vigilante in a case of mistaken identity.

That was why he became a cop.

TWENTY-SEVEN

Tuesday
Los Angeles Interagency Gang Task Force

Lee had worked late into the night, sorting through the multiple gang-related homicides requiring investigation. It had been a few days since the blackout, and the city was being restored to normalcy, to an extent. The looting and vandalism had become minimal. The mayor's office, with the assistance of the governor, was working overtime to absorb the massive influx of refugees. Food and supplies were being brought in from around the country, as the blackout was taking its toll on the supply chain.

Meanwhile, life went on, and there were crimes to be solved. First thing that morning, the detectives of the task force gathered to go over the reported murders within their purview. The lower-level soldiers in the CPA-13 and Vineland Boys were assigned to the newest members of the task force. Lee took the three cases involving upper-level lieutenants within the two brutal gangs.

For many years, Lee had played an important role in maintaining the balance of power between the two major rivals in the drug trade that infected the San Fernando Valley. Only Nicole was aware of what Lee did behind the scenes. Not because she was his wife. But, rather, because she'd been a beneficiary of the artful, invisible hand he waved over the drug gangs.

From his early days in law enforcement, Lee was able to look at gang activities as a business, albeit brutal and illegal. To the leaders of the gangs and their cartel backers in Central America, their operations were all about earning. Not unlike the mafia's golden years arising out of Prohibition in the 1920s until the explosion of gambling in the fifties and sixties, the drug gangs of LA pushed their products for profit.

Lee's goals were twofold. Don't let either side gain the upper hand. A strong rivalry kept them focused on each other, which helped him achieve the second goal—containment. Lee had zero tolerance for the gang's street dealers pushing drugs to children and in the schools. He often mused about the only difference between McDonald's with their calorie-loaded Happy Meals and the drug dealers was whether the child grew up obese, with a shortened life due to medical issues, or in the case of drug use, grew up at all.

One of the reasons he and Nicole never had children was because of what he'd experienced in his job. He couldn't imagine trying to bring up a child in this world. Not even away from a major metropolitan area, although his kid's odds might increase.

Lee's tried-and-true methods of leveling the gang warfare battlefield could've resulted in his termination from the force, imprisonment, or being murdered. The game he played was dangerous but quietly rewarding. Not even Nicole knew about the lengths he undertook to achieve his goals.

It was for that reason that he'd cherry-picked the highest-profile homicides that took place in the West Valley during the blackout. The deaths of these three high-ranking lieutenants in the rival gangs would prompt calls for revenge and retribution. He couldn't stop their emotional rage, but he could redirect it to further his purposes.

He stood alone in the conference room dedicated to his team of detectives covering the West Valley. Four white walls were covered with photographs and note cards held in place by stainless-steel push pins. On one wall, known members of the CPA-13's leadership team were arranged in a hierarchical order. A similar organizational structure was created on the opposite wall for the Vineland Boys. The wall adjacent to the hallway had smaller gangs working within pockets of neighborhoods in the San Fernando Valley with loose connections or agreements with the two major gangs.

Lee picked up a red Sharpie off the conference table and marked an X through the faces of the murder victims. He opened their files on the table and studied them for a moment. Then he perused the roster of other gang members killed to cross-reference their time and location. He made several notes to determine a pattern based on the locations of the killings.

He sighed as he flopped in a chair at the head of the table. It was apparent the Vineland Boys had fired the first shots. They'd sent a hit team to a well-known hangout of CPA-13, a construction company's complex barely five blocks from LA Metro Police's Division 8 station. They'd crashed their cars through the padlocked, chain-link gates and opened fire on the group of a dozen rival gangbangers. All were killed except two, who were taken to a nearby hospital. Lee planned on speaking with them first if they were still alive.

Less than an hour later, CPA-13 had retaliated against the Vineland Boys. They'd gathered at a chop shop they controlled in North Hollywood. The encounter was nothing short of a bloodbath, with numerous civilians in the densely packed neighborhood hit by stray bullets. However, the Vineland Boys had been prepared for the expected retaliation. When the blackout ended and the sun rose Saturday morning, CPA-13 had lost four times as many soldiers as the Vineland Boys and two high-profile, upper-level lieutenants.

Lee needed to get a handle on this situation. The balance of power had clearly shifted in favor of the Vineland Boys, who'd use their past successes to request an even larger contingent of street soldiers from the Sinaloa drug cartel. He was deep in thought when there was a knock on the open door.

"Detective Wong?"

Lee turned in his chair, annoyed by the intrusion. "Yeah."

"Detective LaRon Johnson. Metro Homicide. Gotta minute?"

"I guess I do," said Lee, who gestured for the man to take a seat. "Are you working a crime related to the task force?" Lee wanted to get to the point.

"No, actually, it's closer to home. Your home, actually."

Great, Lee thought to himself. *Why is homicide involved in this? The guy deserved what he got.*

"Okay," said Lee.

Detective Johnson opened his file, intentionally allowing the glossy photos of the victim to spill out onto the table where Lee could see them. Johnson referred to the police report, not bothering to arrange the photographs. *He wants them on display*, thought Lee.

"Do you recognize this man?"

"I do not."

"Did you look at his body before you came into work on Saturday?"

"Nope. The local HOA president and his security head were first on the scene, I believe."

"You called it in, right?" asked Detective Johnson.

"I did, but I probably wasn't the only one."

Johnson furrowed his brow and nodded. Then he pressed Lee a little too hard. "As a homicide detective, you weren't even a little bit interested in examining the body or the crime scene?"

Lee wasn't stupid, and he was insulted that this detective from Metro thought he was. He leaned back in his chair and stared at the man, who locked eyes with Lee.

"I had nothing to do with his shooting. I didn't inspect the scene, nor did I have a duty to. I know nothing about who he is or what he was doing in our neighborhood. And before you bother to ask, I didn't kill him, and I don't know who did. Now, anything else before I get to my own investigations?"

Johnson jutted out his chin and nodded as he continued to study Lee. He pulled out another photo from the bottom of the file folder. It was an eight-inch-by-eleven-inch glossy of Dean's official Pepperdine photo.

"Do you know this man?"

"I do. Dean Winchester, professor at Pepperdine."

"Former," interjected Johnson.

"What?"

"Former. He was suspended for carrying a loaded firearm onto campus. In fact, he told school administrators that he was prepared to use it on the gunman who'd been in the corridor of his classroom one day. Am I right?"

"He was protecting his students from a mass shooting incident that turned into murder," Lee said out of anger and frustration. He immediately regretted it.

"Oh, so you know Mr. Winchester."

Lee tried to keep his facial expressions and demeanor calm. "I do. He's a good man. Why are you asking about him?"

Johnson lied. "No particular reason. I'm just looking into this case, if there even is one. Mr. Winchester's name was brought to my attention, so I thought I'd ask you about him while I was here. You know, looking into the case."

Lee tried to shed his open hostility and refusal to cooperate. "Has this been opened as a murder case? Our neighborhood was swarmed that night by people who broke into our homes and terrorized the neighbors."

"Don't know yet," Johnson replied. He suddenly stood and gathered up the photographs. He closed the file folder with its contents sticking out haphazardly from all sides. "Like I said, just looking into it."

As he made his way to the door, he asked one more question.

"Detective, other than your service weapon, do you own any other firearms? Pistols? Rifles? Shotguns?"

"One, a nine-millimeter Glock." Lee would have to hustle home to clean up the mess in the front yard. He hoped Johnson wouldn't send out a forensic team to dig up the NATO rounds out of the lawn before Lee did.

Detective Johnson studied him for a moment longer, then left without saying another word.

Lee sat there in stunned silence. First Dean got suspended for protecting his students. Then Judson got accosted by the FBI for an email sent to a J6 suspect. An email that innocently mentioned Lee's name, resulting in him getting called into Internal Affairs, where he was ambushed by the feds. Now, a piece of crap who had it coming got lit up before he could kill Judson and Liza, and a Metro detective was nosing around looking for someone to pin it on.

Johnson had made an error, Lee noticed. He'd claimed he was just looking into the case. Yet he'd only asked about Dean, who lived on another street and wouldn't have a reason to get involved. That said, what made matters worse was that he was looking in the logical direction. However, it was the wrong direction, not that it mattered to a detective who'd established a working theory and set out to find facts to prove it.

Lee knew. He was one of them.

TWENTY-EIGHT

Thursday
Vintage Grocers
Malibu

Liza picked up Nicole and drove to Emmy's house, where she was waiting in Dean's G-Wagoneer. The vintage truck had been put through the paces that week as the three women traversed most of the San Fernando Valley in search of out-of-the-way grocery stores to stock up on more food. They coupled their efforts with learning a long-term storage method for dried foods like beans, rice and oatmeal.

Using mylar food storage bags, food-safe oxygen absorbers, and an iron, they were able to transfer the dried goods from their store packaging into the mylar bags. Then, after inserting a couple of the oxygen absorbers used for pulling any moisture out, they sealed the open end with an iron. A day later, a rock-solid block of food was ready to store for many, many years, if necessary.

Vintage Grocers was an iconic Malibu retailer of fresh meats, seafood and produce as well as unusual grocery staples not found in the national, big-box grocery stores. Vintage Grocers was fairly expensive by comparison, but it provided an excellent array of food products for Malibu locals. Plus, it was close to the Colony.

Word had spread among residents that the store would be reopening at nine a.m. on that Thursday morning, so the ladies decided to organize a shopping trip. With Dean in tow, they'd spent the first half of the week in areas adjoining downtown LA they'd never entered before and most likely never would again. They'd had some success, especially with respect to dried goods. Each of their homes was beginning to have a decent stockpile of provisions to last many weeks, if not months.

Shopping at Vintage Grocers would be a pleasure considering their past experiences. Not to mention, all three of the women liked kombucha, a sweetened black tea drink that was a specialty of the grocer's coffee and tea bar.

Dean wanted to go with them to provide security. Grayson had suggested it during their first gathering following the blackout, and the ladies had willingly brought the dutiful Dean and Judson along as they shopped outside of Malibu. Today, they pined for a girls' day out. Vintage Grocers was barely ten miles away on the PCH. Since the number of refugees descending upon LA had dissipated, the potential for trouble had decreased as well. Or so they thought.

Liza led the way with Emmy following close behind. The ten-minute drive was uneventful, and the ladies pined for a return to normalcy in their idyllic community. Emmy rolled down her windows and took in the smell of the salt air pushed in from the Pacific. At that hour, there were very few people on the public beach at the Malibu Makos Surf Club. The ocean had calmed, as the last of the atmospheric rivers moved through the Bay Area across the Sierra Nevada mountain range, dumping many feet of snow as a last hurrah. The calmness was a reminder of how beautiful and serene Malibu had been before the power grid failures on the West Coast.

When they pulled into the parking lot of the Trancas Country

Market shopping center, they immediately noticed others had the same idea. While the small shops remained closed or boarded up, Vintage Grocers was the only outlet prepared to open for the day. And they'd drawn quite a crowd. All the spaces in front of the store were full, forcing Liza to guide Emmy toward the side parking lot adjacent to the Drill Surf & Skate, a barnlike building where visitors could rent surf gear.

After they parked, the women commented on the crowd. "Did you see the line?" asked Nicole.

Emmy nodded. "Thirty people. Maybe more?"

"Yeah," said Liza with a scowl. "If my body weren't screaming for kombucha and a scone, I'd say we go grocery hunting elsewhere." The women didn't call it shopping. Hunting was more appropriate, especially since they all carried their pistols per Grayson's order, their field general.

He'd spent free time during the week to teach the women some advanced firearms training. Using a dry-fire technique, Grayson taught them how to defend themselves inside their homes and applied it to any building they might find themselves in during a gunfight. He focused on night-time hours with little or only ambient light. The women were fast learners, especially driven by the events during the blackout.

They accepted the length of the line and decided to wait their turn. When the three garage-style rollup doors were opened in unison, patrons muscled their way inside. Ordinarily, tables and chairs were set up just within the roll-up doors for people to enjoy a beverage and a pastry. Potted flowers would be for sale as well. Today, Vintage Grocers was a bare-bones operation, dispensing with the customary ambience that had endeared the retailer to Malibu residents.

Inside, the store looked the same with the exception of the produce department. Local suppliers had been contacted by government agencies, which paid more than double above normal for their harvest. The fresh produce had been sent under armed escort to regional distribution facilities that in turn delivered them to local food banks for the refugees. Other than changing the look of the store once inside, it didn't affect the ladies' shopping priorities.

They were the only customers who stopped at the coffee and tea bar for a drink. While the kombucha was prepared for them, they noticed the other shoppers swarm through the store, throwing foods into their baskets as if they were competing on the old game show *Supermarket Sweep.*

"They're taking all the refrigerated foods," whispered Liza.

Emmy nodded. "Short-term thinking. I guess they've already forgotten about the blackout. Or they think it was a one-off."

"Hello? San Francisco, anyone? Half the city came to LA because the grocery stores are totally empty."

Nicole was anxious to get started. "Come on, ladies. It's starting to fill up in here. I don't know if they can handle all of these people."

As if on cue, two customers started to fight over bottles of orange juice in the refrigerated section of the produce department. There were only a few jugs left, and two women laid claim to them. Shouting turned to shoving before store employees intervened with a case of Califia Farms orange juice, bottled in California.

The ladies knew the store well, so it was easy for them to split up to fill their lists. Emmy started with the bulk foods to make snacks of high-protein, high-energy granola. These ziplocked treats would serve as meal replacements if they had to conserve their propane fuel used for cooking in another blackout.

The perimeter of the store's interior was lined with refrigeration units. Meats, cheeses, dairy, and prepackaged meals were on display. The velociraptors, as Emmy called the ravenous shoppers, were filling their buggies at the deli section. She, along with Liza and Nicole, focused on products in the aisles. It was the ordinary, boring foods that were a necessity, but not nearly as attractive as the grocer's extensive deli selections.

The trio was methodical and thorough. All the families comprising the Friday Night Club realized they were draining their financial savings to acquire food that might take them a year or more to eat. As Grayson had put it, this was like buying insurance for your home. You hope you never have to use it.

The same concept applied to food storage. It was akin to insurance coverage for that mind-blowing catastrophic event like a prolonged power outage lasting a month or more, during which grocery shelves would be emptied. Rather than paying expensive insurance premiums, they bought food to survive. The worst case, as he put it, was that they'd have to eat beans and rice for a while.

Recalling his explanation reminded Emmy she needed to stockpile a variety of spices. Beans and rice without Cholula or Tabasco would get old fast. She finished her shopping in the baking and spice aisle. She emerged at the front of the store, where Liza and Nicole waited. Long lines had already formed at the checkout, while even longer lines of people outside the store produced angry glares at the shoppers who'd overfilled their carts.

They were weighing their checkout options when all hell broke loose. Three masked gunmen burst through the exit closest to the cashiers. They fired their pistols into the air, shooting out fluorescent lights, which rained small pieces of glass and dust onto those checking out.

"*Dame el dinero, ahora!*" one of the men shouted, his voice somewhat muzzled by the black surgical mask he was wearing. "Give me the money, now!" he repeated in English.

The screams from the primarily female crowd were deafening. The enclosed space trapped the reports of the pistols and screams of the patrons, adding to the chaotic feel. Many stormed the entry doors in fear for their lives. Those would-be shoppers in the line outside the doors knocked each other down in search of safety.

Emmy, Liza, and Nicole were trapped between the gunmen, a large kiosk holding the floral department, and the stampede of fleeing customers.

Liza reached into her handbag and drew her weapon, but Nicole gently placed her hand on Liza's wrist. "Careful," she said in a loud whisper. "Don't let them see you, and don't make any sudden moves."

Emmy crouched down behind the shopping carts. Liza and Nicole did as well.

More shots were fired. A man, a would-be hero with a gun of his own, groaned in pain and fell into a Valentine's chocolate display. His body twitched as he died.

His dead eyes were facing Liza, who immediately froze. She began to shake. Emmy wrapped her arm around her friend and whispered reassuring words into her ear. "This will be over in a minute. Hang in there with me. They'll get their money and leave."

Nicole surreptitiously took the handgun from Liza and shoved it into her jeans' waistband. Her eyes were focused on the gunmen. One of them was responsible for emptying the register; the other kept a wary eye on the customers and any approaching law enforcement.

Nicole really wanted them to get the money and go. The cops' arrival would only complicate matters. And she was right.

Sirens were blaring in the distance as sheriff's deputies descended upon the grocery store. The robbers immediately became nervous. Nicole knew they could be trapped inside, suddenly turning from shoppers to hostages.

The shooters became more agitated. A second robber forced a dilatory cashier to the ground and pistol-whipped her. He frantically rummaged through the register drawer to empty the contents.

The sirens were closer, and the sound of squealing tires told Nicole the responding units had arrived at the scene. It was now or never.

She turned to Emmy and Liza. "Look at me. Trust me. We've gotta get out of here."

"But the cops are here," protested Liza.

"They're gonna get pinned down, and then we'll be hostages," said Nicole. "Please follow my lead."

Emmy nodded, but Liza was still frozen in place. As Nicole slowly backed away from the back side of the register station, Emmy led Liza with her. A dozen customers stood in place, too frightened to move away from their close proximity to the gunmen. Outside, the cops began to stage behind parked vehicles. Nicole knew the procedures. Lee had discussed them over dinner many times.

She was now crawling through some floor displays in the direction of the produce department, which had already been emptied of customers. Emmy and Liza followed, staying low to avoid detection as they crawled toward the entry doors. Once they reached the shopping carts within the alcove of the store, Nicole paused.

She studied the line of sight the gunmen had toward the three open rollup doors. She looked toward the parking lot to determine how many deputies were on the scene. She could only identify four but heard more sirens in the distance.

The men were shouting to one another in Spanish. Even with her knowledge of the language, she had difficulty understanding them in the chaos. There was the sound of shuffling feet and customers begging for their lives. Nicole took a risk, looking around the stacked tables and chairs to observe the cash registers. The gunmen were forcing the hostages deeper into the store, down the same aisles where the three women had just been shopping. If the ladies had lollygagged in the aisles, they might've been hostage victims. If they'd skipped the coffee and tea bar, they might've been checking out the moment the gunmen burst into the store.

Regardless, Nicole saw an opening. She grabbed each of her friends by the wrist. "We're gonna run for it. Do you understand me? Stay low. Run through the door on the left and don't stop until we're at the cars, okay?"

Emmy nodded and looked to Liza. Her friend had put on a strong front following the blackout. It didn't last. Emmy couldn't blame her for that. She wasn't sure how much more her friend could take.

"She'll be okay. Right, Liza?"

Liza's eyes were wide open and filled with fright. She managed to nod her head.

Nicole didn't want to wait any longer. "Okay, stay low. Ready? Go!"

In unison, the three women rose to a low crouch. They ran into the open-air patio entrance of the market and raced around the side of the building. They crashed through a group of onlookers who were too stupid to realize a firefight could ensue at any moment.

By the time they reached their trucks, more police had arrived, and the grocery store was embroiled in a hostage standoff that would take hours, and multiple deaths, to end.

TWENTY-NINE

Friday
Dean and Emmy's Home
The Colony at Malibu

It was Dean who suggested Liza and Judson move in with them until the chaotic world around them settled down. Liza was not doing well. Her exposure to the dark underbelly of what the world had to offer in the throes of societal collapse had taken its toll. Grayson even suggested she might be suffering from PTSD, post-traumatic stress disorder, following the shooter's attack on their home.

They discussed it over breakfast. "Here's the thing," Dean started the conversation by considering the logistical aspects of the subject. "We have three extra bedrooms. One is used as a wardrobe closet for you."

"Hey! You have stuff in there, too."

"A few Pepperdine sweatshirts don't count."

"Well, I can't help it. These people send me free clothes to wear to events. You know how it is. I make you take pictures of me when we're out shopping to post on Instagram. I tag the company, and they send me free stuff."

"I never get anything for taking the pictures."

"Not true, Dean. Birkenstock sent you some shoes."

Dean rolled his eyes and laughed. "I gave the ugly things to Judson. He actually wears them all the time. But we're getting off track. The other two bedrooms are never used. As in, once in a blue moon when one of your friends from the show comes over and has one too many."

Emmy cleared the table of dishes and set them gently in the sink. It was her turn to clean after Dean had cooked up biscuits with sausage gravy, a rare indulgence of Southern comfort food. Since *General Hospital* wasn't filming at the moment, she could afford an extra pound or two. In Emmy's mind, a temporary muffin top was wardrobe's problem to cover, not hers.

"We'll have fun," said Emmy as she hugged her husband around the neck. "I love those guys."

"Me too," he added. "Do you wanna walk down there to tell them the good news? I'm certain they'll take us up on it. Judson said it was pretty depressing around there even before yesterday's debacle."

"Sounds good, darling. Let me get a Juicy tracksuit on and some walking shoes. Maybe we could hit the streets after we see them. I'm sure Liza will want to take time to pack some clothes."

"Whatever they want," said Dean. "Judson knows it could take weeks to get replacement windows. He's concerned for their safety and the supplies they've accumulated. I'll suggest they bring it all here, and we'll sort it out."

Thirty minutes later, the couple exited the front door into a beautiful springlike day. The last of the atmospheric rivers that had rollicked Northern California had moved on, replaced by a high-pressure system that would return Southern California to normal temperatures and precipitation.

As they walked, Dean took Emmy's hands. It felt good. Normal.

Despite everything they'd been through, he internally hoped the dark clouds that had hung over their lives for the last several weeks had moved on.

Despite this somewhat euphoric feeling, Dean was still keenly aware that they faced challenges within their neighborhood. Toby and Zelmanski had held another board of directors meeting on Tuesday without inviting Emmy or Nicole. They were now operating in secret, making decisions without input from anyone who might disagree with them. It was a reminder that Dean and Judson needed to get to work on identifying like-minded neighbors. If enough of them could band together, they could stand up to the bullies in charge.

He looked ahead and saw Mrs. Javitz having a conversation with one of the uniformed security patrols. It was not the block captain who'd been hounding Dean for information. He hadn't come around since the blackout, causing Dean to wonder if the man had quit.

Mrs. Javitz noticed Dean and Emmy first. "Good morning," she greeted them. Her voice was full of trepidation, which stood in stark contrast to Dean's conversation with her the other day.

"Everything all right?" Dean asked. He glanced back and forth between the security guard and Mrs. Javitz.

"This young man claims he has a right to ask about how much food I have and whether I have a gun. I just told him for the hundredth time it's none of his damn business!"

Emmy addressed the security guard. "Why are you bullying her like this? She's right. None of that is any of your business."

"Who are you, ma'am?" he asked as he pulled a small notebook out of his pocket. He began thumbing through the pages.

Emmy looked at Dean. "I'm so sick of these people asking me for my name."

Mrs. Javitz straightened her back and adopted her best German accent with her New Yorker dialect. "Show me your papers!"

Dean managed a smile. She never ceased to amaze him. "Sure sounds like that's what he wants."

Mrs. Javitz was emboldened by Dean and Emmy's presence. She turned to the security guard. "Now you listen to me, mister security guard. I don't care if your boss told you the HOA requires this information. You, and they, can kiss my arse! My ancestors went through this kind of treatment when the Nazis took over Germany. They barely escaped tyranny. I'll be damned if I succumb to it in Malibu, California! Now, you can march your jackboots out of our cul-de-sac!"

The guard scowled and left. He was making notes as he walked away, glancing over his shoulder once before writing more notes. Dean and Emmy turned their attention to Mrs. Javitz.

"I'm sorry he treated you poorly," said Emmy, who was concerned for the elderly woman.

She began to laugh. "He's a bully. They all are. There is a difference between persistence and bullying. He, and the others, are bullies. Plain and simple."

Dean took a deep breath. "Karen, would you like to come over to our house this afternoon? Our friends Judson and Liza Pryce will be there. Well, temporarily, they're actually moving in with us."

"So terrible. Their house was destroyed. It's a beautiful place today. I saw that the man responsible for that mess got what he deserved."

"You know about that?" asked Emmy.

"Of course. I heard the shoot-out. Then it suddenly stopped. I expected one side or the other won the battle. When I saw those teenagers and two other men running down the road, I figured the man with the shotgun bit the dust."

"You could see all of that?" asked Emmy.

Mrs. Javitz looked around to make sure nobody could overhear their conversation. She patted Emmy on the arm. She spoke with a sly grin on her face. "I've got night-vision binoculars, dearie. Nothing slips past this old biddie."

Dean and Emmy burst out laughing. If nothing else, Mrs. Javitz was entertaining. Soon, they'd learn how valuable she could be.

THIRTY

Friday Night Club
Dean and Emmy's Home
The Colony at Malibu

Other than Lee, who'd been working overtime, everybody had taken an extended leave of absence from their work following the blackout of a week ago. Dean, who was still in limbo after being suspended by Pepperdine, had received a phone call from Sara Brewster, the provost and chief academic officer, to discuss his future. They wanted him back, but he had to commit to leaving his handgun at home. At first, Dean scoffed at the idea, especially in light of the wave of violence that had swept over LA in the wake of the regional black-outs. However, he wanted to get back into the classroom and promised the provost he'd give her an answer by early next week.

That afternoon, the group spent time moving Judson and Liza into the guest bedroom. Dean and Grayson focused on securing the Pryces' home while Emmy and Nicole assisted the couple in moving their most valuable possessions, from jewelry to stored supplies. An extra bedroom had been dismantled, and furniture was pushed up against the walls, and the center of the room began to look like a stockroom at a convenience store, as well as an armory. Food products mixed with ammo cans and weapons were stacked throughout the room. The two couples committed to organizing the mess as part of their Saturday projects.

After the move was completed, Dean invited Mrs. Javitz over to meet everyone. It was close to the time Dean would ordinarily convene the Friday Night Club. Lee had already phoned Nicole to say he'd be late and to begin without him. He gave his approval for Mrs. Javitz to be a part of the evening discussions, to a point. He was naturally skeptical of anyone else in the neighborhood but acknowledged they could use her help to identify some like-minded allies.

"Karen, how about a margarita?" asked Emmy as she finished preparing the first pitcher.

"I don't know. I'm kind of a beer gal. My Bernie and I would meet up with other cop families at Cheap Shots in Flushing. It's a dive bar, but the food was cheap, and the beer was cold." She rapped her knuckles on the bar. "Let me give one a go."

The ladies laughed as Mrs. Javitz took a quick sip from the salt-rimmed margarita glass. She winced a little, and then her smile told the story, as did the next, much larger gulp of the Friday Night Club staple.

"Welcome to the club, Karen," said Liza, who had become smitten with the older woman's wit and humor. And honesty, as they'd soon learn.

She pointed toward Nicole as she spoke. "Here's something I bet you and I both know. You may have sold all of the people their homes, but I've watched how they live their lives in them."

"I don't doubt that," added Nicole. She'd been told the primary purpose of inviting Mrs. Javitz to this social gathering was to determine whether to bring their neighbor into one of the outer rings of their inner circle. "I think it would be interesting to compare notes on what people told me when they were looking for a home and whether they lived that dream once they were settled in. You seem to be very observant of the comings and goings in the Colony."

Mrs. Javitz finished her first margarita and slid the glass toward Emmy. "Hit me again, counselor." Mrs. Javitz laughed and then asked, "Do people ever come up to you on the street and refer to you as your character name, Reagan Sutton, mafia attorney?"

Emmy nodded as she emptied the pitcher into her glass. "All the time, Karen. I've never decided if that's a good thing or a bad thing. They don't remember my real name."

Mrs. Javitz turned on the swivel bar stool back to face Nicole. She took a sip before speaking. "You wanna know something, missy. Knowing a secret in this neighborhood is like having a loaded gun ready to shoot. All of these people have secrets. Some are readily known, others not so much. However, knowing those secrets can help you manipulate people if necessary."

Dean sensed she was trying to make a point. "What are you driving at, Karen?"

"This HOA mope, Davenport. He's real trouble. I've seen the likes of him when we lived in New York. This HOA is no different than any organization or government that has the ability to exert power over people. People like Davenport corrupt the power given to them. In fact, it's that very prospect of being able to exert power over others that draws psychopaths like him to run for office, even if it's just the president of the HOA.

"Without question, he and his henchmen, led by this new guy, Zelmanski, are canvassing the neighborhood in order to find out who their friends are, and who are threats to their power. For some reason, they are also trying to determine what kinds of food and weapons we possess. They act like they have a right to this information. Or, as I believe, there is a more nefarious purpose.

"I watch the news. I've seen the food riots taking place in Seattle, Portland and San Francisco. I've lived through shooting sprees in New York City long before America went bankrupt, morally and financially. If I were a bettin' man, I'd say Davenport and Zelmanski are preparing for some eventuality similar to the power outage last weekend. They want to know whose homes to break into first. Or which residents they can strong-arm."

Dean exchanged a glance with Grayson, who'd been studying Mrs. Javitz the entire time she spoke. The intensity of Grayson's face spoke volumes of how seriously he was taking her presence in their group. He was making sure she was a good fit.

"Karen, as you undoubtedly know, Nicole and I are at odds with Toby," said Emmy. "We have always been the two members of the board who voice opposition to his proposals, not that it mattered. The rest of the voting block would override our objections or suggestions."

"I think you're entirely correct, Karen," added Nicole. "Toby's actions, and the hiring of Zelmanski, have concerned all of us."

Mrs. Javitz finished her margarita. Emmy made a mental note to double their tequila supply if she was gonna be a regular attendee. The woman could hold her liquor, too.

Karen asked Emmy for one more. "I know things," she blurted out. "Things that nobody is gonna disclose to Zelmanski or his guys. Which marriage is on the rocks. Who is having financial trouble. Who has a cache of weapons. Who is storing food like you guys. I may not know about every resident, but I know about most."

"Very interesting," mumbled Nicole.

Mrs. Javitz laughed as she swallowed half of her last margarita at once. "More than interesting, right, Nicole? I mean, isn't that why I'm here?" She paused to look at Dean and then returned Grayson's stare. She pointed at him. "You are what's known as a deep thinker. It's somewhat disconcerting, you know. Those dark gray eyes are, too. I have my ways of dissecting people as well. You try to look into people's souls. I observe what their soul outwardly produces as they live their lives. I would say my method is better, and yours is guesswork."

She sat a little taller in her chair, swigged down the last of her drink, and aggressively slammed the glass on the bar top. She never took her eyes off Grayson during the entire process.

For two seconds that seemed like an eternity, the two locked eyes until Grayson broke the silence. "You remind me of my grandmother. She practically raised me and made me the man I am today."

"A gorgeous hunk of brooding mystery?" she asked. "You know, like those guys on the covers of the half-naked-men books I see these housewives pluck out of the lending library box next to the mailboxes."

Mrs. Javitz was an expert at breaking the tension of a conversation with humor. She was also capable of disabling a man with her words, a trait she'd learned when she was quite the looker attending the City College of New York.

Grayson didn't know how to respond. He began to wonder what she knew about him. He decided to keep her close to the group. It was better to have her on their side instead of against them.

Mrs. Javitz slid off the barstool. She was both the oldest and shortest of those in attendance.

"I want to thank all of you for inviting me here tonight. I hope that you know we think alike, and I can be an asset. I'm old, but not weak. I'm vulnerable, but not afraid. Most importantly, I have something to offer the group, information. All I ask is that you have my back like my Bernie used to. It's not an easy task and will take all seven of you to fill his shoes."

Mrs. Javitz hugged the women. She shook hands with the guys, saving Grayson for last when they locked eyes again. Then she left without another word spoken.

THIRTY-ONE

Friday Night Club
Dean and Emmy's Home
The Colony at Malibu

"Wow, I need a drink!" Judson exclaimed.

"You already have one, you mope," Liza fired back, using her new favorite word.

Judson swallowed his whiskey and shook the glass in a circle. "Not anymore. And I'm not a mope."

Liza playfully teased her husband. "I think you are. Mrs. Javitz probably thinks so, too."

"Hey, what is a mope, anyway?" he asked.

"Look in the mirror, mope!" Liza replied.

"I'll show you a mope, Mrs. Pryce." Judson feigned chasing Liza as she quickly ran toward the couches. She flipped him the bird as soon as she was out of his reach.

The group let out a collective deep exhale, as Mrs. Javitz had overwhelmed them during their brief conversation. After Judson and Liza quit playing around, Dean began the conversation.

"I told you. She's a whirlwind."

"Quite the philosopher," added Emmy. "Here's the thing about people who are Karen and Judson's age. They've experienced a lot."

Judson immediately protested, "Hey! Why am I the punching bag tonight?"

"Because you are our mope!" replied Liza. Then she raised her glass to toast. "Cheers to the official mope of the Friday Night Club!"

Their usual serious conversation about world affairs and preparing for the worst had been set aside for the moment. It was a welcome relief to them all.

"Darling, I'm beginning to think we made a mistake inviting these two to stay with us," said Emmy in jest.

"Yeah," agreed Dean. "Grayson has more room than we do. Right, buddy?"

Grayson vigorously shook his head back and forth. "Hell. Damn. Nah. No way. In fact, let's help them break into that jerk's house from Denver. He's not gonna come out here anyway under these circumstances."

Judson looked through the window at the neighbor's house. It was a beautiful home and a real waste, as it remained empty for most of the year.

"I'm sure he wouldn't mind. We could become squatters. Write up a phony lease and make ourselves at home. It takes absentee owners nearly a year to get an eviction order with any teeth in it."

It was Nicole who put the kibosh on the playful banter. "Let's get down to business, guys. I need to tell you what Lee has learned."

"Are you talking about the dead guy in your cul-de-sac?" asked Dean.

"Yes," Nicole responded. "Naturally, Lee thinks this is a nothing investigation. Open-and-shut case of self-defense."

"Those cops saw our house," added Liza. "We told them we feared for our lives."

"Well, the first group of deputies seemed to understand what we went through," said Judson. "It wasn't until the detective came from homicide that the questioning got intense. Sure, he wanted to know how it all went down. Really, he seemed to be most focused on the shooter."

Liza addressed Grayson. "Don't worry. We didn't give him any inclination it was you. I believe we said *don't know* a couple of dozen times."

"Here's the problem." Nicole nervously paced the floor as she spoke. "Lee said this detective has worked in homicide for a long time. Apparently, his father died at the hands of a vigilante. He's investigating the case from that angle because there are no witnesses who can place a shotgun in the hands of the dead man."

"Therefore, he might not be the shooter, right?" asked Emmy.

"Exactly," Nicole said as she continued, "Plus, the shotgun went missing. Either Toby and Zelmanski took it, or someone else in the neighborhood. It complicates the investigation because they can't connect the dead man's prints to the shotgun used to obliterate the front of their house." She nodded toward Judson and Liza, who were shaking their heads side to side in disbelief.

Judson asked, "What if I tell them I saw the man using the shotgun and fired back at him? I mean, they know we shot back."

"No," replied Grayson. "That would be a major change in your story."

"Well, we have the same problem," added Nicole. "Regarding changing a story, I mean. Lee thought this shooting would be swept onto the trash heap like all of the other senseless killings during the blackout. Instead, this particular detective wants to make a big deal about it. When he was questioned about what he saw, he lied and didn't say he'd shot at the man in our front yard using the rifle Grayson had given him. He knew the ballistics wouldn't match, but the very nature of an AR-10 would raise suspicion and get him jammed up. He was so nervous about it that he pretended to be working in our flower beds, but he was really digging up bullets he'd fired at them."

Grayson popped open another beer and strolled toward the doors leading onto the upper deck. It was a beautiful night, and he wished they could hang out there. However, "the bushes have ears," Judson had said, referring to Zelmanski's men roaming the streets at night undetected. Grayson was certain their group was on Toby's radar, and Zelmanski was scrutinizing his friends more than ever. He turned to Nicole, who spoke before Grayson did.

"The detective did something that bothered Lee. He asked questions about Dean. Nobody else. Lee is afraid Dean might be dragged into this because of what happened at Pepperdine."

"That's crazy!" shouted Emmy. "Dean did the right thing, and these two incidents had no relation to one another."

"Lee agrees, but it is a concern that Dean appears to be on their radar."

"They haven't interviewed me," Grayson interjected. "I'll come forward and admit I killed the guy to protect my neighbors."

Dean set his glass down and held both of his arms up with his fingers spread. "Whoa, whoa, whoa. Let's not get carried away, here. Lee would agree with this, I think. Cops get a working theory, and they set out to prove it. Sometimes they're way off base. Right now, he has a dead guy who trespassed, using force, into the Colony. He was part of a group terrorizing neighbors and using kids as scouts, placing them in danger under frightening circumstances. This detective can't prove the man didn't use the shotgun to blast their house. He also can't come up with any motive for someone to kill the victim other than the obvious one—defense of others."

Nicole nodded. "Dean has a point, and Lee is in agreement. He said everyone should clam up and go about their business. This investigation will lose the wind behind its sails soon enough. Not to mention, Lee learned this dead guy was not exactly a pillar of society. He's a lifelong petty criminal with a rap sheet that matches what his intentions were for our neighborhood. Nobody's clamoring to the media about this being some kind of heinous form of vigilante justice. They've got plenty of other stuff to talk about."

Grayson ran his hand down his face and gently rubbed the scruffy beard he'd grown. He hadn't shaved since the blackout.

"All right, let's move on."

"I agree," said Dean. "What about Mrs. Javitz? In or out?"

"Is there a category we could call just outside the inside?" asked Liza. "Don't get me wrong, I like her, and she has a wealth of information that can help us. However, forgive me if I have trust issues right now."

"How about an information-sharing arrangement focused solely on finding more friends like us in the Colony?" asked Nicole.

"That would work," Dean replied. "But nothing about our preparations or weapons. I believe she'd be good with that. Mainly, she wants protection if the shit hits the fan again."

Judson looked to Liza, who nodded. "Stamp it. She's in, just outside all the way in."

The group agreed, and Mrs. Javitz would become a part of the group for those purposes. Everyone agreed to check in with her on a daily basis to make her feel included and to see what information she could share.

The topic of conversation then turned to geopolitical affairs. Grayson relayed what he'd learned. He unintentionally brought the group's jovial mood down.

"China sees our weakness exhibited in the Middle East and allowing Russia to invade Ukraine in the first place. After the Taiwanese people elected a pro-independence leader, Beijing appears ready to make their move while Washington is distracted.

"These cyberattacks are viewed as a shot across the bow. They're not done yet, as they provide a military advantage to China. If our ports on the West Coast are shut down, resupply of our forces in the Asian theater will be significantly delayed. Logistically, we don't have the time or resources to prepare for a potential long-term conflict with China in their backyard, especially if we have to send our ships through the Panama Canal. They know this, and that's why I believe they're working overtime to take down the power grid serving the ports around LA."

"Which would bring ours down, too," said Dean. "I had some time to review military websites the last few days. China has been war-planning a D-Day type of invasion across the Taiwan Straits."

"It would require a massive amphibious assault that our intelligence agencies would surely pick up on," said Grayson. "That said, China has seen how we've abandoned Israel in the Middle East and cut back funding to Ukraine. Our pledge to, quote, defend Taiwan may be seen as hollow." Grayson used his fingers to create air quotes as he spoke.

Dean agreed. "Well, somebody took down the grids in these other West Coast cities. And maybe China wasn't actually responsible for our blackout. Maybe we did it to ourselves to see what would happen, or to bolster poll numbers. Either way, the bottom line is, as a group, we have to operate under the assumption that it's gonna happen again. Let's get down to some details of what else we can do to get ready."

PART 4

"That light you see at the end of the tunnel is just an oncoming train."
~ Robert Lowell, American poet

THIRTY-TWO

Monday
LA County Grand Jury
Clara Shortridge Foltz Criminal Justice Center
Los Angeles, CA

A part of Sheila Harrison was eager to serve on a grand jury to see how the criminal justice system worked. Her chest was thumping with anticipation as she sat in the Grand Jury room at the Clara Shortridge Foltz Criminal Justice Center. She was desperate to make small talk with her fellow grand jury members, curious as to what their backgrounds were and whether they were excited about the opportunity to be a part of the system that pulled criminals off the street.

She didn't work, so the two-week-long commitment didn't bother her. She was certain there were others who were looking for ways to get out of their civic obligation. She was easily able to discern who they were after a clerk of the court entered the room.

The clerk called their names, asking them to respond with the words *serve* or *application*. *Serve* meant you were ready to be a part of the grand jury. The response *application* meant you would apply to the court to defer to another date for some reason or another. Sheila imagined that group had scoured the internet, searching the phrase "best way to avoid grand jury duty" on Google.

When the first several responses were *application*, the clerk stopped the process and chastised the group. "Listen, you're going to serve, now or two months from now. Yes, you will be here a full two weeks. No, it doesn't matter if you're opposed to the criminal justice system, or your brother was a convicted axe murderer. You will serve eventually."

It was ironic that Sheila's name was the next to be called. She proudly replied, "Serve!"

The clerk grinned as if she'd been responsible for Sheila's decision. She had not, but she changed the clerk's otherwise sour demeanor.

Two hours later, a grand jury bailiff walked the grand jury members into a room with twenty-three seats, a table and a podium. It resembled a courtroom. Once they were seated, the bailiff brusquely ordered the grand jurors not to speak to anyone. No cell phones. Always sit in the same seat, as you no longer have a name, only a number. The jurors were allowed to take notes, but they could not leave the room. Be quiet, above all. "Quiet!" she repeated with emphasis.

Sheila remained stoic as the district attorney entered the grand jury room, carrying a stack of files, with two assistants following close behind. They also toted binders and files, struggling to keep up with their boss. They dutifully waited behind him until he organized his workspace; then they sat down next to him.

The DA was smartly dressed but with no evidence of flare or flamboyance. He seemed very businesslike. When he spoke, his diction was clear and crisp and easy to understand. Sheila appreciated that, as she'd lost hearing in her left ear, relying upon a hearing aid when in public.

He stood and addressed the twenty-three members of the grand jury. "Ladies and gentlemen, my name is Charles Folsom. I am one of several attorneys in the district attorney's office who do nothing but handle grand jury proceedings on behalf of the state. That means, for starters, that I know what you've sacrificed to be here, and I want you to know the state of California and the victims who've suffered the criminal acts I'm about to prove to you appreciate your help in this process.

"The grand jury process is a power vested in the state's attorney to be used as a sword and a shield. A sword in the sense the state will accuse or indict those who there is valid reason to believe have committed a crime. It acts as a shield to protect the innocent against unfounded accusations.

"Today, I will be presenting two kinds of cases to you. One kind is designed to seek indictments to arrest and take to trial a felon. The other is to present to you the facts as we know them relative to a criminal matter. In these cases, the state needs more information in order to investigate the case.

"Sometimes, if the matter is minor, law enforcement investigators ask our office to present the evidence to a judge, who will issue a warrant. Other times, when more invasive methods are required to gather evidence, under newly enacted laws designed to protect innocent people from false accusations, we have to come to the grand jury to present the facts. Then if you agree more investigation is warranted, we will have the authority to issue search warrants and gather more evidence by any means allowed by the Fourth Amendment to the Constitution.

"Does everyone understand the purpose of the grand jury in California?"

Everyone nodded. Sheila was beginning to understand the magnitude of the task she'd been asked to undertake as a citizen. She would help determine if someone's freedoms would be taken away or their privacy shoved aside in the name of justice. She was glad she wasn't a criminal or the subject of an investigation.

The DA continued, "Good. We have a number of cases to present to you today, although only one of them involves a search warrant. Because it wouldn't result in the arrest of anyone, I thought it would be a good opportunity for you to go through the process before we get to the felony indictments. Sound good?"

"Yes, sir," Sheila replied. She opened her notebook and got her pen ready. Over the next half hour, DA Folsom brought in several witnesses, from the investigative detective to residents of the Colony at Malibu. There were students from Pepperdine and news reporters who'd witnessed an incident involving the target. After the testimony was completed, DA Folsom summarized the evidence and his request.

"The night of the blackout was chaotic, to say the least. In light of other power outages on the West Coast, some presumed the LA outage was permanent. It was not, only temporary. So what happened in the early morning hours of that Saturday at this upscale Malibu enclave? Well, for one, refugees seeking shelter and food asked for the community's help. They became frustrated, and when threatened by security personnel at the enclave's gated entry, they chose to approach the residents directly. That was when things went sour.

"The security guards were shot at. That is not in dispute. They returned fire and even shot someone in the back, which is the subject of another criminal investigation not before you today. During the chaotic moment, many refugees attempted to seek shelter. There were some break-ins, and those individuals will be found and arrested.

"However, you cannot paint every refugee with a broad brush. There was at least one refugee wielding a shotgun. He, along with two teenage boys and two other men, approached the front doors of several homes on the cul-de-sac we've identified earlier. We have evidence that one homeowner, seemingly unprovoked by nothing more than fear, began firing shots at the group of five refugees. One of the teenage boys received a superficial wound. He was treated at a hospital and released before the investigation even began. One of the three men accompanying the boys was his father. Acting out of love and protection for his child, we believe he fired back at the homeowner.

"Then another person entered the scene. Lurking in the shadows of a home he did not own, this newcomer fired upon the man holding the shotgun and his companions. In a brazen act of vigilante justice, he riddled the man's body with powerful bullets shot from an assault rifle in rapid succession, killing the refugee instantly. Naturally, the alleged shooter in possession of the shotgun and the teens fled."

The DA paused to circulate photos of the victim. They were gruesome, causing several of the grand jurors to glance at them but turn their heads away quickly.

He continued, "The homicide detectives conducted extensive interviews in the neighborhood to determine who might have a weapon of this type and be willing to use it. One name was given to the detectives over and over again.

"Dean Winchester. A professor recently terminated from Pepperdine University for illegally carrying a weapon on the campus in a blatant violation of school policy. A professor who wielded said weapon and admittedly was prepared to use it against a troubled young man who was in the midst of committing suicide. He was prepared to take the law into his own hands. Just like a vigilante would.

"Then, to bolster this man's frame of mind, Dean Winchester later made the following statements to reporters covering an attempted carjacking involving his wife." He took a piece of paper from his assistant and read it aloud.

"When asked if his wife should've been allowed to use her handgun on the would-be carjackers, here's what he said.

"You're damn right she would've used it! That's what they're for. Self-defense."

The DA paused. "He was then asked a question about pulling his handgun during the incident at Pepperdine." Again, he read Dean's exact words.

"I don't care if they were frightened. They'd be alive if that gunman had come into my classroom to shoot us all. I'd rather be alive and frightened than dead and stinkin'!"

DA Folsom placed a special emphasis on the final sentence, so he repeated it. "I'd rather be alive and frightened than dead and stinkin'!" He allowed the words to hang in the air so the grand jury could take them in before continuing.

"Dead and stinkin'," DA Folsom repeated for the third time. "Those sound like the words of a vigilante to me. Ladies and gentlemen, vigilantism cannot be tolerated in a law-abiding society. We have a criminal justice system for that. Based upon the LA County homicide division's thorough investigation, we believe Dean Winchester may have been the one who took the law into his own hands and gunned down an innocent refugee in cold blood. We are one step away from confirming this. We are asking for a search warrant that enables LA investigators led by a SWAT team for protection to enter the Winchester home to look for evidence to prove his guilt, or innocence, as the case may be. We are not seeking an indictment against Mr. Winchester yet. Only your approval to search his home. Thank you."

Sheila Harrison joined the other grand jurors in the deliberation room. Grand juries have taken as long as an hour to debate whether an indictment was appropriate. For search warrants, the decisions are made much faster.

Once inside, a man spoke up first. "It's not like they're gonna arrest him for any crime. They just need to look inside his home before he destroys any evidence. Do you agree?" He surveyed the other grand jurors. Most shrugged, indicating their indifference. Others nodded in agreement.

"He might try to hide the gun," added one.

"If he's innocent, he should cooperate," said another.

Sheila wasn't so sure. She had several misgivings regarding the reasoning for singling out Mr. Winchester for a vigilante murder. He had no criminal record. Plus, he was a professor at Pepperdine. Professors don't gun down people in cold blood. However, Sheila was ready to get onto the juicy stuff, not some run-of-the-mill search warrant request. She agreed so she didn't go against the grain or waste time unnecessarily.

Minutes later, Detective LaRon Johnson had his search warrant and approval from the DA's office to serve upon Dean Winchester and Emmy Foley. When he discussed the circumstances of the case with the warrants division, the captain suggested a SWAT team was necessary to protect the deputies and detectives involved.

Detective Johnson went back to the DA's office and discussed the overall situation with the prosecutor who'd actually be handling the case if Dean was later indicted. He thought about it and made the decision to approach a judge to modify the grand jury's approval of the search warrant.

Dean Winchester, the DA advised the judge, had recently been suspended from his job. He'd made statements threatening physical violence. And under the totality of the circumstances, he would possibly be a danger to law enforcement officers executing the warrant. Therefore, a no-knock entry and service of the search warrant was justified.

The judge, out of an abundance of caution, agreed. Detective Johnson immediately reached out to his contacts in the media to give them a heads-up about the timing of the raid. He got everything he'd hoped for. Dean Winchester was in for a helluva perp walk.

THIRTY-THREE

Thursday
Dean and Emma's House
The Colony at Malibu

"What the hell have you done, Dean!" exclaimed Emmy as she rushed through the front door into the yard. Her husband was briskly walking up the driveway to greet her.

"Okay. Okay. Let me explain." His voice trembled, as many husbands' do when they think they've done something that might get them exiled to the couch by their missus.

Emmy stood with her hands on her hips, her eyes darting between Dean and his G-Wagoneer parked in the cul-de-sac. She pointed towards the truck, her mouth opening, but she couldn't manage to vocalize her astonishment. Dean approached her, gently took her by the hands, and kissed her on the cheek.

"You know I love you, right?" he asked sheepishly.

"Dean, seriously?"

"Yes, I know. It's technically an RV."

"It's a tow-behind camper. But it's tiny. Like a miniature version of the A-frame chalet we used to stay in at Big Bear."

"Here's what I was thinking—" he began before she cut him off.

She pulled her hands away and began walking toward the rig. As she did, Dean trotted alongside like an anxious puppy excited to show his mommy the hole he'd torn open in the sofa.

"You were actually thinking when you did this?" she asked.

"Yeah. Grayson talked about looking for camping gear this week. Well, I found a camper."

"Yes, you did," she said dryly.

Dean's shoulders slumped, and his chin dropped to his chest. Emmy noticed the sudden change in his demeanor and decided to stop teasing him. She could see the benefit of having something like this if the worst-case blackout scenario came to fruition. She'd used her acting skills to give Dean a hard time, but seeing his reaction, she dropped the ruse.

"I love it!" she exclaimed.

"What? You do? Really?"

"Yeah, it's kinda cute," she said as she leaned over to reward him with a kiss on the cheek. "So, um, tell me about it."

Dean adopted his best impersonation of Cousin Eddie in the movie *Christmas Vacation*. "Well, Clark, this here is an RV. Yup, except I'm callin' it a bug-out vehicle."

"Bug out?" she asked. "Like, bugging out of town for a romantic weekend?"

Dean laughed. Partly because it was funny and partly out of a sense of relief. He didn't want to sleep on the couch, especially with Judson and Liza home, who were now moseying down the driveway with their morning coffee.

"Holy crap!" exclaimed Liza. "My parents had one of these when I was a kid."

"It's a bug-out vehicle," said Dean.

"Bug out to where?" asked Judson.

"Anywhere we want," Dean replied. He proudly strolled around the A-frame-shaped camper and admired its features. The tongue of the trailer holding the camper included a large front deck made with iron mesh for storage and two propane tanks attached. He opened the door and, with a touch of grace, stepped back to allow everyone to peek inside.

"You'll never be a *Price is Right* girl," said Judson with a chuckle. He stuck his head inside to look around. The small camper included a galley complete with a sink and gas range. A microwave was built into a cabinet as well. "How many does it sleep?"

"Okay, here's the thing," began Dean, who was proud of his purchase. Judson exited to allow the women to go inside. "It has a flip-up bed that sleeps two. A dining seating area that converts to another bed for two. And the floor would allow for three sleeping bags. All seven of us could sleep in here if we had to."

"And this is for when we bug out?" asked Judson.

"That's right. Here's the best part," Dean began in reply. He eased closer to the door so Emmy could hear. "I bought it on the Facebook Marketplace for only $4,000. The guy had lost his job and really needed the money. I felt bad for him, but he assured me the cash was more important to his family than the camper they couldn't use."

Emmy and Liza emerged from inside the camper. "Girls got dibs on the beds."

"Deal," said Dean. He pointed to the roof of the A-frame. "Look, skylights and solar panels too. There are racks attached for bicycles or a kayak. The large green containers will hold sixty gallons of fresh water."

"Hey, where's the potty?" asked Liza.

Judson pointed his thumb over his shoulder toward the bushes. "Nature, sweetheart. This ain't the Four Seasons on wheels."

Emmy wrapped her arm through Dean's and snuggled close to him. "Grayson will be proud. When does he come home, anyway?"

"He called and said he had to make another stop in Flagstaff to pick up some more gear," replied Dean. "He said he'd be back tomorrow afternoon."

Grayson had become concerned about their weapons and ammunition supply. He'd always kept plenty for his purposes. Now, he had to bring three other households to a level that would allow them to defend themselves for an extended period of time. As he'd reminded the group last Friday, if China took down the grid for many months, if not longer, they wouldn't be able to shop for guns and ammo anywhere. If the reaction of the desperate refugees was any indication, it would become a far more dangerous world than they were accustomed to.

Emmy gently patted Dean on the chest. "Okay, honey. We all love it. Now, would you mind putting it somewhere besides the front of our house?"

Dean averted his eyes. "Yeah, um, about that. The storage place down the road has a parking spot for it, but I can't take it down there until tomorrow, which is the first. I have to park it here for now."

Emmy gave Dean *the look*, and this time she wasn't acting. "Move it in front of his house, or at least the camper part. He's out of town anyway."

Dean took a moment and circled through the cul-de-sac, parking his bug-out rig so his vintage G-Wagoneer was visible from the house, but the camper was tucked away behind the trees separating the two properties. It was rare for Dean to park his beloved Jeep Wagoneer outside of the garage. At least he could keep an eye on it this way.

Once he was done, he joined the group for a day of shopping. They were going to focus on high-end camping stores to purchase more of what they'd acquired a few weeks ago. The camper would be used to stow the gear in case the group had to leave in a hurry.

By the end of the day, they'd stocked the camper with nonperishable foods, water, full propane tanks and clothing. If necessary, they could hook it up and be on the road before they got trapped in a powerless city of nearly ten million residents, plus the refugees from around the state who caused the City of Angels to burst at the seams.

THIRTY-FOUR

Friday
The Colony at Malibu

At 4:00 a.m. on Friday morning, on-duty SWAT team members met at the LA County Sheriff's Department mobile command center in Woodland Hills. The vehicles carried the team of eight specially trained patrol officers and their gear across the Santa Monica mountains near the Topanga Canyon. The winding road was deserted that morning as the commander of the operation, known only as 30-David, rode in an unmarked SUV along with Detective Johnson and two more detectives from the Metro homicide division.

Once they arrived at the entry gate to the Colony, another sergeant, 24-David, approached the security personnel and confirmed the purpose of the SWAT team and the warrant to be served. Zelmanski was there, as he'd been contacted two hours prior. They were asked to block all traffic in and out of the neighborhood until advised otherwise. He provided the gate guards his business card with his cell phone number to contact him if anyone tried to force their way through the gates.

30-David took a moment to check with the eight-man SWAT team who'd perform the breach and clear the premises. They were ready. They confirmed they'd set up all command vehicles down the street, blocking the entrance to the cul-de-sac. Four men were divided into two-man teams. They would secure the perimeter and then make their entry once the other four SWAT team members, plus two sergeants, breached the front door.

For three days, team leaders worked with Detective Johnson to conduct background checks on the suspect and his wife. They learned from the neighborhood's HOA president that another couple had moved into the home of the suspect. This couple had been involved in the shooting the night of the power outage. Detective Johnson pointed to this new revelation as further evidence the suspect, Dean Winchester, was in fact the shooter of the victim.

For that reason, and based upon the recent behavior of the suspect, he was considered to be armed and dangerous. This fact helped bolster Detective Johnson's argument that a no-knock raid was warranted.

All teams were set for a breach at 5:00 a.m. The two-man teams indicated the perimeter was secure. The four SWAT team officers, followed by 24-David and the three detectives, formed a single-file line often referred to as the snake. This minimized the number of team members who presented an open target to armed suspects.

The point man was at the most risk. He was also the teams' most experienced member, having served nineteen years with LA SWAT. He had nerves of steel, as his job was to enter an unknown room first and neutralize any suspects he encountered. The point man had to make split-second, life-or-death decisions. He held his own fate, and the fate of any one in the home, in his hands. Or his trigger finger.

The point man received the go command. He stood aside to allow an officer who stood six feet, four inches tall room to work. His legs were as strong as telephone poles, and his biceps measured nineteen inches. He needed that strength to wield the *enforcer*, an all-steel, fifty-pound battering ram the team used to force doors open.

With a herculean heave, he pulled the enforcer back and slammed it hard against the door near the bolt lock. The Kwikset bolt lock was no match for the brute force exerted through the enforcer. The officer stepped aside, and the point man took over.

They'd studied the layout of the home by obtaining a floor plan from the county building department. This enabled them to focus on the most likely location of the suspect within the residence.

"Police department!" he yelled as they rushed into the foyer. By prearrangement, the second member of the team, followed by the fourth, peeled away from the snake to quickly clear the living areas, including the kitchen. The remainder of the team moved to the right towards the master bedroom.

A figure appeared in the doorway, barely visible to the naked eye. The point man wasted no time. He retrieved a flash-bang grenade from his utility belt and detonated it in the hallway near the master bedroom entrance.

"Arrrggghhh!" shouted Dean as the grenade bounced off a wall near his face. He was temporarily blinded and stunned, causing him to spin around and fall back into the bedroom.

"Police! Stay on the floor!" shouted the point man.

He pressed forward, automatic rifle raised, pointing it back and forth in search of targets. "Right!" he shouted as he approached a guest bathroom. The next man in the snake line burst into the bathroom and swung his rifle in all directions.

"Clear right!"

Emmy was screaming. She asked, "What's going on? Dean!"

The point man cautiously approached. "Police! On the floor! Now!"

"But why?" Her voice pleaded for an explanation in the midst of her sobbing. She was on her knees and bent over her husband, who was unresponsive.

"Movement upstairs!" shouted one of the members of the team who'd breached the home through the back door.

"Hey! What are you doing?" Judson shouted over the railing. Seconds later, red laser dots bounced around the ceiling above him until they settled on his chest. Instinctively, he swung around to avoid the laser sights.

"Going up!" shouted one of the SWAT officers.

"On your six," said another, a former Army soldier.

The two men rushed up the stairs, one pointing his rifle toward the landing; the other pointed toward the bedroom doors upstairs.

"We don't want trouble!" shouted Liza.

Her request was met with another flash-bang grenade being detonated in the dark hallway. Liza screamed and ran back into the bedroom, where she and Judson huddled in the corner. The two SWAT team members rushed into the room.

"On the floor!"

"But—" Liza tried to protest, but the officer grabbed her by the arm and forced her down.

Judson became angry. "Stop that! You can't do that to my wife!"

Instead, the other officer did it to him. While one officer jammed his boot onto the back of Judson's neck, the other restrained Judson by tying his hands behind his back with plasticuffs.

Liza was sobbing as her body went limp. She allowed the officer to force her arms behind her back and handcuff her as well. She and Judson lay on the floor, trying to see one another in the dark, both crying uncontrollably.

"Second floor clear! Two in custody!"

"Moving to third floor!" Another two-man team ascended the stairs to arrive in the middle of the place where the Friday Night Club had gathered for years. It was a place where the friends could enjoy one another's company and seek refuge from the outside world. In an instant, it would become subjected to a brutal examination by people who didn't care for the sanctity of Dean and Emmy's home or the memories that had been created there.

"We are Code 4!" yelled 24-David.

"Roger that. Code 4," replied the SWAT team commander, 30-David. "Restore power."

Prior to the raid, the SWAT team commander had notified the power company to disconnect the electric service precisely at 4:55 a.m. Now that the premises were secured, they were authorized to reinstate power so the detectives could serve their warrant and search for evidence.

"Suspect secured. In need of medical attention."

"Inbound," replied 30-David.

"Weapons located on second floor in bedroom three."

"Roger that," responded 30-David. "Forensic team en route."

The entire raid took eleven minutes. The nightmare for Dean and Emmy was just beginning.

THIRTY-FIVE

Friday
Dean and Emmy's Home
The Colony at Malibu

It had been a week since the Colony at Malibu residents thought they'd had enough excitement to last a lifetime. The SWAT team raid of Dean and Emmy's house provided the kind of drama the daytime actress could only imagine generating. As the sun peeked over the mountains, the sirens of an ambulance screamed down the PCH and up the ridge to where nearly a dozen law enforcement vehicles blocked the streets. The scrum of vehicles at the entrance to the cul-de-sac didn't deter the curious onlookers from walking through people's landscape beds and manicured lawns to get a look at the crime scene.

Two of the people forcing their way through shrubs and onlookers were Lee and Nicole. They had been unaware of the raid until the ambulance entered the neighborhood with its sirens blaring.

When it passed their street and turned into the cul-de-sac, Lee noticed the police presence. It didn't take him long to realize what had happened.

By the time the two rushed into the yard across the street from Dean and Emmy's, the SWAT team had begun to remove their gear. Uniformed patrol officers were attempting to cordon off the area, demanding residents back up away from the scene.

Lee, who was casually dressed, remembered to bring his detective's shield. In the midst of the chaotic scene caused by the sheer numbers of residents who crowded around, he was able to flash the badge and gain entry inside the police tape, with Nicole close behind.

Judson and Liza were sitting in the back of a patrol car parked in front of Grayson's house. Lee approached the officer watching them and flashed his badge. His demeanor shifted from concerned friend to detective.

"Lee Wong, Interagency Gang Task Force. What've we got?"

"No-knock warrant on the perp," the young officer responded. "SWAT executed it perfectly."

"Who's in the ambulance?" Nicole asked, drawing a stern look from Lee.

Now, the young officer was curious about Lee and Nicole. "Can I see that badge again?"

Lee showed him. He pressed for answers although he expected the young man to be more guarded. "What about these two?"

The officer scowled and hesitated. He gave an imperceptible shrug before he responded, "They were in a guest bedroom. Resisted arrest. I'm babysitting until Detective Johnson gives me the word to take them downtown."

"Who is the ambulance for?" Lee asked.

"The perp. He got in the way of a flash-bang." Inexplicably, the officer laughed and added, "He'll never do that again."

Lee knew the permanent damage the grenades could do. Dean could be seriously injured. He resisted the urge to grab the patrol officer by the throat and let him have it. He turned to Nicole and nodded toward the patrol car. She immediately left his side to check on their friends. The officer watched her go.

"Hey, what is she doing?"

"She's checking on their well-being," Lee replied with a raised voice. "You need to learn to respect the rights of the innocent. You're not dealing with a bunch of gangbangers. These people are respectable and possibly innocent. Treat them accordingly."

"Who are you again?" the officer asked as he reached for the microphone attached to his portable radio unit.

Lee dissuaded him. "Don't bother calling Johnson. I'll deal with him myself."

He began to march toward the ambulance, his shield on full display, prominently attached to his jeans' waistband.

Nicole hustled to catch up to him. "They're scared, but fine."

"Good," replied Lee, who had smoke coming out of his ears. "Check on Dean and find Emmy. I've got something to do."

"What?"

"I've got this," replied Lee, who ripped his badge from his waistband and flashed it at an officer standing at the bottom of Dean's driveway.

He strutted toward the front of the house and approached another officer blocking the entrance. Flashing the badge didn't work with this one.

"Where's Detective Johnson?"

Without responding, the officer pointed over his shoulder toward the house.

Lee tried to move past him, but the officer blocked his access. "I need to see him," insisted Lee.

"Strict instructions, Detective. Nobody inside except his team from homicide."

Lee was pissed. He began yelling, "Johnson! Get out here. I wanna talk to you!"

Detective Johnson was in the living room, discussing his plans to search every square inch of Dean and Emmy's house. They'd already made several startling discoveries to bolster his murder case against Dean.

"Who is that?" Detective Johnson bellowed from inside.

"Detective Lee Wong!"

"We're a little busy, Wong. Besides, this is not a drug task force matter. Officer, escort him off the premises."

The officer took Lee's arm, who quickly jerked it away. It caused the officer to lose his balance. Lee had an opening and took it. He raced up the stairs into the foyer.

Lee wasted no time. "What the hell do you think you're doing?" He shouted his question at Detective Johnson. He glanced at the front door, which had been knocked off its hinges. "A no-knock raid? Are you out of your freakin' mind?"

"Get out of here, Wong. Or I'll have you arrested. Besides, you're a material witness in this murder. Get out!"

The burly officer Lee had scooted around was back and ready to forcibly remove him from the house. Lee kept shouting.

"I know how these things go! You are about to destroy this family's home for no reason. What kind of lies did you tell the grand jury to justify all of this?"

"Enough!" Detective Johnson shouted back. He quickly moved to get in Lee's face. "I told you to get the hell out of my crime scene!" He hissed through his teeth as he spoke.

"There is no crime here, asshole!"

Lee was truly pushing his luck. He would most likely get reprimanded for his actions. It would be just one more of many he'd received over the years.

"Really? Well, I've got two unregistered shotguns and three handguns, so far. Enough ammo to start a gang war. The people whose house was shot at were sleeping in the bedroom right over our head. Coincidence? Hell no. We found a stash of gas and gold coins. And guess what else? A camper stocked and ready to go on the lam. We got here just in time, Detective Wong, before Winchester disappeared."

"That's ridiculous, and you know it!" Lee screamed into Johnson's face. However, he knew better. The circumstantial evidence was beginning to pile up.

"No, it's not. And we're just getting started. Now, last time before I have you arrested for obstruction of justice. Get the hell out!"

Lee scowled and jutted his chin out. "This isn't over."

"It is for you. Go!"

Lee turned and walked away, brushing past the patrol officer who blocked the doorway. When he reached the porch outside, he took a deep breath and exhaled. He observed the scene from the elevated point of view. *What a circus*, he thought to himself. The media had arrived and were filming from all directions. The ambulance was attending to Dean. Emmy was restrained and held in a patrol car nearby. Nicole was arguing with an officer. And just outside the crime scene tape, Toby and Zelmanski stood side by side, having a good laugh.

THIRTY-SIX

Friday
Dean and Emmy's House
The Colony at Malibu

"Man, I couldn't have scripted this any better," said Toby as he leaned into his number one, Zelmanski.

The two men had been aware of the raid in advance, as the SWAT team commander, 30-David, had reached out to Zelmanski to advise his entry gate security personnel of their approach. Zelmanski had immediately brought Toby up to speed so they could get a ringside seat across the cul-de-sac from the house. They had a clear, unobstructed view of the SWAT team's breach of the front door. As the breach had occurred, Toby actually giggled like a young child.

Once the SWAT team gave the all clear, the rest of the officers working the periphery moved into position. First, they cordoned off the scene. Then the forensics unit and other officers moved in to assist the detectives. Toby and Zelmanski did tamp down their enthusiasm slightly when they heard the call over the police comms for an ambulance. Apparently, one person had been injured during the raid.

As soon as the barricade tape was in place, Toby and Zelmanski rushed to get the best possible viewing point, not unlike what golf tournament attendees do when they wanna be closest to a golfer's ball that landed in the rough.

Their elation grew when Judson and Liza were perp-walked out of the house in plasticuffs. Liza was sobbing, and Judson was fighting back tears. Toby and Zelmanski were like two high school boys getting a chuckle out of a common enemy getting the screws put to him. They both were looking around, astonished at the number of residents who'd come out of their homes to watch the spectacle unfolding at Dean and Emmy's home.

Next, Emmy was pulled out of the house in cuffs. She, too, was crying. They'd allowed her to put on a robe, which kept flying open, revealing her silk pajamas. Toby and Zelmanski strained to get a look at the famous actress in her barely there attire.

As the sun came up, the crowd grew larger. Police were working diligently to keep them out of the way of the detectives and the forensics team, who needed access to their vehicle. When the ambulance finally arrived, they physically pushed a large part of the crowd out of the cul-de-sac. Toby and Zelmanski changed their location to avoid being evicted from the crime scene.

Shortly thereafter, Dean was taken out of the house on a stretcher. He had an oxygen mask affixed to his nose and mouth. A moistened bandage was wrapped around his head to cover his eyes. The exposed skin, namely his cheeks and forehead, looked like he'd fallen asleep in a tanning bed for hours.

The two men stared as Dean was lifted into the ambulance. They pushed forward to get a closer look, bending the barricade tape to the point of breaking. Their efforts landed them near Mrs. Javitz, who was fighting back tears of her own.

When a police officer was instructed to remove Emmy from the back of a patrol car so she could see her husband, many in the community began to cry. Emmy was distraught and barely able to stand. She begged the officers to let her ride with her husband. She was refused. She tried to wrestle away from their grasp, and during the struggle, she fell to her knees, tearing open bloody wounds on both kneecaps. Regardless, the sobbing wife was denied access to her husband and was dragged by two burly officers to the back of the patrol car, where a paramedic attended to her wounds.

"You can't feel sorry for these people," said Toby. "This is what happens when you don't cooperate with law enforcement. This is what happens when you don't obey the rules and standards of our neighborhood."

"Absolutely," added Zelmanski. "There are rules that must be enforced by those of us with the authority to do so. It's not up to the likes of a professor to take matters into his own hands. I know it's a lesson learned for him and his friends."

"And the rest of the neighborhood," said Toby.

Zelmanski studied the crime scene and the faces of the neighbors who were watching the police do their job. "I think we need to call a neighborhood meeting. I mean, if not today, tomorrow morning."

"ASAP," added Toby. "We need to capitalize on this to bring into the fold anyone who thought they could avoid being a part of our vision for the future here at the Colony."

Zelmanski nodded and smiled. He shared a fist bump with Toby. "Never let a good crisis go to waste. Right?"

"Damn straight!" responded Toby.

The two men backed away from the police barricade tape, whispering back and forth as they studied the faces in the crowd. There was one face, however, standing in close proximity to them that they missed because she was short in stature although large in her convictions—Mrs. Javitz.

THIRTY-SEVEN

Friday
Los Angeles Sheriff's Department
Inmate Reception Center
450 Bauchet Street
Downtown Los Angeles

The concussive effect of the flash-bang grenade came as a result of its detonation near Dean's face. The point man had been overzealous in tossing the stun grenade too close to Dean. In baseball parlance, the point man had thrown a fastball high and tight.

Flash-bang grenades have long been used by law enforcement to temporarily disable a suspect during an arrest or as a tool to control crowds in a riot. When the grenade detonates, its sound reaches one hundred seventy-five decibels. By comparison, a jet engine is about one hundred forty decibels.

The closer the target to the stun grenade, the more dangerous it becomes. Temporary deafness and ear-ringing are expected. Too close, as was the case with Dean, and disruption of the inner ear fluid occurs. This can cause permanent damage to the hearing and disorientation, resulting in loss of balance. Further, as was the case for Dean, nearly being struck in the face resulted in flash blindness and burns to his skin.

Rather than taking Dean to the nearest hospital, the ambulance driver was instructed to drive directly to deliver the detainee to the Los Angeles County and University of Southern California Medical center's open ward, where injured criminal detainees were treated. Known as the LCOW, there were full-time deputies on duty to deal with the securing of criminals while they were treated.

Because Dean had not been charged with a crime, his personal information had not been entered into the Los Angeles County Sheriff's Department, or LASD, database. The watch commander at the hospital became irritated when he was unable to find any of the normal criteria for assigning a security level to Dean, such as his inmate or booking number, threat assessment relative to his danger to the community, or even the arresting agency's jurisdiction.

As a result, Dean was treated as a John Doe for purposes of medical treatment until the watch commander was provided a copy of the Automated Jail Information System, AJIS data, relative to the patient.

For the next eight hours, Dean was attended to by a combination of hospital personnel, including University of Southern California students. The LAC & USC Medical Center was an inner-city public hospital that was required to take all injured people regardless of their ability to pay. Even before the blackout of a week ago, the facility had been overwhelmed, as unrest had been rampant throughout LA. With the influx of refugees, the demand for medical attention had quickly resulted in a health care crisis.

By six that evening, Dean was ready to be released by the hospital staff into the care of law enforcement. His hearing was partially restored, and his vision, although blurred, was sufficient enough to find his way to the stainless-steel sink-toilet combo in the holding cells at the nearby Inmate Reception Center.

After Dean became more coherent, his brain fog having dissipated from the near concussion he'd sustained, he peppered hospital personnel and the occasional deputy who came near his bed with questions. None of them responded to his questions, and they certainly did not comply with his demands for a phone call. He was told he'd get his phone call when he was booked into the jail. When he demanded to know what his charges were, the deputies would shrug because they honestly had no idea.

At 10:00 p.m., Dean was transported in a small bus that made runs back and forth between the medical center's jail ward and the Inmate Reception Center. Housed within the Twin Towers Correctional Facility in downtown Los Angeles, the IRC, as it was known, was responsible for the intake classification, processing and release of inmates who were in the custody of the LASD.

The IRC was also responsible for the storage of inmate property. Dean did not have any. He'd slept in a pair of pajama bottoms and nothing else. At the hospital, his clothes had been removed, and he was provided a bright-orange jumpsuit with the letters LASD emblazoned on the back. He was issued a pair of blue imitation Keds sneakers, white boxers and a pair of socks. That was it.

First, the deputies processed the inmates transported by the medical bus because they'd been assigned AJIS numbers. Dean was still an anomaly within the sheriff's department. He was simply being detained on a forty-eight-hour hold per the instructions of Detective LaRon Johnson in homicide. Protocols required someone of Dean's status to be held in protective custody, separate from the general population, because he had not been charged with a crime.

The Twin Towers also housed the central jail. Its overcrowded conditions were legendary. In 1990, the building had been renovated to increase its capacity to fifty-three hundred. Today, it held just under nineteen thousand criminal detainees, all men.

Due to the large number of detainees, isolation cells were nonexistent. The intake supervisor placed Dean in a medical-designated cell with seven other inmates, which included violent offenders. It was the only available bunk on a Friday night.

Dean persevered. He was aware of the dangerous conditions at the Twin Towers facility. He was keenly aware that his injured state would make him vulnerable to the inmates around him with violent tendencies.

By midnight, he was settled into the medical cell. He'd expected something akin to the medical ward at the hospital. Instead, the floor was littered with trash. One of the two sink-toilet combos was stopped up and overflowing with feces. The smell took his breath away. The shower curtain had been ripped off the bar and lay in a heap near the overflowing toilet. He wondered what the rest of the jail looked like if the medical-designated cell was this unhygienic.

Eventually, he found himself on a top bunk, staring at the ceiling, afraid to sleep. His mind wandered as he calculated the number of hours he'd been in custody, which he hoped was nineteen. In his mind, he had been raided by SWAT at five a.m. It was now midnight. Nineteen hours, leaving twenty-nine more to go.

He could do this, he kept trying to convince himself. He recalled what he could of the SWAT raid before the flash-bang grenade had blown up near his face. He had no memory of being transported to the hospital. When he had been awakened from the mild concussion he'd suffered, he had been handcuffed to a hospital bed, surrounded by the dregs of society.

Now that he was settled, to an extent, Dean fought back tears as he tried to process the events of the day. He'd read of many cases of mistaken identity committed by police and SWAT teams. He wouldn't be the first innocent homeowner to be attacked by such a brutal method of police tactics. He presumed this was the reason nobody was able to tell him what he was charged with. Having never been arrested, he was not familiar with any of the procedures he was being subjected to.

All he knew was that he was on a forty-eight-hour hold for some reason. Dean lay in his bunk, listening to the sounds echoing through the concrete and steel surroundings, praying Emmy was safe and another hour had passed. It would be the longest forty-eight hours of his life, until the next forty-eight.

THIRTY-EIGHT

Saturday
Los Angeles Sheriff's Department
Inmate Reception Center
Downtown Los Angeles

Dean's mind and body finally succumbed to exhaustion. When he was awakened by the sound of inmates assigned to the jail's kitchen staff making their way to the medical cells with breakfast trays, he immediately asked his cellmates what time it was. "Five a.m.," one of them finally responded. Dean thanked the young Hispanic kid, whose right shoulder and upper arm were heavily wrapped.

Dean tried to befriend the man by asking, "What happened to your shoulder?"

"Got shot, man. Whadya think?"

The guy was rude, so Dean didn't further the conversation. Moments later, he learned how rude the gang member could be when he snatched Dean's breakfast tray out of his hand. He lowered his eyes and stared Dean down, daring him to protest. Even with a gunshot wound and a heavily bandaged shoulder, Dean imagined the guy could administer a helluva beatdown. Besides, after catching a glimpse of the watery flour gravy poured over a biscuit, commonly known in jail parlance as shit on a shingle, Dean decided the meal wasn't worth risking his life over.

An hour or so passed, and Dean tried to relax. His mind had difficulty resting, as the pain to his face and the ringing in his ears took a toll. Then he heard his name called out.

"Winchester!" a guard bellowed as he waddled down the corridor. "You got a visitor."

Dean was excited. He thought for sure Emmy would be coming to see him. His emotions took over, and he began to shed a few tears, drawing ridicule and mockery from his cellmates. Anxious, Dean stood at the gate, waiting for the guard to unlock it.

"What the hell are you doin'?" the guard asked with a gruff.

"Um, you said I had a visitor."

The guard laughed and looked at the other inmates. "So, do you think I just unlock the door and let you stroll through the jail to the visiting rooms? Turn your dumb ass around and stick your hands through the tray slot. You gotta get cuffed, man."

Dean's shoulders slumped as he turned around. One of his cellmates took his plastic spoon and slung a soggy piece of biscuit that smacked him on his burnt cheek just as the jailer closed the cuffs on him. Dean vigorously shook his head to get the gross hunk of food off his face.

The door opened with a clank, and the guard squeezed Dean by the back of the arm and pulled him into the corridor. "Stand there with your back against the wall. A detective is here to see you. I want you to hear my words. Don't screw with me. Feelin' me?"

Dean nodded. "Yes. Okay."

He was trembling as the guard led him by the arm through two steel doors, which were opened and closed by an officer sitting in what looked like a toll booth. The small space was full of closed-circuit monitors and a console of buttons that operated several doors associated with the medical detention section of the jail.

Dean was dejected at first. He'd hoped to see his wife and an attorney that he was certain Emmy would've gotten for him. Then his anxiety rose to a fever pitch as he wondered if Emmy had been taken into custody as well. Was she being held in a shithole like this one? Was she injured? What about Judson and Liza, innocent bystanders in this. Whatever *this* was.

Dean was led into a small cell-like room that contained a stainless-steel table and a stool bolted to the concrete floor. A steel ring protruded through the table. The guard unlocked his cuffs and deftly brought Dean's arms around to the front of his stomach. In a matter of seconds, he was handcuffed to the steel ring and forced to sit on the steel stool.

"Cool your jets, Winchester. The detectives will be here shortly."

"Detectives? More than one?" asked Dean. He'd expected Lee, who'd probably use his contacts within the LASD to determine Dean's whereabouts.

He fidgeted on the hard seat, trying to make himself comfortable. His face itched from the burns he'd sustained. He struggled to bend over to rub his cheeks and forehead against his handcuffed hands. Occasionally, he'd look up at the one-way mirror, the partially reflective glass that was often used in interrogation rooms like this one to observe a criminal defendant during questioning. He wondered if he was being watched.

Only, Dean reminded himself, he was not a defendant, nor was he a criminal. They might have questions for him, but he had questions of his own. If Lee or his attorney didn't walk through that door, then he was prepared to give these detectives an earful.

He worked himself up, imagining the back-and-forth that would take place between himself and the detectives. However, nearly an hour passed, and Dean lost his will to fight. He became sleepy and relaxed, somewhat appreciative of the opportunity to get out of the cell. The air was cleaner. The noise was muted. And he was safe.

He was nodding off when the steel door suddenly opened, and two men walked in. He was jolted out of his relaxed state of mind as he heard his name.

"Dean Winchester, my name is Detective Johnson with Metro homicide. This is my associate Detective Jones. We have a few questions for you."

The two men pulled folding chairs in front of the table. Johnson opened a file folder, and the other detective had a yellow legal pad with a pencil in front of him. He would never use it. Nor would Dean.

"What's this about?" asked Dean. Rather than being combative, he elected to take the calm, innocent approach because he was.

Detective Johnson did not answer his question. He opened the file folder and removed the gruesome, gunshot-riddled body of the victim. He turned it and shoved it toward Dean until it lodged against the steel ring where his hands were cuffed.

"Recognize this man?" Detective Johnson asked.

Dean glanced at it for a moment and then averted his eyes. He had not eaten since Thursday evening, as the hospital had failed to feed him. He could feel bile rising up in his throat.

"No."

"Are you sure, Mr. Winchester? Perhaps you'd like to take a closer look?" Detective Johnson picked up the eight-by-ten glossy of the victim's body and held it in front of Dean's face. Dean immediately turned his head to the side.

"Look at him, Winchester!" the other detective shouted, startling Dean to the point he almost urinated in his jumpsuit.

"I already told you. I don't know this person." Dean's voice was stern, but weak. He was exhausted. "Why are you doing this to me? To us? Where is my wife?"

Detective Johnson continued, "Where were you at approximately three in the morning last Saturday, the evening of the power outage?"

"Home," Dean replied. "With my wife."

"Mr. Winchester, during the course of our search, we discovered two shotguns, three handguns, and several military-issue ammunition cans filled with shotgun shells and nine-millimeter bullets."

"Nearly a thousand rounds, by our count," said the younger detective. "Are you planning to start a war, Professor? Or do you consider yourself some kind of one-man police force?"

"What? No. I'm not starting a war or a police force. Those are for self-defense."

The younger detective broke out in a fake laugh. "A thousand rounds? I don't think self-defense is the only thing on your mind, Professor. Just admit it, you've got some superhero complex. I bet you watch a lot of cop shows on TV. Is that, like, some kind of fetish for you, Professor cop-wannabe? Do you think it turns on all of those pretty co-eds you pretended to protect that day at Pepperdine?"

"Screw you, asshole!" Now Dean was pissed off. "I did protect my students from that murderer. I wasn't going to allow them to be victims."

"Okay, Mr. Winchester," began Detective Johnson calmly. "Is that what you did the night of the power outage? Protect your neighbors and friends. Um, Judson and Elizabeth Pryce." He referred to his notes to confirm the names before he studied Dean for a response.

"No. I was home, like I said. I had my own house to protect from the people who busted through our security gates and raided our neighborhood."

The young detective began to laugh. "There we go. Now I get it. Those refugees were raiders. Marauders. Barbarians at the gate. And you, Professor, are the protector of neighbors. The good guy when law enforcement isn't around. What are you, some kind of doomsday prepper?"

"Huh?" asked Dean.

"Well, let's see, Professor. Your home had enough food stored to last a month of Sundays. I mean, how many forty-pound sacks of pinto beans do you need, Professor?"

For what seemed like the twentieth time, the young detective mocked Dean by using a sarcastic tone of voice when referring to him as a professor.

"I'm not a professor. At least not at the moment."

"Why is that, Mr. Winchester?" asked Detective Johnson.

"I was temporarily suspended because of the incident on campus regarding the gunman."

"Yeah, sure. The incident," the young detective interrupted, using his fingers to provide air quotes around the word *incident*. "Is that what you call brandishing a weapon? Scaring the crap out of your students? All in violation of university policy, which could've gotten you fired. You got lucky and received a suspension, although lawsuits are flying around, aren't they?"

Dean took a deep breath and exhaled. The fight had left his body, not because he wasn't up to the task. Lack of food, worry over Emmy, and being the brunt of ridicule coupled with false accusations had taken their toll.

Detective Johnson spoke softly to Dean. "Mr. Winchester, let me tell you what I think. I believe you are otherwise a good man who has gotten caught up in the news headlines of the day. Listen, I get it. You should see what I see every day. I can understand why you might feel the need to protect your students and your wife. Even your close friends who have moved into your home. I can't argue with any of that.

"That said, we have to draw the line when people try to take the law into their own hands. I don't know for certain what happened in your neighborhood that night. It could be our victim had it coming. I don't know how a judge and jury would feel about that argument. I do know this, based on years of experience. When people who are in a pickle admit what they've done early on in an investigation like this one, it goes a long way in the eyes of the DA's office and a judge when it comes time to address your future."

The younger detective slowly slid the legal pad and the pencil until it touched Dean's forearm resting on the table. He spoke in a calm voice, completely opposite of his bad-cop demeanor earlier.

"Do the right thing, Mr. Winchester. Write out everything that happened that night. Tell us what happened. Tell us what you did with the rifle that killed this man. It'll help you down the road, and it's the right thing to do."

Dean flexed his fingers and studied the notepad. He knew what had happened. So did Judson, Liza and Emmy. Grayson had shot and killed that man. The gruesome photo revealed the precision marksmanship that had struck the man over and over again in his chest. Dean had a lot of questions to ask Grayson about that night, and other things that had surfaced of late. But for now, he was finished with the questions.

He locked eyes with Detective Johnson. "I want a lawyer."

THIRTY-NINE

**Dateline: Los Angeles – Office of the Mayor
Associated Press**

In a move mirroring decisions made by the mayors in New York, Chicago, and Detroit, Mayor Carla Blass has requested the National Guard to be deployed to governmental buildings and transit systems throughout the City of Los Angeles.

In the last week following the blackout that temporarily beset the city, an explosion of crime has swept across LA. Murders, violent assaults with weapons, and home invasions have spiked forty-five percent.

The mayor's edict includes suspension of her own policies against stop-and-frisk and racial profiling, policies many of her critics claim contributed to the problem. Now, over one thousand redeployed National Guardsmen will join existing law enforcement officers, who are now authorized to conduct random bag checks, frisk searches, requests for identification, and interrogation of those citizens engaging in suspicious activities.

During her press conference, she refused to answer questions. However, it was clear those in attendance sought answers to what standards the Guard or law enforcement officers would be required to adhere to during the course of their duties. Afterwards, her press liaison acknowledged that the next step in battling the crime wave could include curfews and lockdowns. The press liaison also confirmed enhanced security measures, including surveillance, possible social media controls, and movement restrictions, were not off the table.

FORTY

Saturday
The Colony at Malibu

Toby and Zelmanski spent most of Friday preparing for the neighborhood meeting he'd called for Saturday morning. They'd printed flyers and distributed them to every neighbor, even practicing redundancy by handing them out to residents as they passed through the entry gate. Because they hoped for a large number of residents to be in attendance, they chose a point in the center of the neighborhood where everyone could walk to equally. It was calculated, yet outwardly happenstance, that the chosen location was the entry to the cul-de-sac where the shooting had taken place during the blackout.

"Good morning, everyone!" Toby raised his voice to direct everyone's attention to where he and Zelmanski were standing in the bed of a pickup truck acting as a makeshift elevated podium. The vehicle was flanked on both sides by several of Zelmanski's uniformed security guards.

While Toby allowed the residents to settle down and halt their conversations with one another, he tried to estimate the crowd size. He mentally divided them as to where they were situated, whether in the center of the street, in someone's yard, or far in the back to avoid being noticed.

Later, he shared his count with Zelmanski, and the two men were nearly identical at eighty. Half of the adult population in the neighborhood. *Not bad*, Toby thought to himself, since there were a lot of second homeowners who wanted nothing to do with the LA area under the circumstances. The count of eighty adults also represented the number of residents who'd willingly cooperated with his block captains when they interviewed homeowners about their firearms and food supplies.

Before he started, he nodded to the security team, who waited dutifully for his command. They slowly moved through the crowd and handed out a four-page packet of materials. He began his presentation by addressing the printed materials.

"Thank you all for coming. We have quite a bit to discuss today, and I'm sure you have questions. To quicken the meeting, I've taken the liberty of passing out a summary sheet of what Mr. Zelmanski and I continue to implement to enhance security measures to protect all of us.

"Then you'll see a list of people who are either out of town or who've been unresponsive to our block captains as they undertook to gather basic information about their households. I hope that you'll find the time to reach out to any of these folks, whether they're close neighbors or acquaintances, and urge them to cooperate with Mr. Zelmanski's team."

Toby paused while the materials were handed out. He allowed himself a smile. First, he'd gotten his standing army. Now he had an army of snitches. The neighbors were thumbing through the pages, focused primarily on the list of residents who'd not complied with a request most in attendance thought to be reasonable. He saw several comparing notes, tapping on the page while their heads shook with disapproval. *Us versus them*, he thought to himself.

He continued, raising his voice at first until the whispering amongst the residents stopped. "Okay, everyone. Let me discuss a few matters with you. What happened in our neighborhood during the blackout could be a sign of things to come. Mr. Zelmanski and I have reached out to our contacts in local law enforcement as well as in Sacramento. The possibility of future rolling blackouts is very real. If what we experienced that evening is any indication, the next major power outage could be far more dangerous."

"What can we do to help?" asked one of the residents, strategically planted in the middle of the crowd by Toby.

"I'm glad you asked. Mr. Zelmanski's team risked their lives to protect our neighborhood during the power outage. While mentally prepared, they were outmanned by the horde that stormed our gates. And they were outgunned. What we learned from that incident is we need people to step up as volunteers to assist in the neighborhood's security. Let Mr. Zelmanski's trained security personnel handle the entry gate, where intruders are likely to challenge our privacy and safety. We need street patrols to observe our homes at all times of the day and report back to Mr. Zelmanski's security team if they see anything out of the ordinary."

Zelmanski stepped forward. "See something, say something."

"That's right," added Toby.

A man raised his hand near the front of the crowd. He spoke softly. "I'd love to help, but I don't have a gun."

"Can't hear!" shouted a woman standing at the rear of the attendees next to Mrs. Javitz, whose presence was obscured by a large man standing in front of her.

"Okay," began Toby. "He was saying that he was willing to volunteer but doesn't own a firearm. Let me address that. Volunteerism is the bedrock of any society. It takes a village, as they say. We all need to come together as an entire community to help protect one another and to support our neighbors in their time of need. Volunteering will fill that need.

"Now, with respect to guns. We actually do not want you to carry weapons while volunteering. Many of you recall the shooting of young Trayvon Martin by George Zimmerman. Then there was the lynching of Ahmaud Arbery in Georgia by a trio of white men. And closer to home, one of your neighbors is being investigated for the alleged vigilante murder of an unarmed man that occurred during the blackout."

Toby paused, allowing the correlation between the allegations against Dean and the other famous killings of a similar nature. He turned to Zelmanski and gestured for him to speak.

"My goal is to get twenty-four seven coverage on every street. I realize the so-called graveyard shift will be the most difficult to fill. Unfortunately, this is also the time when these types of crimes occur. I ask that all of you please consider this urgent request by our HOA president." Zelmanski appeared pensive as he paused. He lowered his head, the silence drawing everyone's attention.

He continued, "We don't know everything. Mr. Davenport and I have reached out to all of our resources in government. Let me say this, however. Just before our gathering this morning, the Los Angeles mayor has announced her intention to deploy the National Guard to the streets. She has ordered advanced security measures that some will claim are overbearing and even unconstitutional.

"Although, just like during the pandemic when the city was on lockdown and safety restrictions were put into place, all of those who pitched a fit against the use of masks stood to benefit from the mayor's actions. They called the vaccine mandates draconian. But the shots saved lives. Likewise, the additional security both behind the gates of our neighborhood and beyond them will serve to protect all of us, not just those who've complied with Mr. Davenport's reasonable requests.

"That is why volunteering to join my team of security personnel is vitally important. In addition, asking your neighbors to cooperate, to become willing participants in our security measures, is just as important as well."

Zelmanski stepped back to allow Toby to speak, but as he did, those in attendance spontaneously began to applaud. Several cheered while others thanked Toby and Zelmanski for their efforts.

Toby had more to add to convince the neighbors to fully embrace his measures, but any further rhetoric was unnecessary. He knew fear was an often used means to influence others, and this gathering had just proved this to be true.

FORTY-ONE

Saturday
IRC
Los Angeles

"Detective Wong," said Lee unemotionally despite how he felt inside. He slid his badge and identification into the security slot within the bulletproof window separating the intake officers and visitors. "I need you to pull an inmate for questioning. Dean Winchester. Malibu address."

The intake officer studied Lee and then his credentials before tapping on the keyboard. He scowled as he pushed Lee's identification back through the slot.

"This is a homicide case, Detective Wong. I see nothing in the intake records of a task force correlation. You might need to speak with Detective LaRon Johnson to gain access."

"Winchester hasn't been charged, has he?" asked Lee, unsure of the response.

The intake officer studied the screen again. "No. It looks like he's on a forty-eight."

"Okay, so what's the problem? I have a couple of questions of my own regarding the vic."

The intake officer was still skeptical. He turned his swivel chair around. "Hey, Sarge. Gotta sec?"

A burly sergeant approached the intake window. "Whadya got?" He studied Lee as he awaited the answer.

The officer pointed at the monitor as he spoke. "Winchester is a forty-eight for Metro homicide. This one, Detective Wong, is Interagency Gang Task Force. He wants to question Winchester. Not his case."

The sergeant looked at Lee, who held his shield and credentials close to the window. "True, it's not his case, but Wong here ain't the inmate's old lady here for a quickie, either. You can let him in."

Lee nodded his thanks and waited near the solid steel door with a tiny porthole window at eye level. A loud clank followed by the mechanical sound of the door opening came next. The intake officer gave Lee instructions.

"They're just finishing up chow time. Inside, they'll assign you a visitation room."

Lee nodded. "I know the drill." He walked through the door and continued down the corridor. He'd interviewed suspects and witnesses many times in the facility, but somehow, he'd never dealt with this particular intake officer. It was a sign of the times with the LASD, as personnel were being moved from desk jobs to the streets to combat the rampant crime and rioting. Attrition was at an all-time high, as many rank-and-file deputies were taking early retirement.

He had to wait for half an hour before Dean was brought into the interrogation room. Lee immediately caught Dean's attention and held his index finger to his lips, indicating his friend shouldn't react to his presence. After Dean was handcuffed to the ring on the table, the officer left, leaving the two men alone except for anyone who might be eavesdropping on the other side of the one-way mirrored glass.

Lee leaned forward to speak in a loud whisper. "You okay?"

Dean mimicked Lee's method of conversation. He nodded and leaned forward. "This is a load of crap. They think I'm some vigilante hunting down intruders in our neighborhood."

"Hang tight, Dean. I checked the intake records. You're forty-eight-hour hold expires at five in the morning. If they don't charge you this evening, most likely you won't be."

"Then why doesn't this jerk, Detective Johnson, just tell me that?"

Lee took a deep breath and exhaled. "It's part of the game, Dean. We, um, I mean detectives can't put you in a sweatbox with lights shining in your face anymore. So we make life uncomfortable here. Make you think we're waiting for the last moment to charge you. Reality is, in my opinion, they don't have enough to charge you. Maybe obstruction of justice, which seems to be a common tool used by prosecutors nowadays to get a conviction of some kind if they can't use the crime they're trying to pin on you."

"Dammit, Lee. They broke into our house and hauled me away after blasting a grenade in my face. I'm starting to remember some of it."

"Have you been interrogated by Johnson?"

"Yeah, and some young guy playing good cop, bad cop. The young guy was trying to intimidate me. Make me mad. I tried to keep my composure, but it wasn't easy."

"Did you give them anything?"

Dean leaned back in the chair. "Nope, I lawyered up. It took forever to get a phone call, and I used it to call my attorney, a college classmate of mine. Trust me, I desperately wanted to call Emmy, but I knew it would involve a lot of conversation that might get me in more trouble. I have to trust and believe they'll release me tomorrow morning."

"Have you talked to your attorney?" asked Lee.

"She's coming this afternoon. I hope she can find out what my bail is."

Lee frowned and shook his head. "There is no bail on a forty-eight-hour hold. It's either charge or release."

"At five in the morning?"

"Yeah."

"I don't have any clothes," said Dean. "I was wearing my damn pajama bottoms when they carried me out on a gurney."

"Emmy will bring you some discharge clothes. It may delay things a bit in the morning, but know they can't hold you past five. I'll come with her to make sure there are no hiccups."

"How about Judson and Liza? Are they okay?" asked Dean.

Lee was intentionally curt. He held up his hands and barely nodded over his shoulder. "They're fine, and it's not necessary for you to worry about any more of your friends. Understand?"

Dean nodded. *Don't ask about Grayson.* Message received, loud and clear. Throughout the ordeal, Dean was keenly aware that he was protecting his friend from a murder charge. They had no inkling of Grayson's involvement unless Dean gave him up in order to get released. He would not do that to his best friend.

"Otherwise, things are going pretty well for me. I was kinda challenged at first by some of the guys in the cell with me. I'm in a medical-designated location with only eight bunks. Half the guys were moved out early this morning after breakfast. That left me with only three to deal with, all of whom are cool."

"Don't tell them anything!" Lee raised his voice before catching himself. He leaned in to whisper, "They cleared the cell to allow snitches to have one-on-one time with you. Johnson knows you don't belong here and would divulge information to anyone who appeared friendly. These criminals are experts at, as they say, getting up under you. That means they befriend you to get you to talk about your crime. They go to their attorney with the information and ask for a deal in exchange for testifying about your jailhouse confession."

"I haven't—" began Dean before Lee cut him off.

"I trust you, Dean. Just be very careful. They're experts around here at piecing together seemingly innocent statements and getting the truth out of you. Trust me. I have snitches everywhere."

Suddenly, the door was flung open, and Detective Johnson rushed into the room. "What the hell are you doing, Wong?"

Lee stood and returned the man's glare. "Conducting my own investigation."

"Bullshit! How does obstruction of justice sound? Tampering with a witness? Coaching a perp? There's a long list of what you are really doing."

Lee was angry. "Yeah, well, look in the mirror, Detective! What kind of lies did you spin to the grand jury to get a no-knock warrant? Huh? Does this man, a respected member of the community, look like he's dangerous? With no freakin' record? Maybe that's what needs to be investigated!"

"Screw you, Wong! We're still processing the evidence we discovered. Maybe I'll drop a resisting arrest charge on him right before the forty-eight ends."

"Resisting arrest!" Dean shouted. "You blew my face up with a grenade." Dean stood and tried to wrestle his hands out of the ring welded firmly to the table.

"CO!" shouted Johnson. "Take Winchester back to his cell. Seems like he's fully recovered from his injuries."

"That's a bullshit charge, and you know it," hissed Lee as he continued to remain in Johnson's face.

"C'mon, you know how it works. Gimme a name, and I'll find a crime. Right? You do it all the time, I'm sure. Now, you need to go before I contact IA."

Lee glanced at Dean, who revealed his frustration in the returned look. Lee was afraid he'd made matters worse for Dean, as he'd overstepped by visiting with him. Berating Detective Johnson probably didn't help either.

As he left, he realized how helpless the situation was. The only way to get Dean released early was if he was charged with a lesser, bailable offense. If he was charged with murder, or even manslaughter, the preparedness supplies and camper would certainly justify a ridiculously high bail, one that Dean and Emmy couldn't afford.

He glanced at his watch. It was approaching two on that Saturday. Fifteen hours to go.

FORTY-TWO

Saturday
Dean and Emmy's Home
The Colony at Malibu

The group came together for what had been a social occasion in the past. Now it was far different. Emmy had been too distraught to consider entertaining. All she could think about was the pain and suffering Dean was enduring. Judson and Liza had picked up the slack with a trip to a Vons grocery in Thousand Oaks whose shelves had been rumored to be receiving regular restocking. The couple had loaded up on nonperishable foods and some party trays for tonight's meeting of the Friday Night Club.

While Dean was unable to attend, Mrs. Javitz was. She had information to offer on several fronts. After Lee provided the group an update on his conversation with Dean and the subsequent argument with Detective Johnson, Mrs. Javitz was given the floor. Like their prior gathering of the Friday Night Club, she excused herself to return home before dark. She asked to go first this evening for the same reason.

"Toby has rallied the troops. People are afraid after the blackout, and the SWAT raid only made matters worse. Nothing like that has ever happened in the Colony."

"It shouldn't have happened this time," mumbled Lee. "Have you noticed anything else this afternoon?"

She sighed before responding, "As we expected, he's effectively dividing the neighborhood. With everything going on, you've probably noticed that Zelmanski or his people haven't come down this cul-de-sac looking for volunteers. I contacted them, and they flat out told me I was too old. Fine, I was just trying to do it to be on the inside. Anyway, all I know is they've assigned one of Toby's favorite board members to coordinate the watch on our street. A lawyer, I think."

Nicole nodded. She glanced at Emmy, who was mindlessly poking at the ice cubes in her drink with a straw. "We've butted heads with him before. Seems like he was handpicked for that reason."

Mrs. Javitz shrugged. "Also, I have taken all the information given to me by Judson and Lee. I've developed a pretty good list of who is potentially naughty and nice. Can I just say we're outnumbered by more than two to one?"

"Wow!" exclaimed Liza. "I thought our neighborhood was evenly divided, politically."

"I think, under the circumstances, political thought has been overshadowed by fear," added Grayson. "Many people are only marginally interested in politics. Unless they have strong feelings about one issue or another, they don't participate in the process."

Emmy looked up from her glass and studied Grayson. "You sound like Dean."

Grayson provided her a knowing smile. He knew she was hurting. "Where do you think I learned it?"

Emmy beamed. The exchange seemed to bring her out of her shell somewhat. "Karen, if I hear you correctly, it's possible Toby and Zelmanski have developed a list of their own. What do you think?"

"You bet. It's the shit list, and we're all on it."

"Not my first time," said Nicole as she toasted with Emmy, who laughed for the first time.

"It's probably called the nonconformist list," added Mrs. Javitz.

Judson had another name. "The noncompliance list. We have refused to comply with their demands."

"I'd rather die on my feet than live on my knees," said Grayson, who moved around the bar to get another beer. He was taking Dean's incarceration as hard, if not harder, than Emmy. He'd insisted on joining Emmy and Lee the next morning when it was time to pick Dean up.

Mrs. Javitz stood and left the list she'd created and the handout from the neighborhood meeting on the bar. "I'll leave this for you to review and draw your own conclusions without my input. All I can see is we are way outnumbered. What does that mean in the scheme of things? I don't know. You guys are the strategists. Just let me know what I can do to help."

Liza stood and hugged Mrs. Javitz. "Is there anything you need? We make frequent trips to the grocery store."

"I order online from Vons and have it delivered," she replied. "I add extra stuff every few days, trying not to make it obvious that I'm filling up my pantry and a guest bedroom." She got tickled at herself.

Mrs. Javitz left, and the group took turns passing around the lists of residents she'd compiled. There was definitely a pattern as they cross-referenced Toby's noncompliant list with the information obtained by Lee and the online searches conducted by Judson.

"The best approach is to divide up this list, first approaching people we have some form of connection to. Then we need to come up with a game plan to casually run into the others, make small talk, and feel them out about the overall situation."

"We can't make it obvious," said Lee. "Nicole and I routinely jog the neighborhood, so that's a good cover. Grayson and Dean are the same way. However, if Judson and Liza suddenly take up jogging. Um, well."

"Yeah, yeah," said Liza with a laugh. "We'll find a way that doesn't involve huffin' and puffin' up a hill."

Lee turned to Emmy. "Did you hear back from the attorney after she met with Dean this afternoon?"

She nodded and smiled. "She said he looked good except for the extreme sunburn. She took copious notes as she met with him and planned on pulling his medical records. She thinks we have a great case for a police brutality claim."

"A 1983 lawsuit," interjected Lee. "Civil rights lawsuits against police usually involve denial of due process under the Fourth and Fourteenth Amendments. I think the grand jury proceedings leading to the no-knock warrant should be challenged. Then there is the violation of Dean's civil rights, 42, United States Code, Section 1983. The detective and SWAT team members will likely claim immunity from suit. However, this is LA County, and juries are very sympathetic to victims even if they end up being convicted felons."

Emmy sighed. "Well, honestly, that's down the road. I'm sure Dean will consider it. Most likely, he'll be glad to have this nightmare behind him. As will I."

"Okay, that's understandable," said Lee. He changed the subject to Dean's release. "If I drive, I can get us parking around the Twin Towers restricted parking areas. Beats walking around downtown LA at night. Even near the biggest jail in the region, crime is rampant on the streets."

"Okay, pick me up around four in the morning?" Emmy asked.

Lee nodded. Then Grayson asked, "Emmy, may I come? I feel I owe Dean a huge apology for putting him in this situation."

Emmy smiled and shook her head. "You didn't put him in this situation, Grayson. I believe Toby and Zelmanski are responsible for this. But, yes, please ride along with us. He'll be glad to see you, too."

"I'll have the coffee pot ready for you guys," said Liza. "Tomorrow will be a big day!"

She was right.

FORTY-THREE

Saturday
IRC
Los Angeles

Dean heeded Lee's warning about avoiding unnecessary conversation with his fellow cellmates. Another inmate had not been given the good advice. A young, frightened black kid who was barely eighteen years old was being mentally worked over by two Hispanic inmates, one of whom was the guy shot in the shoulder who'd taken Dean's breakfast tray that morning. The young man had been badly injured by a K-9 unit in the course of his arrest. Even Dean overheard enough of the young man's story to get time off his sentence. Assuming Dean was eventually wrongfully convicted.

He listened to the conversation as his mind wandered to the discussion he'd had with his attorney just before their dinner trays were served. She'd confirmed what Lee had relayed to him. Emmy and his friends were fine. In the simplest terms, she'd laid out the possible charges against him, the worst of which was murder.

Fortunately, with the crime wave taking over the entirety of Los Angeles County, Dean's arrest barely made the midday news on Friday before the networks moved on to something else. This was to his benefit. Based on her conversations with Emmy and Dean, she felt confident the forty-eight-hour hold would pass, which meant he'd be released before dawn Sunday morning.

This was welcome news to Dean. She'd cautioned him that the wheels of justice moved slowly. His jailers were quick to process criminal defendants and get them into inmate housing but were far more reluctant to release those who'd made bail or were innocent, like himself.

Finally, after taking notes from Dean about the events, she'd brought up the various civil remedies available to him, including a civil rights lawsuit. Dean hadn't thought about that much, but when he caught a glimpse of his face in the reflection of a window, he was beginning to think it needed to be done if for no other reason than to deter similar behavior in the future. There had to be a better way to undertake a search warrant besides tossing flash-bang grenades around.

First things first, he'd told her and himself. As the lights turned out in the cellblock at eleven that night, Dean tried to count minutes so he could be ready for that five-o'clock release time. He was feeling better, and the attempted countdown, akin to counting sheep, made him drowsy. Now that the three biggest snorers in the cell had been relocated or released, the quiet enabled him to drift off to get some much-needed sleep.

Dean was in a deep slumber when a boisterous guard smacked the steel bars of the cell with his hard rubber nightstick. "Winchester, roll it up!" he yelled.

Dean was startled, and he bolted upright in his bunk. He wiped the sleep out of his eyes a little too hard, causing them to sting. The pain was so great he forgot about the burns immediately below and above his eye sockets.

"What?" he asked, unsure the guard had called his name.

"Roll it up, Winchester. Let's go!"

Dean's heart leapt out of his chest. He scrambled out of his bunk and slid down the metal ladder until his bare feet smacked the concrete. He located his blue faux-Keds sneakers and slipped them on.

"I'm ready," he said as he swiftly turned and stuck his arms through the food tray slot, presenting them to the jailer to handcuff him. He'd fallen into a deep sleep and assumed he was being released although it didn't feel anywhere near five in the morning.

"What's wrong with you, Winchester? I said roll it up. That means get your bedding and pillow and personal shit and come with me. Jesus!"

"Wait, I won't need that stuff. I'm being released, right?"

"Nah, man. You're being transferred to genpop."

"What?"

"Sweet mother of—" the officer groaned. "Genpop, Winchester. General population. You've been cleared by medical to transfer out of here."

"I haven't seen any medical personnel," argued Dean.

"Look, man. I ain't got time to mess with you. Get your stuff, or don't. I couldn't care less, but you'd better be ready to sleep on the floor without a mattress. Or maybe a pretty boy like you might make a friend to bunk with. I could give two shits less."

His cellmates, even the young man who'd spilled his guts in the first hour he'd arrived in the cell, were getting a hearty laugh out of Dean's lack of knowledge and confusion. He made his way back to his bunk, stripped his sheets, and grabbed his pillow. The officer escorted him out of the cell and slammed the door behind him.

"Listen up. You hold that stuff tight and hug the wall with your right shoulder. If you wander or try anything, you're gonna get the stick. Are we clear?" He slapped the hard baton into his hand for emphasis.

"Clear," said Dean.

As they traveled the hallways, the relatively serene confines of the medical cell block were replaced with a deafening roar of yelling and laughter. He was certain he was being transported into one of the seven gates of hell. As they approached the final set of steel doors, he was kicked into what appeared to be an insane asylum full of hyperactive, homicidal maniacs. Dean paused and caught a glimpse of the jailer's watch.

It was five minutes 'til midnight.

He took a deep breath and opened his eyes wide as the jailer pushed him in the back until he stumbled into the madhouse.

Five hours. He had to survive five hours.

PART 5

Some days are like shadows.
They stretch on too long.

FORTY-FOUR

Sunday
IRC
Los Angeles

Dean would never forget his experience in genpop. From the second he entered the open pod of the cell block housing hundreds of inmates who had recently been brought into the jail on charges or who were awaiting trial, he knew that he was different.

Certainly, he was not the only one who maintained his innocence. As a professor of public policy, Dean knew *innocent until proven guilty* was a guiding principle of the U.S. Constitution, universally understood by most Americans, except those in the sensationalist media.

Undoubtedly, all of the nearly three hundred men in this particular cell block out of the nearly nineteen thousand housed in the Twin Towers Correctional Facility maintained their innocence. Some even until after they were sentenced to life in prison. Certainly, famed actors and television personalities Paris Hilton, Harvey Weinstein, and Ron Jeremy, to name a few, had claimed their innocence during their stays in the jail.

No, it was Dean's age and demographic that stood out. Dean was not a racist as that term had been used so often as of late. He also wasn't blind. He was one of only a few white men in the cell block. The vast majority of the inmates were black and Hispanic. That didn't mean that white people weren't arrested. Clearly, they were. He was exhibit A. However, the disparity in numbers was shocking to Dean. What that meant was something he'd reflect on another day. For now, he had to survive the next five hours in the midst of the mayhem.

He stood with his arms tightly wrapped around the only belongings he had inside the IRC. A pillow made of hard plastic, held together by a few threads before the stuffing came out. A pillowcase and two sheets, stained from bodily fluids Dean didn't want to think about. And his attire, the orange jumpsuit paired with blue faux Keds. The only things he had in common with his fellow cellmates. And his incarceration, of course.

His mind raced as he scanned the open common area, where dozens of stainless-steel tabletops and stools were affixed to steel supports bolted to the concrete floor. Like the medical cell he'd been confined to, the pod looked and smelled like a dumpster.

He considered sitting at a table, except all of the seats were taken by inmates playing cards or dominoes. A couple of men were playing chess, substituting the ends of plastic spoons with letters written on them to identify missing pieces. From the excitement of the onlookers who frequently razzed one another, gambling was popular inside the jail.

He noticed some men were snacking on generic potato chips or peanut butter crackers, tossing the empty packaging on the floor when they finished. These inmates had been in the cell long enough to receive commissary funds from loved ones, which allowed them to make purchases.

Less than five hours. Dean laughed to himself. *No commissary for me.*

There was a bank of eight telephones. They had been shut off at ten o'clock when the guards came through the cell block to perform a head count of the inmates to confirm nobody had escaped or gotten lost in the constant shuffling of prisoners from one level of classification to another. Out of the eight phones, three had the handsets torn off. Had it been done by an inmate angry at a loved one or an unfaithful girlfriend? Or had it been used to bash in the skull of someone who cheated at cards.

Oddly, Dean felt unnoticed. Unremarkable. He thought he would be swarmed by men who, as Lee suggested, wanted to get up under him. Whether to gather information, take commissary, or for forced sex. Yes, his mind went there. He glanced up at the ceiling, where dim lights provided the inmates just enough illumination to play their games all night. Within the cells themselves, it was pitch black. What could happen in there?

Around the perimeter of the pod, men slept on the floors. A few had mattresses; most did not. He imagined that the kingpins of the cell block took any mattress they wanted to make their steel bunk more comfortable. Dean had done the same after some of his cellies, as they were called, had left for other locations within the Twin Towers.

Feeling vulnerable, he decided to blend into the walls. He made his way to an open space nearest the steel doors where he'd entered. Subconsciously, it was a self-preservation decision, hoping he could get to the door and scream out for help in the event he was attacked. Outwardly, he managed a smile as his signature sense of humor recalled the accounting method of cost flow assumptions known as LIFO. Last-in, first-out. He doubted that applied to the prison system, but it worked to calm his nerves on this night.

Because Dean had been so concerned about interacting with the inmates in the cell block, and therefore remaining close to the steel door, he never noticed the clock mounted high above it. Instead, he tried to estimate the minutes he'd been in there. Nothing worked, as he frequently lost count of the Mississippis and potatoes, as he'd recently read in a novel. He pulled his knees to his chest, sat on his pillow, and gently fell back against the concrete wall. Rarely blinking. Certainly not sleeping.

Dean's mind wandered to Emmy and his friends, especially Grayson. He didn't blame Grayson for not coming forward. In fact, he was glad he didn't. No amount of inconvenience, if that was all that came out of his nightmarish ordeal, warranted putting his friend through Detective Johnson's vendetta because Grayson had done the right thing. Dean felt like he was hours away from release, and it would all be over.

The minutes passed, and Dean became intrigued by the interaction between the inmates. At the end of the day, they were people just like him. No better, no worse. Their economic situation and demographics had likely led them to the predicament they found themselves in. Undoubtedly, poor decision-making and common greed were mostly to blame. Now, because they were comfortable living around their fellow inmates, it had become one big party. Dean had always fashioned himself to be a people-watcher. In airports, however. Not prisons.

Unexpectedly, the outer door to the pod opened, and a deputy came to the small, barred opening located within the inner door. The noise level immediately decreased, which was as disconcerting for Dean as the suddenness of the guard's appearance. The guard began shouting out names.

"Ramirez, Jesus! Jones, Lamarcus! Alvarez, Julio! Navarro-Santiago, Mateo! Roll it up!"

Dean's heart sank, as the four names called did not include his. He'd been in the process of standing, presuming his FIFO theory was correct or, at least, might manifest itself. Elation turned to dejection as the deputy stopped reading his list. He slumped back against the wall and sighed.

The lucky few who were being moved or released shuffled to the door, their arms full of prison-issued items. The rest, commissary, was tossed around to friends within the pod, who readily munched down the snacks. All of them appeared to be anticipating their release that morning.

As they arrived, the deputy's radio squawked to life. "Pod four hundred, intake. Over."

"Go for pod four hundred."

"Pod four hundred, go ahead and bring us Winchester, Dean."

"Copy." Then the guard shouted, "Winchester, Dean! Roll it up!"

Dean's eyes grew wide, and he jumped to his feet, leaving his bedding on the floor behind him. "Here! Ready!" A few of the inmates laughed at his response before turning back to their table games.

The guard began to process the other men through the door, comparing the intake photo with their faces. When Dean arrived, he couldn't stop smiling.

The guard scowled. "What's wrong with you, Winchester? Are you high or something?"

"No, sir. Happy to be getting out."

His eyes roamed from Dean's feet to his face. "You're not going anywhere without your bedding. Roll it up means roll it up."

"Oh, um, sorry," said Dean. He rushed back to where he had been sitting and immediately noticed someone had already stolen his pillow. He came back with a wadded mess of sheets. "This is all I have."

The guard smirked and waved him through. He led the five men through the corridors until they reached an elevator, where two armed deputies waited inside. Their utility belts contained stun guns, mace and night sticks.

"Two at a time, gentlemen," the escorting guard said. "Act out, you'll catch another charge and a well-deserved beatdown. Comprende?"

None of the inmates responded. The first two entered the elevator. Dean was anxious. He tried to catch a glimpse of the guard's watch until he was busted trying. The man shot him a nasty look and a scowl. Dean decided it wasn't worth the effort.

The elevator finally returned, and the next two men entered. Dean tried to follow, having forgotten the two-men-at-a-time rule. It earned him a stiff rebuke from the escorting guard.

"You're a special kind of stupid, aren't you, Winchester?"

The doors closed, leaving the two of them alone. Dean replied softly, "First time in jail."

"Shocker," the guard said sarcastically. He waited a moment before speaking again. "What are you in for?"

Dean paused before responding, wondering if Lee's admonition applied to the prison guards as well. "They called it a forty-eight-hour hold."

"Suspect," the guard mumbled. "Suspected for what? Shoplifting?" He began to laugh.

"Yeah, um, something like that." Dean had stalled long enough for the elevator to return. He quickly stepped inside and let out a deep exhale once he was on his way to the ground floor. It was almost over.

The ride down the elevator was excruciatingly slow. The deputies made small talk, relaxing somewhat, as Dean was not the kind of threat they were used to keeping an eye on. He let out a long exhale in attempt to flush the tension out of his body.

Then, without warning, the lights flickered, and the elevator shuddered.

"What the hell?" asked one of the guards.

"This thing is old, man. It gets a workout, you know?" the other replied.

Dean nervously balled his fists, slowly rubbing his fingernails against his sweaty palms. His eyes darted from the LED display above the elevator doors to the buttons on the panel, each of which required a key to activate.

The elevator shook again as the lights flickered.

No, please no, he begged to himself. *This cannot be.* Dean closed his eyes, focusing his senses on the sounds of the elevator and its motion. Then he was shocked back into the present by the elevator landing hard at the bottom of its ride to the ground floor.

"I hate this thing," one of the guards muttered.

"You and me both, brother," said the other before addressing Dean. "Let's go, pal. Walk slowly and keep your right shoulder against the wall."

Dean was relieved to have survived the ride. Another blackout would be bad enough. Getting stuck in the elevator of a prison would be the cherry on top of a really crappy ice-cream sundae.

He was placed in another holding cell while the intake deputies took their sweet time releasing the five men. Lee had warned him that this was possible. As Lee put it, they move slower than a postal worker during the peak of Christmas shipping. No rush, no worries was their motto.

One additional factor was that the LASD had come under fire recently for allowing two inmates to be released by mistake. Both gang-related murderers, the men closely resembled two other inmates who willingly allowed them to stand in their stead in exchange for the promises of payment to their families in Central America. Neither of the men had been apprehended.

While waiting, Dean anxiously paced the floor of the holding cell. That was when he caught his first glimpse of a clock near the intake personnel's window. It was ten minutes until two. He had three hours to wait. He presumed these other four men would be released before him, as one was already gone, and a second was being processed. He was a whole elevator ride away from the danger of pod four hundred and one step away from freedom.

FORTY-FIVE

Sunday
Dean and Emmy's Home
The Colony at Malibu

Emmy tossed and turned, trying to find sleep so she'd be somewhat rested when she picked up Dean from the jail. Although Lee wasn't arriving at her house until four, she wanted to shower and make herself beautiful for her husband. For Dean, that didn't mean glammed up in a sparkly dress and heels. He loved her the most when she was her casual self, dressed in one of her many jogging suits and exhibiting her natural beauty. Dean loved her unconditionally. On that day, Emmy imagined, he wouldn't care if her hair was matted and she had bags under her eyes. Just the same, she was gonna do her best to look nice for him.

She'd set the alarm on her Apple watch for both vibrate and a barely audible beep. In her light sleep, the first hint of motion on her wrist caused her to open her eyes wide with excitement. Staring at the ceiling, she listened for movement in the kitchen, hoping that Liza had fulfilled her promise of starting the coffee. There was no shuffling in the kitchen, nor was there the aromatic scent of coffee floating down the hallway.

Liza must've overslept, which was fine. Coffee would've been nice. Not that Emmy needed it. She shrugged it off, glad that her friend found sleep. As she awakened fully, she leaned over to turn on the lamp.

Click-click.

Nothing.

"Seriously?" she mumbled. Emmy tried it again.

Click-click. Click-click-click.

She jerked her hand away from the lamp. "Not funny. This is not a good time to have a burned-out bulb." She sighed and fell back against her pillow, staring at the ceiling for a moment. It was oddly dark in the bedroom. She sat up and leaned on her elbows, her eyes roving the entire room.

Emmy shuddered as beads of perspiration formed on her forehead. She jumped out of bed, dragging the covers onto the floor in the process. She raced to the window and pulled the curtains open. Because their bedroom was on the first floor, surrounded by trees and landscape, she couldn't get a good look at any of the homes in the cul-de-sac.

Panicked, she ran to the bedroom door and flung it open; it slipped from her hand and crashed hard against the doorstop. Too panicked to try the light switch, she stared down the hall toward the foyer and living room.

The silence was deafening. The darkness was blinding.

"No! No! No!" Emmy shouted, running down the hallway, smacking at any rocker switch within her reach. None of them were responding.

"Emmy?" Liza's sleepy voice called down to her from the balcony above.

Emmy ignored her and unlocked the bolt lock on the front door.

She pulled it open and rushed into the chilly darkness. Bounding down the steps without regard for her bare feet, she found herself standing at the bottom of the driveway, mouth agape.

There were no lights illuminated on anyone's porches. No faint blue circles emanating from their Ring doorbells. She couldn't hear the hum of heat and air units maintaining a constant sixty-eight degrees indoors.

Nothing.

"Emmy?" Judson called out for her. "Honey, come back inside."

She whirled around. "The power's out! Judson, the damn power is out again!"

A faint light could be seen in Grayson's house. The beam of a flashlight darted around from wall to wall. Inside her own home, the yellowish flicker of candles being lit in the living room provided an inviting glow. Yet Emmy was unable to calm herself. She stood in the driveway, her arms wrapped around her midsection, shivering from the fifty-degree windchill.

Grayson reached out and gently touched her arm. She started at his touch, as she'd neither heard nor seen his approach. She jerked her head toward his face and squinted her eyes to confirm it was him. Even the late-February snow moon was not providing sufficient light for her to see.

"Emmy, it's me." His voice was soothing, calming as he approached. "Let's go back inside, okay?"

Grayson had arrived by her side. Emmy looked back and forth between her two friends. Her knees began to buckle as she became distraught. The guys quickly supported her by holding her arms, then wrapping their arms around her back.

Now Liza had joined her. She tried to provide her words of encouragement. "This is probably temporary, like before. Let's go inside and talk about it."

Emmy's eyes were full of tears. She couldn't blink. She couldn't breathe. She could barely comprehend the words spoken to her. All she could think about was her husband sitting in that godawful jail with murderers, rapists, and violent felons.

She wrestled away from the guys as her adrenaline kicked in. She turned back toward the cul-de-sac.

"We have to get Dean!" she shouted. "He'll never survive in there. Please, we have to go."

The trio chased after her. It was Liza who was able to get through. "Listen to me, honey. We're not gonna let Dean sit in that jail one second more that he's supposed to. We'll still get him, with or without the lights on."

"How, Liza? How? If the power is off, um, the doors may not open." Distraught, Emmy had become irrational. "What if the power never comes back on? Is he gonna sit in there to rot away? Starve to death? If he even makes it that long." She began to sob again.

The group was given a jolt when the sound of a vehicle approaching preceded the headlights washing their homes at the end of the cul-de-sac. All of them held their arms up, using their forearms to shield their eyes from the blinding light in the pitch darkness. The driver, seeing their reaction, immediately turned off the headlights as the car pulled to a stop.

It was Lee.

"Hey, guys," he greeted them as he poured out of the car. Nicole exited and ran to Emmy's side, hugging her friend and crying tears of despair with her.

Judson turned to Grayson as Lee reached the group. "Whadya think?"

Grayson looked around to determine if they'd drawn anyone's attention. He checked his watch. It was three twenty.

"Let's go inside." He spread his arms wide and encouraged Liza and Nicole to assist Emmy.

Judson walked ahead and made sure nobody tripped up the stairs despite Grayson illuminating them with his flashlight. Once inside, he closed the door behind them to keep the cold, damp air out.

"Lee," began Grayson, "what is the jail's protocol when the grid goes down? Do you have any idea how they handled the blackout last weekend?"

Lee took a deep breath. He wished Grayson hadn't asked that question in front of Emmy. She probably wasn't gonna like his answer.

"The Twin Towers has massive backup generators designed to do two things. One, maintain power to jail operations. You know, administration, communications, intranet, etc. Two, maintain food service to feed the inmates. You can rest assured the ACLU will find a judge in the middle of the night to sue the LASD if the inmates aren't fed or provided medical attention."

"What else?" asked Emmy, her voice hopeful. "Will they let Dean out at five?"

Lee paused to choose his words carefully. "The sheriff will have to make a decision as to whether this outage is temporary like before or not. I imagine he's already been on the phone with Sacramento and his contacts at Homeland Security."

"I would agree with Lee's assessment," added Grayson. "The grid went down a few minutes before two."

"How do you know?" asked Liza.

"My solar-powered battery array switched to auxiliary at that moment. I glanced at the digital display indicating how long auxiliary power had been in use as I came out of the house."

"Okay," began Lee. "I'd be willing to bet within fifteen minutes, the jail was on the phone to the undersheriff, who in turn made the decision to wake the sheriff. Ordinarily, the sheriff would've waited for a while to determine whether it was a short outage. After the blackout and the night of chaos the county endured, I'm sure he took nothing for granted."

Emmy paced the floor, hands on hips, at times nervously running her hands through her hair. "What does all of this mean for Dean's release?"

Grayson glanced at Lee. The flickering candlelight reflected his troubled demeanor. Clearly, the longtime member of law enforcement was struggling to find an answer that was truthful without sending Emmy spiraling out of control.

Lee approached Emmy and took her hands. "A lot of times, events like this cause the jail administrative operations to come to a screeching halt. It happened when they threatened to burn the city down over George Floyd's death. The LASD learned from that."

"Are you saying they might not let him out?" Emmy grew concerned.

"No, they have to." Only the distraught Emmy bought the lie. The last thing of concern to the deputies operating the Twin Towers facility, which was overcrowded by four hundred percent, was releasing some guy on a forty-eight-hour hold.

"Okay, we should get down there," said Emmy, who pulled away to rush to get ready.

"Emmy, hold on," cautioned Lee. "That said, for Dean's safety, they might wait until the sun is up. Under these circumstances, I would imagine they wouldn't want to release Dean onto the streets of downtown LA."

Yet, that was exactly what they did.

FORTY-SIX

Sunday
IRC
Los Angeles

Dean found a seat on the bench near the corner of the holding cell and sat with his legs crossed in front of him. He was settling in for the three-hour wait until five a.m. when his forty-eight-hour hold expired. For the first time, he was able to relax, feeling comfortable that the other inmates awaiting release wouldn't be stupid enough to attack him when they were on their way out the door. Within minutes, his mind had been cleared of what he'd endured thus far. Visions of Emmy. The thought of her touch. The laughter they shared. All came back to him as inmate Dean Winchester began to transition to a human being again.

Then the forced air from the air handlers stopped. The bright fluorescent lights in the corridor turned off. Only the glow of the intake officers' computers provided ambient light.

"What's going on?" one of the intake officers could be heard asking the other deputy working the desk.

"Hang on," he replied. "Phones are out."

"The computers are working," the other added. "Internal comms, too."

Several audible dings could be heard by Dean and the other two men as they stood grasping the bars, their faces pressed against the cold steel in an attempt to see the intake officers.

"Oye!" shouted the inmate to Dean's right.

"Hey, man! Whassup with the power?" asked the other.

Dean focused on listening rather than asking questions that wouldn't be answered. The two intake personnel lowered their voices as they compared messages being received on their computers. A loud clank followed by the steel door being manually opened distracted the three men in the holding cell. A sergeant came rushing past, ignoring the other two inmates' requests for information. He addressed the intake personnel.

"Captain wanted me to let you know the backup gennies are up and runnin'. Keep your comms to a minimum as they try to maintain order upstairs. The entire facility is on lockdown."

"Yes, sir," one of them responded. "What do you want us to do with those three? Return them to genpop?"

Dean heard that and screamed NO in his head. He turned his head and tried to stuff his right ear, the one that wasn't still ringing, through the bars.

"What's their release status?" he asked.

"Two made bond, so they're an immediate release. The third guy is on a forty-eight."

"What time does it expire?"

"Five, sir."

The sergeant stepped back a few paces in the dim emergency lighting; he studied the three hopeful faces staring back at him.

"All right, release the two who bonded out. Let me see if I can reach anyone in Metro homicide."

"At this hour, Sarge?"

"I know. It's a long shot. If I can't, he'll just have to sit there and wait."

Dean heard the entire conversation. The two men who'd been bonded out stepped away from the bars and exchanged high fives. Dean tried to get the sergeant's attention.

"Sir, please. I don't have any charges. Please don't make me wait."

The sergeant stopped, realizing he didn't know the forty-eight's name. Rather than replying to Dean, he turned back to the intake desk.

"What's this inmate's name?"

"Winchester, Dean."

The sergeant turned and marched away without another word.

Over the next thirty minutes, the other two men who'd made bail were processed and released. Dean sat alone in the holding cell, alternating between crying and getting his hopes up, when the steel door that the sergeant had come through earlier opened.

Nothing changed.

He sat with his elbows resting atop his knees, hands buried in his face, rocking back and forth. Unaware that a deputy had approached from the intake window. He was startled into the present by the sound of the jailer's key manually unlocking his cell door.

"Let's go, Winchester."

Dean hesitated before standing. His eyes darted around as he tried to determine whether he was being returned to the general population cell block or being released. The guard seemed to sense his apprehension.

"Come on, let's go. Unless you wanna stay? We'd be glad to send you back upstairs."

"No. I mean, yes. I wanna go home."

"Good, then move it."

Dean hustled out of the cell a little too fast for the guard, who instinctively moved his hand onto his stun gun. Dean abruptly stopped and then, as he'd been previously instructed, pushed himself against the wall so his right shoulder touched it. As the guard led him to the intake desk, Dean marveled at how quickly he'd become indoctrinated by the authority imposed on him by his jailers. In just a short time, he knew exactly what to do to avoid suffering their wrath.

The intake deputy began to ask Dean some simple identification questions to confirm it was him. The other deputy returned to the desk and motioned toward Dean.

"I couldn't find anything," he said with a shrug.

The intake deputy looked up at Dean. "Were you naked when they arrested you or something?"

Dean shook his head. "Um, no. Just pajamas, which they took at the hospital. He leaned closer to the glass so the deputy could see his face.

"Too much time at the beach?" he asked sarcastically.

"One of your flash-bang grenades," Dean hissed in response.

The deputy took another look, momentarily fixated on Dean's wounds. He didn't have a witty comeback for what he saw.

"Do we have any release clothing?" he asked his partner.

"You're joking, right? Everything is on a full facility lockdown. Only COs are moving. No inmates or orderlies."

"This guy's in a jumpsuit. We could get hammered if we let him out of here like this."

"Don't you have some clothes for me?" asked Dean. He thought about telling them his wife would bring clothes at five but thought better of it. They might keep him in the holding cell until then.

"This ain't Brooks Brothers, pal. Do you wanna go or not?"

Dean tried to help by chiming in. "I don't care. I'll change as soon as I can."

The deputy shook his head in disbelief and turned back to his partner. "Whadya think?"

"Let him bear the consequences, then," the other replied as he turned to the computer to search for information on the power outage.

"All right, Winchester. You'll be on your own, buddy. I suggest you keep these discharge papers I'm about to give you. If a black-and-white sees you, they're gonna scoop you up and bring you right back."

"Yes, sir. I understand."

Minutes later, Dean was walking through a side entrance to the jail, clutching his paperwork. He was immediately hit with a gust of cold wind and the sound of gunfire in the distance. Several people were running in all directions along Bauchet Street in front of the jail, screaming for no apparent reason.

Dean stopped and took it all in. Then he asked himself aloud, "Now what?"

FORTY-SEVEN

Sunday
Los Angeles

Lee turned on his lights and siren, using them as an audible and visual ramrod to force his way through traffic. Grayson rode in the passenger seat, listening to Lee's police radio embedded in the dash. Emmy was buckled up in the backseat, flanked by the men's rifles, clutching Dean's change of clothes as if they were a security blanket.

It was thirty miles from the Colony to the Twin Towers in downtown Los Angeles. On a good day, it was an hour drive. With no operating traffic signals and vehicular traffic that seemed to have forgotten the rules of the road the moment the grid went down, Lee had to carefully force his way east on the PCH toward the Santa Monica Freeway leading into the city.

As they entered Pacific Palisades, the first signs of looting were evident. The beaches had been filled with refugees camping out on the white, pristine sands of Palisades Beach. Now the displaced were having their way with local restaurants and businesses. Dozens poured in and out of the entrance to the Beach Club, a beachfront hangout featuring outdoor dining and live music. Most carried food, and a few carried electric guitars. At least the looter with the snare drum had an instrument he could play.

The scene was the same when Lee drove past the Santa Monica Pier. The restaurants were under siege, as were the gift shops. The Hilton Santa Monica hotel was surrounded by people trying to force their way inside to get shelter. Security guards had barricaded the revolving door with furniture, prompting the refugees to break out the large plate-glass windows to gain entry.

Sirens wailed in the distance, and the occasional gunshot could be heard as Lee pulled onto the Santa Monica Freeway. At that point, the late-night drunks from Saturday engaged in a deadly game of bumper cars on Sunday morning.

Inside his unmarked car, conversation was kept to a bare minimum so Lee could focus on navigating his Dodge Challenger through the dangerous traffic conditions and Grayson could listen to the police chatter on Lee's two-way radio. Emmy resisted the urge to ask Grayson to speculate about the power outage, or for Lee to opine, for the fifth time, about whether Dean would be released. She did stare at the LED display of Lee's dashboard unit to watch the minutes tick away. By her calculations, they would arrive at the jail about fifteen minutes before five, just in time for Lee to take Dean's release clothing inside before he was released.

By the time they crossed through South Central LA, fires were burning out of control. At the massive, three-level cloverleaf interchange where the Santa Monica Freeway and Interstate 110 met, traffic was at a crawl. An eighteen-wheeler had jackknifed and was partially hanging off an overpass. The spectacle caused rubbernecking drivers to run into one another. Fistfights had broken out while other motorists shut off their engines and began to walk home, some carrying bottles of liquor to keep their buzz going.

Once past the cloverleaf, Lee elected to race through the Fashion District, using the normally busy neighborhood, which was devoid of traffic at this time of night. It was a well-chosen shortcut to avoid the interchange where Interstates 10 and 5 met. He raced down Figueroa Street and took multiple rights and lefts until he was in the heart of Chinatown. Minutes later, with the help of Grayson, who guided him around the security arm blocking the parking lot designated for LA County Pretrial Services, he parked the car directly across from the Twin Towers.

He shut off the engine to catch his breath. The roar of people screaming outside the main jail was unsettling.

Undeterred, Emmy tried to open her door, but it was locked, as was customary in a detective's assigned vehicle. "Let me come with you," she begged.

"No, Emmy. No way. Didn't you see those crazed fools? Let me get Dean, and we'll get the hell outta here before the city burns."

"She's right, Emmy," said Grayson calmly. He reached over the seat and asked for Dean's clothes.

She gave Grayson a genuine pout before handing the clothing to him. She knew her protests would be denied.

Lee glanced at his watch and took the change of clothes. Seconds later, he was jogging through the parking lot, clothes under one arm and his other hand on his service weapon.

Grayson tried to calm her nerves. "Not much longer, Emmy."

"This is killing me, Grayson. I'm so worried."

"I know. Dean's strong. You have to be strong for him."

The two stopped talking, opting instead to look through the car windows at the growing mob of people who'd taken to the street. Grayson pointed out a structure fire in the direction of Chinatown, where they'd just driven through minutes ago.

More gunfire nearby jolted Emmy. Tears ran down her cheeks once again. She leaned forward in her seat and tried to get a look at Grayson's face. He stared straight ahead, his eyes shifting from one side of the car to the other.

"How can you be so calm?" she asked.

Grayson didn't turn toward her. He didn't want her to see his expressionless face.

"Practice."

FORTY-EIGHT

Sunday
Downtown Los Angeles

.

Lee turned the corner in front of the Twin Towers and approached the Inmate Reception Center lobby. The chandelier-style lights were dimly lit, an indicator the facility was on auxiliary power, which did not surprise him. What did shock him was the number of people crammed into the small, public lobby. A few people were stuffed outside the entry, holding the doors open, which drew vociferous rebukes from those inside who were cold.

"Dammit," he cursed when he realized the predicament he was in. He couldn't force his way in. These loved ones, concerned about their family members, would likely beat him to death, and no LEO would be available to save him.

He stood outside the building for a minute to consider his options. During that time, more people crowded into the lobby, causing pushing and a scuffle. He paced the sidewalk, alternating his attention between the front door and his car, where a distraught Emmy was certain he'd be returning with her husband. She'd lose her mind if he came back empty-handed.

He took a deep breath and gathered the courage to return to the car. What he had in mind might get him fired. Then the old saying "better to ask for forgiveness than permission" came to mind. He wasn't sure it applied in this instance, but he imagined the LASD would have more important matters to attend to when this was all over. Assuming it came to an end. *The jury would be out on that*, he thought to himself.

He returned to the car. Emmy noticed him first. She slid across the backseat to frantically try the handle, forgetting she was locked in like a perp. Lee could see her face pleading for an explanation, tears streaming down her cheeks. He quickly opened the driver's side door to explain.

"Emmy, Emmy, please calm down and listen."

The questions came flying out of her mouth. "Where is he, Lee? Are they not gonna let him out? They have to. It's almost five!"

Lee caught his breath. "I don't know. I mean, I couldn't get into the lobby of the intake center. It's mobbed with people looking for answers. There was the start of a brawl when I left."

Grayson calmly asked, "Options?"

"One, maybe. I'll be honest, they may tell me to pound sand."

"Whadya have in mind?" he asked as he snuck a glance at Emmy. Her eyes were wide and wild as she leaned forward in the seat. She tried to stare a hole into Lee's brain.

"I'm gonna try to enter through the booking compound. It's a side entrance over on North Vignes Street. Assuming it's manned, which I'm sure it is regardless of the power outage, I'm gonna claim to be picking up Dean to place into protective custody for a case I'm working. That should get me into the facility, where I can ask some questions. Being on the Interagency Task Force gives me a little higher level of respect than the other detectives."

"Solid plan," said Grayson, a man of few words on this day, reflecting the tenseness he was feeling.

Lee took a deep breath. "I'm gonna need you guys to wait here. Out of sight. With the rifles."

"We can't go with you?" asked Emmy.

Lee turned sideways in his seat. "No, I'm sorry. This has to look like official business. Listen, it's approaching five, and I need to get moving."

Grayson nodded and exited the car. He opened Emmy's door and let her out before reaching in to grab the two AR-10 rifles and the mesh bag of additional magazines. His muscles bulged as he held the heavy rifles and several pounds of ammunition.

Seconds later, Lee was on his way, and Emmy found a spot under an evergreen tree against a retaining wall, where they had a clear line of sight to the intersection of Bauchet and Vignes. For a while, they stood silent as they saw the mayhem that ensued at the entrance to the IRC. It confirmed what Grayson and Dean always cautioned. Societal collapse would be ugly.

Emmy got antsy and began to wander around, hoping to get a look at the entrance to the booking compound. Grayson finally took her by the hand and pulled her next to the wall.

"Emmy, please hold still so we don't draw attention to ourselves. I know the cops are busy, but if they come up on us with these things in our possession, we're screwed."

She could see the serious look on his face as the first sign of sunrise began to wash across downtown LA. "You're right. I'm sorry. I'm not much help, am I?"

"Yes, you are. What you're going through is understandable. We'll get Dean and take y'all home."

She laughed, comforted by his Southern dialect. "Yeah, home. Where we can deal with the likes of Toby and Zelmanski."

Grayson smiled. "Kinda shows how irrelevant those assclowns are, doesn't it?"

"It sure does," Emmy responded with a hearty laugh and a smile. Her demeanor had perked up.

The sun shone a little brighter as they made small talk. Grayson tried not to make it obvious, but he frequently glanced at his watch. A quarter to six. It was taking longer than he expected. Were they holding Dean beyond the forty-eight hours due to the power outage, or worse, had he been charged at the last minute? He tried to put out of his mind what that entailed.

"Look!" exclaimed Emmy. "There's Lee!"

She left Grayson's side and rushed toward Lee's car as it approached the entry gate to the parking lot. He pulled in front of the swing arm and stopped. He jumped out of the car and waved to them.

"Come on! Get in!" he shouted to them.

"Where's Dean?" She shouted her question so she could be heard over the mayhem in front of the jail. Since the trio's arrival, the crowd attempting to force their way into the intake center had grown exponentially. Two National Guard Humvees had arrived to begin the arduous task of crowd control.

Lee replied as he opened the back door for Emmy. "He's been released!"

"Great!" exclaimed Emmy. She almost tripped over the curb as she rushed toward the car. "Wait. Where is he?" Her eyes frantically looked from the front seat to the back and then toward the entrance of the IRC.

Grayson rushed to join her, toting the rifles and ammo.

"Lee?" he asked.

"They let him out over two hours ago," Lee replied.

"Then where is he?" Emmy asked, still searching the streets. She walked away from the car.

"I don't know."

Lee's words both stung and frightened her. Dean hadn't waited for them to pick him up. Had he gotten a ride with someone else? Or had he been hurt when he walked out of the building?

She dug deep, mustering the strong will that helped her navigate the Hollywood world she worked in. She straightened her back and thrust her hands on her hips before spinning around to stare at Lee and Grayson.

Unknowingly echoing her husband's words when he'd walked out of the jail and stood in the identical spot, Emmy asked, "Now what?"

THANK YOU

Thank you for reading *Behind the Gates Two,* the second installment in the Collapse of America series!

If you enjoyed it, I'd be grateful if you'd take a moment to write a short review (just a few words are needed) and post it on Amazon. Amazon uses complicated algorithms to determine what books are recommended to readers. Sales are, of course, a factor, but so are the quantities of reviews my books get. By taking a few seconds to leave a review, you help me out and also help new readers learn about my work.

Sign up to my email list to learn about upcoming titles, deals, contests, appearances, and more!

Sign up at BobbyAkart.com

WHAT'S COMING NEXT FROM BOBBY AKART?

BEHIND THE GATES, Book Three, the next installment in this epic post-apocalyptic survival series. You can preorder by clicking here:

PREORDER BEHIND THE GATES, BOOK THREE

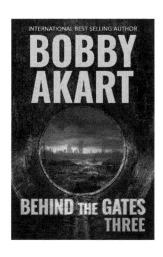

**The grid had collapsed.
But was it temporary, like before?
Or, had America's foes finally succeeded?
Would the lives of the Friday Night Club be shattered as
a result?**

International bestselling author, Bobby Akart, one of America's favorite storytellers, delivers up-all-night thrillers to nearly two million readers in 245 countries and territories worldwide.

"Akart is one of those very rare authors who makes things so visceral, so real, that you experience what he writes."

America's government was on the verge of collapse and her geopolitical foes smelled blood. While the country was destroyed from within, China deals a final blow. It was time to bring the United States to its knees.

Thrust into a world without power, complete lawlessness took over. The Friday Night Club had been divided as they search for one of their own on the streets of Los Angeles. Would the search for one result in the demise of them all?

"You are there. Feeling what they feel. Anger, joy, love, mourning. You feel it all. Not everyone can write a book like this. It takes a special writer to make you feel a book."

An uneasy alliance within the community had finally been endorsed by all. But would it be adhered to? Was it nothing more than a ruse to convince those who were prepared to feed and protect those who were not? Four families remained skeptical and tried to maintain their distance from the neighborhood politics. Until a seminal event threatened to expose their anonymity.

"Akart's fiction becomes reality far too often. Behind the Gates is a cautionary tale of what's to come in our nation."

With seventy novels published worldwide, Bobby Akart delivers intense, up-all-night thrillers that have you whispering just one more chapter.

Pre-order BEHIND THE GATES, Book Three
Available on Amazon by clicking here.

MORE NOVELS BY AMAZON CHARTS TOP 25 AUTHOR BOBBY AKART

The Collapse of America Series
Behind the Gates One
Behind the Gates Two
Behind the Gates Three
Behind the Gates Four

The California Dreamin' Disaster Thrillers
ARkStorm (a standalone, disaster thriller)
Fractured (a standalone, disaster thriller)
Mammoth (a standalone, disaster thriller)

The Perfect Storm Series
Perfect Storm 1
Perfect Storm 2
Perfect Storm 3
Perfect Storm 4

Black Gold (a standalone, terrorism thriller)

Gunner Fox Novels
Made In China (a standalone, terrorism thriller)

The Odessa Trilogy (Gunner Fox)
Odessa Reborn
Odessa Rising
Odessa Strikes

The Asteroid Trilogy (Gunner Fox)
Discovery
Diversion
Destruction

The Nuclear Winter Series
First Strike
Armageddon
Whiteout
Devil Storm
Desolation

New Madrid (a standalone, disaster thriller)

The Virus Hunters
Virus Hunters I
Virus Hunters II
Virus Hunters III

The Geostorm Series
The Shift
The Pulse
The Collapse
The Flood
The Tempest

The Pioneers

The Doomsday Series
Apocalypse
Haven
Anarchy
Minutemen
Civil War

The Yellowstone Series
Hellfire
Inferno
Fallout
Survival

The Lone Star Series
Axis of Evil
Beyond Borders
Lines in the Sand
Texas Strong
Fifth Column
Suicide Six

The Pandemic Series
Beginnings
The Innocents
Level 6
Quietus

The Blackout Series
36 Hours
Zero Hour
Turning Point
Shiloh Ranch
Hornet's Nest
Devil's Homecoming

The Boston Brahmin Series

The Loyal Nine
Cyber Attack
Martial Law
False Flag
The Mechanics
Choose Freedom
Patriot's Farewell (standalone novel)
Black Friday (standalone novel)
Seeds of Liberty (Companion Guide)

The Prepping for Tomorrow Series (non-fiction)
Cyber Warfare
EMP: Electromagnetic Pulse
Economic Collapse

Made in the USA
Columbia, SC
29 March 2024

33814471R00174